Sexy Shorts for Lovers

A collection of short stories

Edited by
Rachel Loosmore

Published by Accent Press Ltd – 2005
www.accentpress.co.uk
www.sexyshorts.info

IBSN 0954489926

Printed and bound in the UK
by Clays PLC, St Ives

Cover Design by Richie Perrott
Desert Point Illustration
www.desertpointillustration.com

This book is dedicated those who tirelessly care for heart patients and to those who support their work.

A special thanks to the authors for generously donating their work.

Acknowledgements

A version of 'Fish In The Sea' by Lynne Barrett-Lee was published in *Image Magazine* (Eire) in August 2003 and *My Weekly* in August 2004. 'Seascape' by Jane Bidder won the Elizabeth Goudge Award 2004, presented by the Romantic Novelists' Association. 'The Guitar Man' by Della Galton was published in *The People's Friend* in July 2003. 'Best Foot Forward' by Sue Houghton was published in *Woman Summer Special* in 2002. 'Second-Hand Rosie' by Christina Jones was published in *Woman's Weekly Fiction Special* in 2002. 'The Dogs Blanket' by Ruth Joseph was published in *Red Stilettos* by Accent Press Ltd in September 2004. 'The Green Man' by Rosemary Laurey was published in *Chat* in May 2004. 'Before I Loved You' by Carolyn Lewis was published in *The Cutting Edge* in July 2002. 'A Racy Little Number' by Carole Matthews was published in *Woman's Own* with kind permission of Ford Fiesta in February 2004. 'The Better Player' by Linda Povey was published in *Take a Break* Fiction Feast in December 2001. 'Heart Cry' by Caroline Praed was published in *Best* in 1995. 'The Association of Bit-Part Players' by Sally Quilford was published on *www.romanceeverafter.com* in June 2004. 'Protesting' by Angie Quinn was published by *Cambrensis* in December 2004. 'Magnetic Attraction' by Ginny Swart was published in *You Magazine* (South Africa) in December 2003. 'Patchwork' by Fiona Walker was published in *Woman's Own* in 2004. 'Remember William Morris' by Jane Wenham-Jones was published in *My Weekly* in November 2002. A version of 'Dancers' by Dawn Wingfield was published by *Mocha Memoirs* in November 2003.

Foreword

I'm absolutely delighted to be supporting the British Heart Foundation by welcoming you to this fantastically entertaining book!

Thank you very much for supporting this great charity by your purchase – £1 from each sale will go towards the British Heart Foundation's vital work in fighting heart disease, the UK's biggest single killer of men and women.

It's a sad fact that each year nearly one in every two women who dies will do so from heart and blood vessel disease. As well as looking after our own hearts by taking regular exercise and eating healthily, it's vital that we all help the British Heart Foundation to continue its crucial work in researching cures and caring for heart patients, through wonderful schemes like their network of Heart Nurses. Once you have finished reading these exciting stories, please take a minute to fill in the donation form at the back!

Have a very enjoyable read!

Nancy Sorrell
Model

Contents

Dream Date	Jan Jones	1
Bedtime Story	Simon Brooke	11
Remember William Morris	Jane Wenham-Jones	23
Patchwork	Fiona Walker	31
Breakfast At Tesco's	Sarah Harrison	37
Best Foot Forward	Sue Houghton	47
Secret Valentine	Lauren McCrossan	55
Swalec Man	Catherine Merriman	65
Protesting	Angie Quinn	71
Before I Loved You	Carolyn Lewis	77
A Lullaby For Micky Marshmallow	Penny Alexander	85
Yin And Yang	Jill Steeples	95
Fish In The Sea	Lynne Barrett-Lee	101
A Racy Little Number	Carole Matthews	115
February Blossoms	Josephine Hammond	121
The Guitar Man	Della Galton	127
The Better Player	Linda Povey	137
Rendezvous	Jackie Winter	141
I'm Not Your PA and I'll Cry If I Want To	Phil Trenfield	145
That Old Magic	Rachel Sargeant	153
Memories	Gemma Forbes	159

Games People Play	Zoë Harcombe	167
Second-hand Rosie	Christina Jones	173
Adonis	Dawn Hudd	183
Breaking The Chain	Rachel Loosmore	187
A Foreign Affair	Kate Roberts	191
Magnetic Attraction	Ginny Swart	201
Dancers	Dawn Wingfield	209
The Green Man	Rosemary Laurey	213
The Spice Of Life	Diana Appleyard	219
Mapping Out The Future	Christina Emberson	227
The Dog's Blanket	Ruth Joseph	231
Mad For Seafood Risotto	Mo McAuley	239
Heart Cry	Caroline Praed	251
Seascape	Jane Bidder	255
Betty Christine, The Thug and James Bond	Suzanne Gillespie	263
The Association Of Bit-Part Players	Sally Quilford	267
Beach Watch	Nina Tucknott	275
Biographies		279
A Message From British Heart Foundation		287

Dream Date

Jan Jones

It's not every day you open your front door to find Fitzwilliam Darcy on the doorstep.

When Chrissie re-opened the door thirty seconds later, he was still there, a little puzzled at having it shut so unceremoniously in his face, but unfailingly courteous for all that. "Chrissie Taylor?" he said.

Chrissie took one look at his swallow-tailed coat, embroidered waistcoat, snowy white cravat and perfectly moulded dark trousers and croaked, "Er – yes –"

His face cleared. "Excellent. I'm your dream date."

You're not kidding, was Chrissie's first coherent thought. God, he's gorgeous, was her second. Her third, sadly, was that it had to be a mistake. In a daze, she took the armful of roses he presented to her. Her eyes went past him to a gently purring car by the side of the kerb. It was sleek, black and very, very long. Anyone else wanting to see her tonight would have to park four doors down.

"You did get the letter, did you? The one telling you you'd won the competition?"

Over the years Chrissie had won many competitions – for everything from a month's supply of breakfast cereal to a set of lacy underwear she didn't dare wear even in the privacy of her own bedroom. "Oh yes," she lied instantly.

It *wasn't* a mistake! He really was her Dream Date! The letter had probably been in the batch of mail that the dog had chewed up a fortnight ago. At the time she had been too furious with her husband for telling her that he'd agreed to go on a team-building exercise in Scotland over Valentine's week (from the safety of the doorstep on his way to work) to do more than sweep the pieces of soggy post into the bin.

"Ah," said Mr Darcy, relieved. "Only you don't seem to be very..."

"What? Oh, *this*!" Chrissie indicated her t-shirt and jeans. She frantically ran excuses past her brain, terrified that he might leave after all. "I, ah, I was waiting until I got the kids out of the house before changing. Won't you come into the lounge and sit down for a moment? I'm afraid it's a bit full of Lego."

He gave her a perfectly wonderful smile. "That's fine. I am yours to command for the evening."

Chrissie's legs very nearly gave way. They nearly gave way even more as he brushed past her in the narrow hall. There were powerful muscles lurking under that linen shirt. She caught herself wondering if 'hers to command' meant that she could accidentally tip the water from the vase of roses over him just to complete the *Pride & Prejudice* fantasy. "Careful where you sit," she warned him. "My daughter tends to leave stickers and glue everywhere."

He took her hand. "Don't apologise," he said and carried her fingers to his lips. "It's a delightful room."

For something so chaste and polite, the kiss sent an astonishing assortment of feelings racing through Chrissie's body. There was 'God, it's really true, I've really won Mr Darcy for the evening' to 'Chrissie, you're *married*, tell him to go away at once' to 'Wow, that felt wonderful. I wonder if he's going to do it again?'

She hurtled upstairs to her son's bedroom without giving herself time to think. "Spike, you are officially ungrounded. On mature reflection, my last remaining bottle of expensive bubble bath was the perfect thing to use to wash the dog and you were absolutely right – the bathroom floor did need cleaning. Grab your stuff and the dog's biscuits and get the pair of you round to that sleepover straight away."

The next stop was Star's room, where Chrissie stuffed an assortment of clothes and cuddly toys into a bag and then dragged her daughter outside with her trainers still unlaced just as her friend turned up to collect her for Brownies.

"My God," said Miranda, looking at the stretched limo. "What's that?"

"It's yours to take the girls to Brownies in, if you'll also keep Star overnight for me."

"I thought Neil wasn't getting back until tomorrow? You were furious about him missing Valentine's Day."

"He isn't and I am. But I've got Mr Darcy sitting in my lounge at this very minute claiming that I've won him as my Dream Date for the evening."

Miranda's mouth fell open. "Mr Darcy? Really?"

"Well, obviously not *actually* Colin Firth. But he's a damn near perfect look-alike with the hair and the eyes and everything and he's wearing a dinner jacket and he's given me roses and he's got this driver and this car *and he's sitting in my lounge.*"

"Give me Star's stuff and don't do anything I wouldn't do. Into the limo, girls. Let's go and knock Brown Owl's eye out."

One down, one to go, thought Chrissie, still ramming her 'but you're *married*' wail down where she couldn't hear it. And on the thought, the dog bounded joyously out of the house in all his fuchsia-and-geranium-smelling glory dragging Spike behind him. "See you tomorrow!" Chrissie called.

In the lounge, Mr Darcy was leafing through Lego instructions.

"I – er – I won't be long," said Chrissie.

He looked up and smiled into her eyes. "Plenty of time," he said. "The table isn't booked until eight. Remember to wear something you can dance in, won't you?"

Chrissie made a faint whimpering sound and dashed back upstairs before her conscience got the upper hand. She'd won the competition, hadn't she? And besides, it was Neil's own fault for not being here on Valentine's Day. And it would only be dinner and dancing anyway. She tried to remember what she'd written on the entry form.

Question: In twenty words or less, what would be your dream date and with whom?

Answer: Dinner in a five-star restaurant with Mr Darcy. Dancing on the lawn. And maybe one parting kiss by moonlight...

Chrissie fanned her heated face, tore off her clothes, leapt in and out of the shower (thank God she'd waxed last week), and opened her wardrobe door.

What did one wear for an evening with Mr Darcy?

Not what she'd worn to Neil's firm's dinner dance. That dress said 'wife of underpaid executive who is willing to work all the hours God sends (*and* get sent on team-building trips to flaming Scotland during Valentine's week) in order to move up the corporate ladder'. The next dress along was her 'dutiful daughter-in-law' one. Then there was 'overweight, but trying not to show it', 'pregnant and trying not to show it'...

There had to be *something* she could wear! She had Mr Darcy downstairs in full Regency gear and a stretched limo outside! Frantically, Chrissie slammed the clothes along the rail. And stopped. She *did* have something that might possibly do but it would have been a lot easier to put it on with a glass or two of wine inside her.

Chrissie murmured an apology to Neil and slid into her sexy lace underwear. From the back of the wardrobe she pulled out an Empire-line nightie given to her by a hopelessly romantic godmother who had no idea what living with two boisterous children and a hyperactive dog did to one's sex life. It was made from heavyweight cream satin, was far too glamorous to sleep in, and consequently had never been worn. From the same godmother, she had a cream pashmina, light as a cobweb and warm as duck's down. Silver roses earrings, matching necklace, and she was ready.

"You look breathtaking," said Mr Darcy, standing up.

He looked pretty good himself, all lean and power-held-in-check. It was no wonder these fashions hadn't lasted – they were far too dangerous to be allowed out! He was pure smouldering male within a civilised exterior. He kissed her hand again, slower this time, then leaned past her shoulder. Chrissie's heart thumped with startled anticipation. Her lips had actually parted before she realised he was stripping the thorns off one of his roses before tucking it with firm, assured fingers into her hair. Down, girl, she told herself shakily.

Inside the limo, there were vast acres of coffee-coloured leather, soft romantic music and an ice-bucket.

"Champagne?" he murmured.

Chrissie's outfit was feeling more like a nightdress with every passing second. "Yes, please," she said, and downed it in one.

By the time they got to the roundabout on the edge of town, she'd had two more glasses and was feeling much more confident about her right to enjoy the prize she'd won. "Do you do this often?" she asked.

"Take beautiful, sexy women out to dinner? Not often, no. Refill?"

Chrissie sighed happily and held out her glass.

She floated into the restaurant on his arm. There was more champagne. Also a photographer from the competition people. Corks popped, light bulbs flashed, and hundreds of streamers and glittery stars showered around them. She was fed slivers of melon and peach, a mouthful of paté, chicken so tender it melted on her tongue and a raspberry sorbet which pierced her alcoholic haze with surprise. Then came rounds of pork coated with Madeira sauce, vegetables to die for and finally spoonfuls of something gloriously chocolaty and trufflish and frantic with cream. In between eating she told him about Neil and Spike and Star and her workaday life and how she didn't really suppose it would have been any different if she'd been born in Regency times except that the clothes were so gorgeous and by the way had anyone ever told him how absolutely spectacular and knee-trembling he looked dressed like that?

The last waiter took away the final dish. Chrissie sighed. "That was the most wonderful meal I have ever eaten." She laid her hand on his sleeve and felt the muscles move underneath the cloth. "Thank you so much."

His sensuous brown eyes smiled down at her. "It wasn't as wonderful as you," he said. "Shall we dance?"

"I'd love to, but I'm not sure I can stand."

He slipped an arm around her waist and drew her upright. "Of course you can. You can do anything. It's your night."

He was right. Chrissie felt as light and insubstantial as gossamer as she waltzed around the room in his arms.

"What about you?" she asked. "What are your hopes? What are your dreams? What do you want from life?"

"To be happy," he said lightly. "To have a home and a dog and two children. To have Lego and stickers all over the floor and a partner who is still cross about my missing Valentine's Day after twelve years together."

Chrissie felt tears prickle her eyes. "That's so beautiful," she said.

"The door to the terrace is open," he replied, "and I think there's a lawn. Shall we dance out there?"

On the way back in the limo, he felt solid and comfortable and warm and not quite familiar. Chrissie stirred sleepily against him. "You aren't Neil," she said.

In the glow of the street lamps she saw him stretch out long legs, saw his mouth flash into a smile. "No," he said. "Neil is one lucky man."

They stood on the doorstep in the moonlight. His voice was husky as he linked his arms around her waist. "One parting kiss?" he said.

She slid her palms up his close-fitting sleeves and over the intricacies of his cravat. "Oh, yes, please," she breathed.

They kissed. He tasted of champagne and melon and Madeira sauce and chocolate. As she responded, he held her tighter, the kiss becoming deeper, less a goodbye than a hello. Chrissie felt empowered, enraptured, beautiful and wonderful and desirable. His hands moved over the heavy cream satin like a lover's, smoothing it to her contours. She rubbed against him and threaded her fingers through his hair. Tiny, glittery stars pattered around them.

She sighed as they came reluctantly apart. "I suppose a wet shirt is out of the question, is it?"

Chrissie woke up slowly, her head muzzy with champagne bubbles and drifting magic. Daylight filtered around the edges of the curtains. How lovely, just once, to wake up slowly and sensuously with a warm male body beside you and no children around to demand attention.

A warm male body? Chrissie's eyes snapped open in shock. Oh God, she hadn't – surely she hadn't–?

Quick. Rerun last night. Champagne, yes. Glorious food, yes. More champagne. Dancing on the lawn. Limo. Goodnight kiss. Sudden inability to stand. Being carried upstairs. Another goodnight kiss. A *lot* of goodnight kiss. Her saying, this is really a nightdress. Him saying, that's handy.

Oh, no! She couldn't have! Could she?

Small tingles all over her body were telling her she had. Her memory had completely gone. Totally, completely and absolutely departed. Dear God, had the limo been parked outside all night?

Slowly, very slowly, with her heart in her mouth, she turned over and slid a hand across the warm, male hip next to her.

"Mmm. Morning, sweetheart."

Neil! Thank God. Oh, thank God. Her heart was thumping so hard she was surprised he couldn't feel it.

He rolled over and pulled her close. "Happy after-Valentine's Day. Sorry I couldn't get back for dinner yesterday."

"It's okay," she said, limp with relief.

He chuckled, nuzzling her neck, his hands moving down to stroke other parts of her. "Although maybe I should go away more often," he said slyly. "That was a hell of a reception you gave me last night."

It was? *It was?*

"I, um, I missed you," she said.

"So I gathered. You want to remind me just how much again?"

Afterwards she dressed slowly, looking out of the window to where the limo had been. She was hopelessly confused now. Had everything after the goodnight kiss been Neil? Or a dream? Erotic, champagne-fuelled imaginings? She'd never know.

Neil came back into the bedroom, towelling his hair dry, naked except for a pair of boxers. His chest was every bit as gorgeous as Mr Darcy's. How had she ever thought a man needed Regency dress to be sexy?

"I see our daughter's been using the shower again," he said. "It beats me why she can't keep her collage stuff on the paper instead of gluing it all over her body. That shower tray was *full* of tiny glittering stars..."

Bedtime Story

Simon Brooke

It was every man's dream, well, every New Man's dream, anyway: quality time alone with my son at a luxury hotel which, by coincidence, was hosting a swimwear catalogue shoot.

The negotiations with my ex-wife to enable me to take Tom away for a week made a West Bank peace summit look like a picnic but we'd finally got there. It wasn't that Jane and I actually fought, it was just that in the nine years we'd been together – four spent thinking about marriage, one when we couldn't quite believe we'd done it, and another four regretting that we hadn't just left well alone – she had decided that I was completely impractical and incompetent and shouldn't really be allowed to go abroad myself, let alone in charge of a hyper-active four year old.

"Mummy says I've got to look after you," said Tom very seriously after he had been dropped off at my flat with a bag that was bigger than him.

"We'll look after each other," I told him, suddenly feeling slightly overwhelmed with the responsibility I had taken on.

In fact we arrived in Corfu and got to the hotel in one piece but when the receptionist explained apologetically that there was a photo shoot taking place in the hotel and so the pool area might be rather busy with models, I got her to repeat her comment to make sure that I had heard it right. Conclusive proof came when the most beautiful woman I had ever seen outside a magazine suddenly appeared beside me. Her long blond hair contrasted with her deeply tanned skin. She ruffled Tom's hair.

"Hallo, there," she said to him in a Scandinavian accent. Tom looked unimpressed and asked me if we could go in the pool now. The girl laughed luxuriously and said: "What a good idea. The water's beautiful. Makes you want to rip your clothes off and dive straight in." Then she picked up her room key, shot me a devastating smile, and left us.

After our swim and some supper I carried Tom up to our room, put his Nemo pyjamas on him and slipped him into bed. He looked tiny in the double bed. Then I took a cold beer from the mini bar and sat out on the balcony listening to the rhythmic scrape of the cicadas.

The next morning Tom was up predictably early and we were in the pool while the guy was still hoovering it. Tom had perfected a kind of manic, absurdly inefficient doggy paddle that I had never seen before and it made me realise how much of his life was unknown to me despite our regular outings.

We had breakfast: muesli and coffee for me and three chocolate croissants for him – well, were we on holiday or weren't we?

By mid-morning the models had materialised at the pool. As they lazed around, waiting for their next shot, I did my best to impress – back flip dive (ouch!) and some shameless posing of my own in my newly-acquired Gucci trunks. I made sure that they saw my reading matter too – a bit of Nietzche and a biography of Peter the Great. Brains and brawn, you see.

Thank goodness Jane wasn't around to ruin it all with comments like 'Your nose is looking very red' and, 'I found the Imodium in case you need it,' as she had on our honeymoon. But it was Tom who was the real centre of attention. As he splashed around in his arm bands or pushed his plastic boat along in the kids' pool, a selection of the world's most beautiful women crowded around him, laughing adoringly. He regarded them with a mixture of nonchalance and indulgence, especially when they admitted they knew nothing about Buzz Lightyear.

I hadn't been in a situation like this since I'd been on the pull at the university bar with my best mate Nick who, unfortunately for me, happened to be not only rather handsome but also something of a wit and a genius at Jim Bowen impressions.

After the first few days I began to forget about work and slipped into that kind of mindless, holiday indolence in which even trying to decide between a drink or a swim becomes too arduous. Tom had further entrenched his position as Number One Babe Magnet. I decided that it was time I saw a bit of the action and so I started making small talk with the girl we had met on our arrival, who had also become the leader of Tom's fan club. She was called Anna and she was Swedish, I discovered. Eventually, I plucked up the courage to ask whether she might want to have a drink that evening.

"Just you and me – no Tom," I found myself explaining, apologetically.

"Sure," she smiled, shaking her blonde hair free of a bandana and slipping her sunglasses off. "That would be great."

We arranged to meet in the bar at seven. As she sashayed away from me towards the lift I found myself overcome with excitement – and guilt.

"It's just for one night," I told Tom as I bathed him a few hours later. "A nice lady will come and read you a story."

In fact, the hotel's baby-sitter turned out to be a sullen seventeen-year-old who looked like she'd be much happier watching repeats of *Friends* and demolishing a packet of Maltesers than entertaining a lively four-year-old. If Anna and I promised to be a match made in heaven, Tom and his prospective guardian were clearly a pairing from hell. But, as I had told Tom, it was just one night.

I gazed at my son who was sitting up in bed holding his favourite rabbit and giving me a mournful look.

"Don't fancy yours, mate, either," I whispered. "But look, if I read you a story will you go to sleep?" It was now five to seven.

After relating two adventures of Thomas the Tank Engine at break-neck speed I kissed Tom gently on the forehead, smiled weakly at his prison guard and got up to leave.

"Daddeee." His chin wobbled and he blinked back tears.

"Just this one night," I pleaded, stroking his blond hair. "Tomorrow we'll... erm... have ice cream for breakfast." Bribery mixed with revenge on his health-freak mother – it seemed too perfect. And it was. "Another storeee!" I checked my watch. Nearly a quarter past seven.

"OK, OK, one more and then you go to sleep." I finally left the room at gone seven thirty.

When I finally found her, Anna was sitting in a chair gazing out at the sea and absent-mindedly stirring the remains of her drink with a straw. She looked more lovely than ever. I dived down on to the seat beside her and gasped: "I'm so sorry."

She looked slightly startled. "Oh, that's okay, I was just enjoying the view. Look, do you think that's a fishing boat out there?" It could have been a UFO for all I cared but I was just relieved that she wasn't cross with me. We speculated for a moment and then a waiter appeared.

"Can I get you another drink?" I asked.

She looked at the dregs in her glass.

"Mmm. Vodka and cranberry, please."

"Make that two," I told the waiter. I sighed, realising how exhausted I was after the last hour or so of negotiations and emotional blackmail.

"Where is Tom? In bed?" asked Anna, turning towards me.

"Yes," I said. "Sorry, that's why I was late. He wasn't very keen on being left on his own. Well, not on his own, obviously. What kind of father would do a thing like that? He's got a baby-sitter with him."

"Oh, I see. Is she reading him bedtime stories?"

"I think she's probably reading him the Riot Act." Anna frowned slightly, confused. "I don't think either of them is very pleased to be left alone together," I explained.

"What's the matter? Shall we go up and see him?"

"No," I said, a bit too quickly. "I mean, he's probably asleep by now. Don't worry. Anyway, how did the shoot go today?"

Anna rolled her large blue eyes. "I think they finally got the pictures they wanted but it's just so boring I nearly finished a whole book today."

"What were you reading?"

"Oh, it's about the development of Restoration comedy in seventeenth century England."

I must have looked so surprised that she laughed. "I'm doing a degree in English literature."

"Really?"

Our drinks arrived.

"Yes, I only do the modelling thing during the holidays."

I tried to think of something to say that didn't sound patronising. I failed. "I didn't realise, I just assumed… that...you were..."

"A complete air head."

"Oh, no, God no. I assumed that you were just a full time model."

"Oh, I'd go mad with boredom," said Anna, taking a sip of her drink. "I'm what you'd call a mature student. I've been a primary school teacher and then an au pair in England."

"Ah, that would explain your perfect English."

She laughed and sipped her drink. "You flatter me. But, tell me, what do you do, for work, I mean?"

"I'm a graphic designer," I explained. "I work for a small consultancy in Leeds. You know, in the north of England."

"Oh," she said. "How interesting." She pointed to herself. "Words," and then to me: "Pictures."

"Oh, yeah, I suppose we sort of complement each other," I said.

There was a pause after this clunky chat-up line until she leaned further towards me and said, "I'm always fascinated by people who think visually." Her lips were now inches away from mine and I could smell her perfume and the remains of suntan lotion on her flawless, tanned skin.

"Depends how your brain works," I whispered. "Just like a talent for words, I suppose."

"Two such different ways of looking at the world," she said, her eyes darting over my face. We studied each other for a moment and I was just contemplating making a move when she asked: "Are you hungry?"

We ate sea food and drank ice-cold Retsina on the terrace, the night breeze catching gently at the table cloth. Then I suggested a stroll along the beach.

The sand was still warm from the sun, and powder soft. She put one hand on my shoulder as she slipped off her sandals. I took mine off too and we walked along in silence.

The waves slapped gently at the shore and then pulled away slowly, as if reluctant to leave it. Lights from cafés and restaurants sparkled along one side. I don't know how far we walked but eventually they petered out and finally we came to an outcrop of rock that prevented us from going any further.

I hated it for ending this magical, silent promenade but then Anna turned to me. I cupped her face in my hand and kissed her. She led me by the hand to a sandy cove which was hidden from view. We had become shadows in the moonlight. She lay down on the sand and I lay down next to her. We kissed again as she ran her fingers down my back. But then she paused. I looked down at her. Her eyes were wide and inquisitive. Of course, she was right –

"I'm sorry, but I was just thinking about the little fella," she said. As I hovered over her she pushed my dark, unruly mass of hair away from my forehead and traced a line down my cheek to my mouth. I bit her finger softly. But when she laughed gently I knew that we weren't going to carry on.

"Sorry," she said. "But it's just that you looked so much like him for a moment then. You know – when he's about to jump in the pool with his arm bands on and he's concentrating so hard."

Oh, right. That 'little fella'. Thinking about your parents is supposed to be ultimate passion killer but I found that Tom had the same effect. To be honest Tom and sex are probably the two things I think about most on a daily basis – apart from Leeds United, that is – but, until now, never they'd never entered my mind simultaneously. The combination clashed horribly. It was weird, disturbing. I rolled over on to the sand next to her. We lay in silence for a moment looking up at the stars.

"Are you cross?" She was leaning over me now.

I smiled. "Of course not," I said, truthfully. "How could I be cross with you?"

She looked embarrassed. "It suddenly occurred to me… here we are, having such a... such a nice time and poor little Tom is on his own." A nice time? I wasn't having a nice time, I was having one of the most erotic experiences of my life.

"Oh, I'm sure he's okay. He's got someone looking after him."

Anna chewed her lip for a second. "But he does not like her, you said."

"I didn't say that, she's just..." I could suddenly see Tom's little face again looking up beseechingly at me as I backed out of the room.

"Shall we just go and see how he's doing?" asked Anna.

"Oh, he'll be fine," I said, running a hand down her arm. "I told the girl that if there was any problem at all she should ring my mobile."

I reached over to pick up my shirt and produce the supporting evidence for my consideration and ingenuity. Except that it wasn't there. I checked my trouser pockets but every one seemed cruelly flat. Amid the fuss of leaving the room I must have forgotten it or, worse still, it had fallen out onto the sand. I gazed around desperately but it was just too dark to see anything.

"Have you lost your phone?"

"Erm, yes, it must back in the room – or somewhere."

She leapt up. "Quick, let's go back and check." I was torn. The air was scented with pine needles and wild oregano and Anna had looked so stunning in the moonlight. And yet Tom was in his cell with no way of contacting me. Oh, no!

"Come on," I said, getting up. We walked back in silence again but slightly faster. "You wait there," I said when we got back to the terrace of the hotel. "I'll just dash up and check on him."

I sprinted for the lifts and moments later I was slipping my key card into the door and opening it. The babysitter looked round at me forlornly, a handful of Pringles suspended mid air as she watched the near silent TV. I looked over at Tom. He was coiled up in the sheets, sleeping soundly.

"Hi," I said.

"Hi," she said. "Everything okay?".

"Just looking for my mobile." Glancing round I saw it on the dressing table. "Here it is," I said, a little unnecessarily. I grabbed it and made for the door. But as I turned the handle I heard: "Daddeee."

I sighed deeply and turned round. His eyes were narrowed with sleep – and resentment.

"OK, soldier," I smiled. "See you in the morning." I turned back again.

"Daddee, where're you going?"

Oh, Tom, darling, please. Just this one night. "I'll, er, be back in a minute – now go back to sleep."

His mouth turned down at the edges and his chin wobbled. I read him more Thomas followed by extracts from a book about dinosaurs. I was just pointing out a stegosaurus when I noticed that his eyes were closed. I stood up, cast the baby-sitter an apologetic glance and slipped out.

Anna was staring out at the sea again only this time without a drink. She looked beautiful but tired and when she said that she was going to bed I was hardly surprised. I didn't even drop a hint about joining her.

"I'm sorry about tonight," I said. I'd buggered up her evening as well as Tom's. I waited for a reaction and then said: "I just wanted to… "

"Have sex with a model?" She carried on looking straight ahead.

"No," I said, horrified. What the hell was I hoping for then?

"Discuss restoration comedy?" she asked helpfully. I opened my mouth to say something but gave up. We sat in silence for a while then I found myself saying: "Aghh, what a mess. I'm sorry."

The sound of the waves that had been so beautiful earlier now seemed harsh and desperate. Eventually Anna said: "Tough having a kid around when you're trying to score."

Looking round sharply I thought I saw a smile flicker over her lips. Was she teasing? I had to believe it.

"Especially when he's so much more popular with women than I am," I muttered. She was now smiling gently. She reached out and curled my hair thoughtfully in her fingers.

"You're a good father," she said.

"Oh, God, no, I'm terrible," I wailed. "Really, really crap." If only she'd seen Tom's face a moment ago.

"Listen, don't worry about tonight – it was just one of those things. I had a lovely time, anyway." I must have looked rather sceptical. "No, I meant that I've seen the way you play with him in the pool and look after him all day. Really, you're so patient. You give him your time which is more than so many fathers do. When I was au pairing I met fathers who thought that buying their kids some movie spin-off toy every week was all they had to do."

"I know but I really wanted to spend some time with you."

"I wanted to, as well." She smiled, obviously knowing exactly what I was thinking. "But I couldn't bear to think that I was coming between you and your son."

"Oh, but you weren't," said the irresponsible father.

She hushed me with a finger. "It felt like it," she said. "As soon as I saw that look on your face I began to think of Tom and, you know, I sort of missed him." I looked at her in silence. "You're a good father but you must accept that you do have responsibilities." I loved her even more for her common sense. Then she gave me a quick kiss on the lips, stood up and yawned. "Shoot's over. I'm leaving tomorrow." I was stunned. "But not till lunch time."

She smiled at me. "I'll see you at the pool before I go."

"Yeah," I said. "We'll both be there."

"He's a lovely kid," she said. "You're a very lucky man." I stood up too, thinking about what might have been and now never would be. "Yes," I said. "I know."

Remember William Morris

Jane Wenham-Jones

Remember William Morris. That's what the article said. Have nothing in your home that you do not know to be useful or think to be beautiful.

"Well then!" I said aloud, trying to ignore the pang I felt at the memory of Daniel lounging on my sofa. I grasped the lime-and-pink patterned teapot his mother had given me, and spoke to it severely. "And you can go too!"

I'd read the magazine at just the right time, while I was curled up with an empty wine glass in a sea of soggy tissues and chocolate wrappers, feeling that my life was irrevocably in ruins. I was ripe for the power of the life-changing moment, the reversal of my fortunes, the quick fix that would give me a sparkling new future.

And it seemed – according to the aptly named Hester Barren, thrower-away of useless-and-ugly articles extraordinaire – that the only things standing between me and such fulfilment were two dustbin-liners and a cardboard box. 'They will change your life!' Hester's words rang in my ears as I rooted about in the cupboard in a vain search for either.

For once you started 'decluttering', her article assured me, your whole life changed. Freed from the restriction of emotional baggage in the form of unnecessary possessions, you felt brighter, looked younger and rediscovered joy. The entire world became your oyster, with exciting new challenges just waiting to present themselves…

Make Space! That was the motto. Create space in your mind, bring light to your life and anything can happen…

As all that had happened since I'd found out that Daniel's 'Media Studies' evening class consisted of studying the bedroom of a red-haired stick-insect, was that I'd spent a lot of time crying and wondering why my life was so dreadful, anything seemed worth a try. If throwing away a few superfluous ornaments would bring back happiness, I was only too willing to give it a whirl.

Hester recommended starting by throwing out your laddered tights (mine ran to three carrier bags) and then building up to the things you thought you held more dear. Here you had to be honest. 'How often do you read those books on your shelves?' she asked bossily.

Clearly not often enough, I thought picking up the *Seven-day Guide to a Smaller Bottom,*

'…use those casserole dishes?' Never, I admitted, pushing the pizza packet into the bin.

'…watch those videos you recorded years ago?' I scowled as I dropped *Love Story* on top of *It's a Wonderful Life* and yet another photograph of the traitorous Daniel.

'You will start to feel more positive from the first fully-filled sack,' said Hester. (So far my back simply hurt.) But I kept trying.

"New beginnings," I chanted to myself as I hurled a vile green dress I'd always hated into the charity bag. "Let go of the past," I repeated as I dropped a pink padded photo frame containing a picture of Daniel with sunburn into the rubbish sack. "And open yourself to fresh possibilities," I quoted as I lowered the hideous gold dinner service presented by Auntie Betty into the Try-to-Sell box.

Hester recommended a small personal reward when one had been steadily throwing away for a week. A small bunch of flowers or a glass of wine, were her suggestions (I drank most of the bottle). She also urged telling others about the new you. 'This is a good moment to share your new feelings with someone else. Gain validation…'

"You're mad," said my friend Karen when I phoned her.

"Are you over-tired?" asked my mother anxiously, arriving to find me emptying the airing cupboard. "You look a bit pale."

"Blimey!" said the guy in the second-hand shop. "You're having a right clear-out there, love, aren't you!"

"There's more," I gasped as I staggered back from the car with another crate. "I'll be back tomorrow."

For I had to admit that I had got into it. I did feel much less miserable not having Daniel's cheating face leering at me from every surface, and positively cheered by the sight of all the ancient aunts' unspeakable Christmas presents being firmly despatched from my flat.

Hester said one should be methodical. Shelf by shelf, drawer by drawer, a room at a time. Clearing and throwing away anything you didn't really need. I'd emptied the kitchen and couldn't wait to get my hands on the living room.

"Are you sure?" asked Mr Anything-Bought-and-Sold as I fell through his door under a weight of coffee mugs and saucepans. "Won't you need them?" he enquired.

For a moment a lump formed in my throat. "Not when you're back to cooking for one," I said self-pityingly.

"Ah," he said, knowingly. ""Tough, that."

I shook my head, feeling thoroughly sorry for myself. Then I remembered. "I am making Space!" I said smugly. "Physical space leads to mental space leads to positive energies…"

“Certainly got plenty of space in here,” he said the following week, as he walked through my bare kitchen on his way to collect the sofa. “Keep a few things, love, you don’t want to go too far.”

But I didn't want any of my old life now.

That evening I sat on my single bean bag in the middle of an expanse of empty carpet and contemplated the single silver candle I found so pleasing to the eye.

I waited to feel a surge of joy and power.

Nothing happened. Maybe I needed to finish the bedroom first.

“Can’t be much left now,” said Mr Second-hand (call me Andy) when I took in the last of the books. “Feeling any better?”

“Have you sold it all already?” I asked hastily, pointing to the end of the shop where my life’s possessions had been tastefully displayed only a few days earlier.

“Goes quickly, good stuff like that,” said Andy diffidently, fiddling with a purple china cat a well-meaning friend of my mother had given me when I passed my driving test and which had always given me the shivers. “Chap who took it has just bought a new flat,” he said. “And it's hardly got a thing in it.”

“Neither has yours!” shrieked Karen when she found she had to sit on the floor. “Where are all the chairs?”

"This is minimalism," I told her loftily. Daniel had said the stick-insect's flat was minimalist – I shook my head to dispel the image of the two of them entwined on the black futon against stark white walls, the only colour provided by a single orchid…

"It looks like you've been burgled," said Karen. "What about that pot I gave you last Christmas and oh – my god – the TV's gone!"

"Daniel always said I kept too much junk," I said sadly. "That was the problem – I was surrounded by clutter in a stagnant life. No wonder he went off and found someone more interesting."

"Daniel was a control freak," said Karen firmly. "You can't sit in here with just a cushion and a pot plant. "Get it all back!"

"I've sold it to Andy," I said.

"Well go and un-sell it. "

"It's probably all gone – he sold the last lot the same day I took it in. Same bloke bought it all apparently. Andy said this guy had just split up too and didn't have anything. Funny, eh?" I added, a lump in my throat.

"You should have asked for his phone number," said Karen, crossly.

"Andy asked me if I'd like to go out actually," I said shyly.

"And?" Karen demanded.

"I told him we'd be in Paris!"

Karen beamed and leapt to her feet. "Yes, I'd better go and pack a bag," she said. "I suppose you've still got one? Just think, this time tomorrow – Gay Paris!"

I nodded. Karen had made all the arrangements weeks ago and Daniel had been dead keen for me to have a weekend away – no wonder, the Rat! – but what with everything I'd barely given it a thought since. Karen, however, was hopping with excitement. "We'll find a couple of sexy Frenchmen," she said, narrowing her eyes. "Get to bed early – I'll see you at six."

I smiled. A weekend away with Karen would be fun. I looked around my bleak flat – it was beginning to look a bit cheerless even to me.

"And don't forget your passport…" she called gaily as she swung away down the stairs.

"I won't," I called back. I knew exactly where my passport was – in the folder with my driving licence and birth certificate that never strayed from… I clapped my hand to my mouth. The second-hand leather-topped desk Daniel and I had bought for a song from the small ads in the local paper. The desk that I had sold to Andy three days before…

Oh God. I'd emptied all the drawers but completely forgotten about the little cupboard underneath where your knees fitted. Would he have sold it already? I looked at the clock. He would have shut up shop hours ago. But this was an emergency. Karen would kill me if I let her down. I got my coat on.

The lights were all off in the shop. I cupped my hands around my eyes and squinted through the glass. There were various dark shapes of furniture at the back but I couldn't make out if any of them was my desk. I looked up at the window above. A soft light glowed behind the blinds. There was a bell on the door leading to the flat upstairs. Taking a deep breath I rang it.

Andy opened the door in jeans and a floppy T-shirt. He looked startled, then pleased. "Hi," he said grinning. "Changed your mind about that drink?" His eyes looked very green in the hall light.

"Have you sold my desk?" I blurted out anxiously. His face fell.

"Er yes, it um went yesterday."

"Oh god, have you got a number for the person who bought it?"

Andy looked uncomfortable. "Well, no…"

"Oh!" I wailed. "What am I going to do? I must get hold of it."

"Is it sentimental value?" asked Andy sympathetically. "Are you wishing you hadn't sold it?"

"No, no!" I shrieked hysterically. "Karen will murder me!" He looked mystified. "My passport's in it. And I'm getting a train to Paris in the morning." Andy laid a hand on my arm. "You'd better come in."

He seemed ill at ease as he led the way upstairs and pushed open a door. "You can have any of it back…" he said.

I gasped. There, beautifully arranged on a shelf, were a set of glass bottles I'd got last Christmas, next to flowers in a vase that looked very familiar. My desk was in one corner, topped with the green glass lamp I bought when I was a student. My Chinese rug was on the floor. I looked from one of my hand-painted mugs, past the heap of videos I'd seen several times to the ex-cushions on my one-time sofa and noted how much better the throw looked at its new jaunty angle. Everything looked warm and bright and welcoming and I suddenly had a lump in my throat.

Andy had crossed the room and turned the key in the desk cupboard. "Hey, don't worry," he said, seeing my expression. "It's all still here."

I turned to him wonderingly.

"I'd been so busy since I opened the shop, I hadn't had a chance to get anything for up here…" He picked up a jug I'd bought at a boot fair and examined it, not looking at me. "And you've got good taste," he said hurriedly, "and I didn't want to sell it in case you changed your mind and – " he went on in a rush – "I was worried when I saw you sitting all on your own in that bare flat. A lovely girl like you…"

“Bet you didn't keep Daniel's mother's teapot,” I said, trying to joke but finding I was close to tears.

Andy shook his head and smiled. “Would you like a drink?” he said.

“I have to get up ever so early,” I told him. “Yes, please!”

Later he sat next to me on my sofa and poured a little more wine into my glass. “It was a bit drastic wasn't it?”

“I was trying to make a new beginning,” I explained, thinking how lovely my books looked on his shelves. “And Hester Barren…”

“Dreadful dried-up old prune,” he interrupted cheerfully. “Saw her on breakfast TV the other morning, moaning about how she’s never had a man. Kept banging on about that bloke William.”

“Who?” I asked.

He laughed. “Your friend William Morris.”

He put his arms around me and brushed his lips softly across my cheek.

My stomach jolted in a way it hadn't done for an awfully long time and I carefully put my drink back on my coffee table. “What?” I murmured as I snuggled closer. “Never heard of him.”

Patchwork

Fiona Walker

"Jim and I have been going through a bad patch," Babs confessed to her mother.

"That's lovely, darling," came the distracted reply as, on the other end of the phone line, Elspeth anxiously tried to watch *Countdown* with the sound muted.

"We're moving to Cornwall to make a fresh start," Babs told her.

"Mmm – really?"

"I wondered if I can store some things in your house? The cottage Jim's found is tiny."

"What sort of things, darling?"

"Clothes. My old clothes."

Elspeth let out a long sigh and abandoned the conundrum. "Babs, darling, your father and I already have several wardrobes loaded with fashion statements that you refuse to part with."

"I know, I know, and there's honestly not much more I want to bring over," Babs lied, trying not to think of the loft above her filled with rails of tightly crammed hangers, dry-cleaning bags and fabric memories. Then there were the bin-liners full of shoes, drawers of pretty underwear and boxes of costume jewellery.

"Can't you just sell everything?"

"That's what Jim says." Babs' voice was tight with emotion. "But they are my memories. My life."

"You have a life now, darling. You have to let go of the past. It's no wonder poor Jim is so unhappy."

"What about me, Mum? What about my happiness?" Babs rang off tearfully. She went up to the loft and sought sanctuary amongst her lovely clothes – velvet and silk, chiffon and sequin. Here lay all the ghosts of the parties at which she had sparkled throughout her single years, the ravishing Babs Sinclair, society temptress and forerunner amongst 'It' girls. She had been the biggest catch of her generation, feted by eligible bachelors, living a jet set life swathed in designer dresses before marrying for…

…love.

She made her way shakily through the rows of hanging rails to her wedding dress, entombed in cellophane, hanging from the far wall like a chrysalis. Inside was the dress that has transformed her not into a butterfly, but into a dusty moth, the wife of a struggling writer and now the mother of three demanding children.

Lifting the plastic pupa skin, she pressed her face to the cream damask and breathed in the memory of new, true love, her wet cheeks spreading watermarks through the silk.

She still loved Jim with a fierce, rebellious pride that hadn't waned, but she sometimes missed the glamour of her former years so desperately it made her ache. That was why she kept the dresses that reminded her of the past admirers and lovers, an anthology of adulation as descriptive as her husband's prose.

And Jim wrote beautiful books: old-fashioned love stories that had made Babs so humbled by his talent that her heart had almost cracked her ribs with pride. But old-fashioned love stories didn't sell, according to Jim's publishing contacts. They preferred his misanthropic spite – the pre-married, angry young Jim. He'd hardly had a piece of original fiction published in their fifteen years together, surviving instead on soulless freelance work and a succession of dead-end day jobs.

Babs carefully replaced the plastic cover on the wedding dress and drifted between the rails once more, stroking her hand against textiles nostalgically telling of a life – and a dress size – into which she no longer fitted. Her out-of-contextiles, she thought idly.

Here was the red cat-suit she had worn on the rich Arab's yacht the day he'd surprised her with a fleet of dinghies bearing roses. There was the flowered dress she'd worn at Ascot, each bloom hand-sewn by a French couturier. She held it up against her, remembering the way heads had turned as she passed. Even Prince Andrew had raised a beetle brow.

"Mum!" Lizzie screamed from downstairs. "Where *are* you? Granny's here!"

She started in shock, realising that the children were already home from school. She must have been upstairs for hours. And what was her mother doing here?

Elspeth was already helping herself to a gin and tonic. "I bought you a present. Your father's just fetching it in from the car."

"Oh, Mummy." Babs eyes filled with tears as she looked through the window for the inevitable flowers or wine being removed from the Bentley's boot. Her parents were sweethearts.

Instead, she saw a large John Lewis bag.

"It's a sewing machine," Elspeth announced theatrically. "For mending your bad patch – or should that be your cross patch?"

"What *are* you talking about?" Babs glanced at her mother worriedly, wondering whether dementia was setting in.

But Elspeth merely winked a wise blue eye and asked her grandchildren whether they were looking forward to life in Cornwall.

"I'm going to learn to surf," Guy announced excitedly.

"I want a pony." Cora batted imploring eyes at her indulgent grandfather.

"I hope it makes Mum and Dad happy again." Lizzie sighed.

Elspeth hugged her eldest grand-daughter. "Don't worry, darling, they'll patch things up."

Over Lizzie's shoulder, Babs caught her mother's eye and suddenly understood.

The next morning, she unpacked the sewing machine and set it up on the dining room table. Then she took the pinking shears from the dresser and headed upstairs.

Two months after moving to Cornwall, Jim brought Babs breakfast in bed, carefully setting the tray of toast and teacups on the bedspread as she wriggled up on to a pillow.

"You spoil me too much."

"I want to." Jim joined her in bed and poured the tea from the pot. "Which memory did you wake up with this morning?"

"Forgotten," she grinned. "Waking up to you is by far the best thing going."

"Liar," he smiled back, thrusting a piece of toast in her mouth and taking the pile of post from the tray. Amongst it was a letter from his literary agent, expressing interest in the synopsis he had recently sent.

"It's a start." He tried not to look too excited.

Babs chewed madly at her toast, spluttering, "This is the new idea, yes? Harry Potter meets Dorian Gray."

He nodded. "The children's book about a magic quilt made from an old witch's cloaks."

Laughing, Babs threw the toast of her toast slice at him.

"Okay – young witch." He held up his arms. "Young, glamorous, sexy witch with a racy past. Happy?"

She pressed her face to a square of red satin fabric on her beloved bedspread, breathing in the memory of yachts and roses. Curled around her and Jim's bodies was a patchwork canopy of memoirs, a bedspread made from pieces of all her favourite party dresses. It was her anthology of happy, carefree nights and she adored entwining her limbs with Jim's beneath it each night.

"You've weaved magic into our lives one more." He stroked her cheek.

"Sleep carefully because you sleep beneath my dreams," she smiled, pulling several nights of society balls up over their heads and inadvertently knocking their cups of tea over Prince Andrew's admiring glances at Royal Ascot.

Breakfast At Tesco's

Sarah Harrison

I like married woman. I mean I LIKE them, the way other men like blondes or girls in glasses. You might think it would have a deleterious effect on my social life, fancying the unavailable, but it hasn't. I don't let it. To put it at its most brutally simplistic, who'd want to invite all that hassle? I know when I'm well off.

There's just something sexy about women who've thrown their lot in with one man, for life. Leave divorce statistics aside – it's the thought that counts. I don't hide any of this from my girlfriend, Caroline; we do the whole honesty bit. Actually she finds it funny. On more than one recent occasion she's pointed out that if I only played my cards right I could have a married woman of my very own… But that's missing the point. The buzz is admiring from afar.

I'm not talking working wives, either. Jesus, we've got those in the office. Black trouser suits from Next and whingeing for Britain. No, it's the whole *kinder, kirche, kuche* thing I'm into. In a good way. I don't buy that best-man joke: 'Why do brides wear white? Because all domestic appliances are white.' It's offensive. A woman who tends hearth and home for a man – that's sexy.

My office is in north London, but once a week I spend a day at the Milton Keynes branch. I'm driving against the flow of traffic so it's not a bad trip, and I like the change. I don't even have to be in MK till ten, so there's no rush. The first time I stopped off at the out of town superstore it was just to fill up and buy a paper. But I was ahead of myself, so I decided to dive into the café for a Latte and a fag.

What a result! It was nine-fifteen and every young mum you ever dreamed of had come straight from the school gate to do the shopping. I love all that – the toddler in the trolley seat, the scrubbed early-morning face, the furrowed brow, the hair in a scrunchy. Some of them don't have kids with them, and they're in their gym kit – totally gorgeous. There's something totally irresistible about a bit of bouncy un-toned flesh in leggings and a t-shirt. Child-bearing tummy – you can't beat it. And then there are the smart ones – they might be running a little business, or going for a day in town: pearls, jeans, and pointy boots, a sassy look, but teamed with the band of gold that says 'spoken for'…

I know, I know, but it's my little quirk. For fifteen minutes I was in heaven watching these women. All good things must come to an end, though, and MK called. There was one especially nice one, and I managed to help her with her bags to the people-carrier in the car park.

"Thank you so much," she said. "You're a complete star." Single girls don't talk like that. It's as if being married gives women a licence to be sweet. I couldn't get her out of my head.

The following week I timed things so that I was at the supermarket when the café opened at breakfast time. Come on, any six items from the hot menu for £2.50? That's not much to charge the firm who consider me well worth a new

Saab. And what better way to start the day than a good-value fry-up and all those lovely women?

It got to be a habit, a pleasant weekly indulgence. I made sure I did an extra session at the gym to counteract the calories. And I didn't mention it to Caroline. Too specific. Saying "married is sexy" is one thing. "I'm going to this place once a week to watch the married women" is another – altogether too specific. Caroline's gorgeous, an ocean-going babe with a business degree and a great sense of humour – I'd know I was lucky even if everyone didn't keep telling me. No need to rock the boat over what's never going to happen.

It was Week Four that I saw her again – the one whose bags I'd carried. She put her trolley in one of those big lockers – it was absolutely piled high as usual, real hunter-gatherer stuff – and got in the queue for coffee. She was wearing black jeans, white baseball boots, a puffa jacket, nice streaky hair in a pony tail; and wedding ring – I checked. About thirty, probably, but very fresh faced, she could have been ten years younger. Really, really pretty, I'd have noticed her anywhere. She got too warm waiting and took off the jacket. Nice figure in a long-sleeved white t-shirt.

I'd only just begun eating, so there was plenty of time. I was dead chuffed when she came and sat down at the next table! She had a giant cappuccino and an *Independent*. When she took her first mouthful, it left one of those frothy moustaches speckled with chocolate. I watched, and Yess! out came the little pink tongue and swiped the bubbles away. But it must have made her self-conscious because then she picked up a spoon – a full-sized one, because they only do those crap little stirring-sticks – and began scooping the foam off the top. Reading the paper with great attention. Adorable.

That time I did no more than watch. I did notice when she got her trolley out of dock that there was dog food in there, and some of those alphabet potato croquettes. Family sized bubble-bath, Marmite, veg bought loose, not pre-packed, super-economy kitchen towel… it all added up. I followed her out into the car-park and watched her load her stuff into the boot. I wondered what she was thinking. That was one of the attractions – what's going on in a married woman's head when she's doing all that stuff on auto-pilot? Where's the fault line, the join between domesticity and romance? I've always thought there was something heroic about a woman – anyone, actually – who gets on with the unselfish routine stuff every day, without complaint. It shows a kind of nobility, in my opinion, these days, when everyone's hellbent on self-fulfilment and self-esteem and self-you-name-it.

The next week, when I saw her in the queue, I jumped straight in.

"I don't always do this," I said. "But where else can you get a breakfast like this at these prices?"

She laughed. "They should have you in the advertisement – quality and value!"

"Well, it's true."

"It is good. But I have to resist."

I'd have said "You've no need to" but it was a bit early in the game for compliments, so I contented myself with a, "Wish I could."

She was past the cashier first, but I caught her up. "Mind if I join you?"

"Okay."

I could tell she was a bit suspicious. Strange men. Softly, softly. I felt like a horse-whisperer cajoling a nervous mare.

"I'm on my way to work," I said. "I only come out this way once a week, but one sniff of the hash browns and I was sunk."

"Oh well," she said. "Once a week isn't so bad. My diet book says treats are allowed, especially if they keep your morale up."

How right she was. Still, I thought I'd keep the situation safe for her by mentioning Caroline.

"My girlfriend believes in healthy eating, so this is my guilty secret."

"Good for her." I could almost feel the relief, like a rush of warm air.

I took advantage and sent her a grin. "Don't turn me in, will you."

She smiled back. "I won't."

I held out my hand. "Chris Anderson, by the way."

"Gina Lawrence." We shook. Small hand, firm handshake.

I decided to get out while I was ahead, so to speak. Risky strategy, but my intuition was in top form.

"Oh well, better hit the road. It was nice talking to you, Gina. Might see you again."

"You never know," she said. She had that cute, motherly way of speaking.

It became a regular thing. Over the next few weeks I learned that her husband was a GP called Martin. They had a little girl, Sophie, who had just started school, mornings only. Gina came to the supermarket on Thursdays, after dropping Sophie off. She clearly adored her daughter, but I hadn't quite got a handle on Martin. I suspected him of being a boring fart in a sports jacket. Gina had trained as a nurse (be still my beating heart!) and wanted to go back to it eventually, though she said everything had changed even in the few years she'd been out, everything computerised and high-tech, and she'd have a lot of catching up to do. Her favourite film was *The English Patient* and her favourite song ever was 'Fairytale of New York'. She could even forgive Shane McGowan those teeth – any man who could write a song like that would be attractive. The song made her cry even more, apparently, since Kirsty McColl's death. Her eyes actually got a bit teary just talking about it. Her favourite book was *To Kill a Mocking Bird* and she'd voted for it in the 100 Top Books. She liked Italian food, for going out, and Indian food as a takeaway. She didn't shop for clothes often these days, but when she did she always wound up buying another pair of jeans, to which she was addicted. She liked to dance 'properly' as she put it, with a partner, not free-form.

"Does your husband dance?" I asked. I'd seen the husbands at do's, lurking, while their wives boogied up a storm.

"He does," she said, "for me. But it's not really his thing."

"Blokes are more self-conscious than women," I remarked. I was sticking up for myself here, as well as poor old Martin. "And if it's proper dancing we have to lead, and stuff. It's an awful responsibility."

"But if you knew how much we loved it," she said, "you'd try harder. It doesn't need skill, it needs soul."

God, but I liked her.

I suppose I thought it could just go on like that, a little weekly fix of whatever you like to call it – romance, I suppose, as far as I was concerned. I've no idea how she saw it, but she always laughed a lot when we were together, which I took as a good sign. I didn't have any intention of taking it further, I liked the idea of being her little secret, perhaps even her little fantasy. It was fun, and it was nice, and she was gorgeous.

But of course things do change. It was such a cliché. Caroline found the piece of paper in my pocket where I'd written down Gina's favourite stuff.

"What's all this?" she asked. "Your desert island selection…?" Her eye ran down the list. "Hold on, this isn't yours." She gave me a rueful smile. "I don't know whose, but I like her already."

That was Caroline. Not a bit arsey. More in sorrow than in anger. For once I was stuck for words.

"Just tell me something," she said. "Would I be well advised to clear off?"

The more casual and flip she sounded, the more pain she was in.

"No," I said, "she's just a woman I sometimes have a coffee with."

"At work?"

"No."

I couldn't bring myself to say "in Tesco's caff". And Caroline probably imagined an intimate corner of some gastro-bar in Kentish Town. So it was from nought to meltdown in under ten seconds. I began to say something, she said, "No!" and then, "No…" more gently. And then, "Excuse me, Chris, I've got a new life to get on with."

On any normal calculation it was completely ridiculous. One little list, and I'd blown it. If ever I'd needed persuading of a woman's intuition, that did it. Caroline just knew – and she was too proud to hang about for the details.

But I didn't do a thing! I know that. *You* know that. Jesus, Gina could have sworn an oath on the Bible. Nothing but conversation. It was all so sweet and innocent. But then something that sweet is never innocent, that's the trouble, and Caroline knew it. Perhaps any woman knows it. For her, the infidelity was in the head, not the trousers. And she had a point.

I felt a shit. The horse had bolted but I was going to padlock that stable door anyway, just as a penance. You might say I'd have been better not to go back there at all – don't Catholics call it 'an occasion of sin'? – but that was too much to ask.

Funny how things work out. It may be unsporting to kick a man when he's down, but Fate doesn't give a stuff about sportsmanship. You're on the floor? Great, here's one in the goolies for luck.

We were sat there at what I'd begun to think of as our usual table, when who should bowl up but Martin. Tall, rangy, chambray shirt, scrubby little-boy hair and Armani specs… Big smile. Like something out of ER, but English and nicer. Not the least bit fazed by me, either.

"Don't get up, God, but that looks good."

"It is."

She said: "This is Chris, my Thursday morning date."

"Hi Chris. What happened to the other one?"

"I got bored with him."

I realised they were joking, but it wasn't funny. You only had to look at her – her eyes, her smile, her body language – and hear her voice, to know that she adored him, and it was mutual. They were so hot for each other they radiated a little glow.

There was some sort of burble about where he'd left the car and stuff, while I sat there feeling ridiculous with my half-eaten six items. Then off they went. Not touching, or anything, they didn't need to. I know the real thing when I see it.

Didn't finish breakfast. I felt like I used to when I came out of the cinema as a child. The real world would seem so dull and flat and grey I just wanted to crawl under the bedclothes and stay there till I'd readjusted. But when I was back in the car and driving north I had a revelation –

not a blinding flash, you understand, nothing to send me hurtling over the central reservation into the path of an oncoming juggernaut and a James-Dean-style death. No, it was more a sort of slow realisation – an illumination that showed all too clearly what an idiot I'd been.

The reason I liked married women was because they'd committed. And the reason I'd liked Gina in particular was because she loved her husband. I hadn't known it, but that was what gave her her special glow, her charm, her easy confidence. I wasn't bringing a little sparkle to her life, it was the other way round. That glow I'd felt coming off her and Martin, she carried it around with her, and I'd been basking in it. It was love I'd fallen in love with, pure and simple.

But knowing something doesn't help you put it right. Loser takes absolutely nothing. There'd be no more breakfasts at Tesco's. And Caroline had gone. It didn't take long for us to be friends again, she's much too generous to bear a grudge. But she's smart too, and she doesn't believe in going back.

She had the best wedding ever. Country church, red roses, tithe barn, soul band… She looked dreamy, and he's the lucky one now. I bet he knows exactly how lucky he is. I wasn't going to play the sad-eyed ex with regret etched into every line etc., so I took Bethany, whose legs stop just short of her armpits and that's before the Manolos go on. She's okay. All the same, I claimed my ancient right to a slow dance at the reception.

"Good old Chris," said Caroline. "With the most beautiful girl in the room, as usual."

"I am now," I said.

She laughed, and put her cheek against mine for a moment. "You finally did it, didn't you, Chris?"

I breathed in her scent. My heart was breaking, I reckon.

"You got your very own married woman," she said. "But I don't think much of your methods."

'Stand by Me' ended. The new husband showed up.

'You Sexy Thing' started.

I sat it out at the bar.

Best Foot Forward
Sue Houghton

"So, grey's the new black and elbows are the new hips, then," I say, flicking through my daughter's magazine.

Amy pushes her sunglasses hair-band-style on top of her head, rolls over on to her beach towel and sighs. "No, Mum. White's the new black and toes are the new cleavage. Really, it's quite simple."

"Okay. Explain. What's sexy about toes?"

"You won't understand, Mum. You're way too old."

"Oh thanks, love!"

I'm thinking it'd be much simpler if black was black, toes were toes, and bosoms were left to their own devices. I turn over on the sun-lounger to release *my* blessed duo from the pinching elastic of my new and ludicrously expensive bikini top. My upper half is passably fit for unveiling, albeit surreptitiously. Sadly, my hips still bear the tell-tale signs of years of Sunday roasts and family-size takeaways. Hence the voluminous and all-concealing sarong. Whoever invented such a garment – and it couldn't have been a man – should be made Patron Saint of Women. Guardian of the Obese.

I've never been a natural skinny. My genes and metabolism deem I should fit a comfortable size sixteen and yes, I'm perfectly happy with that, thank you very much.

"Voluptuous," Paddy had called me. He said he adored my womanly curves. Said they made him feel comfortable. Too comfortable, as it turned out, because shortly after Amy's sixteenth, he ran off with a size ten waif with boyish hips and no visible feminine attributes. Paddy Harvey – husband, father and breaker of hearts. My childhood sweetheart and, except for Donny Osmond, my first and only true love.

My confidence took a severe battering after we split, but life, as they say, has the habit of continuing, with or without you as a passenger. So, I thought it better to stop on board for the full tour, rather than hop off at the next stop. Time does heal and now Paddy and I get on remarkably well for divorcees. In fact, this holiday was his suggestion. "You're still a very attractive woman, Jenny," he said. A bit rich, considering. "A holiday would do you good. Why not take Amy with you?" He also offered to pay. And why not? He owed me.

So, here we are. Not since giving birth have I exposed so much flesh. Amy, bless her, has no hang-ups about her body. She lies tightly thonged and bare breasted; her sunglasses perched atop her head, only occasionally used for their intended purpose when she wants to covertly clock some golden-toned hunk.

My daughter is beautiful. She has her father's deep-green eyes and copper-brown hair and, most annoyingly, she shares his aptitude for turning a deep coffee-tan on the weakest of sunlit days. Me? If I took suntan oil intravenously, I'd still retain that crushed-raspberry hue of the melanin-deprived.

A young guy in tight black shorts and a skin gleaming as if it's just been rolled in butter tries to attract Amy's attention. He braves her feigned disinterest and bends to offer to oil her shoulders. She smiles, flicking her tongue stud alluringly against her teeth.

Oh God, I think I need a drink. I re-cup my bosom and arrange my sarong into a makeshift dress. "Coming for a stroll, darling?"

"No," winks Amy. "I'll stay under the parasol for a while." She turns seductively on to her stomach giving the 'buttered black shorts' an enviable view of her pert rear. She flicks her hair up into a loose bunch and replaces the earphones and sunglasses. The youth knows he's been dismissed. He smiles self-consciously, shrugs his shoulders, and moves on to the next beach towel.

Confident that Amy can take care of herself, I decide to leave her and take a slow walk up to Dario's Bar. The break's welcome, if only to escape the smell of Ambre Solaire and testosterone. I'm feeling the urge to indulge in a little gratuitous self-pity… and perhaps a large banana Daiquiri or two.

The sand, white hot under my feet, falls away to an equally fiery cobbled path which leads steeply from the tourist mêlée up to the old town. The sun-bleached walls swelter in the mid-day heat, the bougainvilleas entwined thickly beneath their terracotta eaves like a million purple butterflies. The chirring of the cicadas mixes hypnotically with the Salsa music drifting on the breeze from the beachside bars below.

The temperature's soared and my cheap plastic flip-flops, bought in haste at the airport, have taken on a sticky consistency. Like bright pink bubble-gum, they melt and rub until my feet blister. Hopping out of them, I lean against a nearby wall, where an old rusted tap juts out over a broken stone trough.

Giving the tap a quarter turn, I offer up a prayer as a trickle of water hits the hot stone with a hiss. I dip my toes in the stream of cooling water and groan with pleasure.

"You need a swim." The voice comes from above and behind the wall.

Startled, I grapple with the tap and find myself holding a detatched rusting bit of iron in my hand. Water gushes in all directions, soaking me from head to foot, wetting my hair so that it hangs poodle-curled over my eyes.

The owner of the voice emerges from a gate hidden beneath the vines that wind themselves around the top of the wall. "I was trimming the grapes back." He points to the wooden ladder peeking from amongst the vines. "I watched you coming up the hill. You look whacked."

"I'm so sorry," I stammer. "My sandals…the tap…"

"No problem," he says, taking the tap from my hand and screwing it back on to the rusting pipe. "It's old. I should really get it fixed, but, mañana and all that." He runs a wet hand through a mop of plentiful black hair. "The offer was genuine. The swim, I mean."

"No, I'm okay. I'm heading for Dario's, but I think I under-estimated the heat."

"And the direction," he laughs. "You're way off track. Look, my daily can whip us up some iced lemonade. And perhaps she could lend you more suitable footwear?"

"That's very kind of you, but I really think I can manage." What am I saying? It would take two Sherpas and a Yak to get me off this hillside. "Oh, okay, then. I'll just take a breather."

"Welcome to La Villa Concha," he says, as we pass beneath a bower of plump fruit.

The villa's pristine whitewashed walls are reflected in the cool blueness of the modest swimming pool. A mosquito net still covers it from the night before. "I could soon have it ready for a dip," he smiles.

"I'll just sit, I think. I'm Jenny, by the way."

He gestures to a couple of sun-loungers, and a small bamboo table upon which a half-eaten salad's being devoured by a large, and evidently hungry, ginger cat.

"That's Bicky. The cat, I mean. I'm Alex and this is Louisa," he says, as a stout, dark-haired woman appears from what I suppose is the kitchen.

"Señorita. Welcome. Louisa's speciality. Very good," she says, setting down a huge pitcher of juice.

"Gracias, Louisa." I fill a tumbler and gulp it down until the ice-cubes rattle against my teeth.

"Steady on," says Alex. "Don't drink too fast or…"

I come round, spread-eagled on the lounger, with Alex mopping my face with a wet napkin, concern showing in his dark eyes.

"I'm so sorry." I try to sit up, but the walls of the courtyard spin like a fairground waltzer.

"You apologise an awful lot," laughs Alex. "Here. Try again." He holds out the tumbler. "Only this time take it easy."

With strong steadying hands cupped gently around mine, I venture a mouthful and this time I allow myself to savour the deliciously, acid-sweet liquid. As my blood sugar returns to normal and my eyes focus properly again, I take in his appearance. Definitely handsome; his features not ruggedly chiselled like the Spanish, but softer and more relaxed. Laughter lines at the corners of his eyes show he's a man who's enjoyed life. An open-necked polo shirt promises a tanned hairless torso beneath and navy shorts show off long, muscular legs.

From out of nowhere, the sudden memory that Paddy had always looked slightly ridiculous in summer-wear comes to mind. "No yucky sports socks for you," I giggle, staring at his burnished toes stuffed in leather sandals. A look of puzzled concern flashes across Alex's face. *Oh help! I must sound like a mad woman.*

"Would you like to go inside? It's cooler in there."

"No, I'm fine. Honestly."

"If you're sure. Look, could I just try something?" *Oh, please do!* He takes my feet in his hands and gently kneads the soft skin of my instep, exactly at the spot where the arch meets the ball of the toe. "This usually works. Louisa taught it to me."

I close my eyes and let his hands sweep sensually over my skin. *Thank heavens for Louisa!* "You're not a local, are you?" I say, trying to still the Flamenco strumming in the pit of my stomach.

"Yes and no. My mother's Spanish and my father's English. They went back to England a few years ago, but my work keeps me here."

"Have you lived at La Concha long? You and…"

"There's no Señora Alex, if that's what you mean. At least, not any more."

"Oh?"

"My wife Rosa died two years ago."

"I'm so sorry."

"It was an accident. A car…"

Louisa returns with a small cut-glass bottle containing a dark perfumed liquid. "I take good care of Boss Alex now," she twinkles. "Senora? Boss Alex good at massage, yes?"

Absolutely!

Alex slaps her playfully across the bottom. "Louisa has taken it upon herself to be my surrogate mother. Now may I continue?"

"Please do." I close my eyes while he rubs the warmed oil into my blistered feet. He takes each toe between his long fingers and one by one he applies the most delicious pressure. Then he runs both hands around each ankle in turn, long, slow strokes circling and tracing further and further up my calf. Oh God, this is better than sex!

"You ought to do this for a living," I say, breathless.

"Tell me, where are you staying?" he asks, breaking the spell slightly, but still his hands keep up their pressure. "Which hotel? San Rosa? La Vida?"

"San Rosa. Why?"

"One of mine," he says proudly. "I'm an architect. I designed San Rosa. My last commission before my wife died."

"Rosa? Of course. You called the hotel San Rosa as a tribute to your wife."

"It would be a spectacularly romantic end to my story, but no, the owners chose the name."

"What a coincidence."

"Serendipity, I guess."

"Serendipity." *Rather like today.*

Alex reaches for a tissue and wipes the oil from his hands. He leans forward, his face so close to mine that I can feel his breath on my cheek. He touches my hair, brushing it off my face, and the feeling of his skin against mine stays with me for moments after we part. He holds out a hand. "It's getting late. I'll sort out some shoes for you and then I'll run you down to the hotel. Amy must be getting worried."

Amy's sitting in the hotel bar. "Mum! Where on earth have you been? I was so worried. I rang Dario's and they said you weren't there."

"I went for a walk, that's all. I found a beautiful villa where the lemonade was wonderful. And the hospitality was…" I'm remembering Alex's parting kiss.

Amy's gaze falls on my feet. "Mum, what on earth are you wearing?"

Louisa's feet had been a petite size three while I'm a generous size seven. There'd been nothing for it but to borrow a pair of Alex's leather sandals. Funny, they feel deliciously comfortable; like a familiar pair of slippers. I'll tell him that tomorrow, when he comes to take me out to dinner.

I smile at Amy. "You know, that magazine was right, darling. Toes *are* the new cleavage."

Secret Valentine
Lauren McCrossan

Valentine's Day was always a big deal. Even at primary school. I remember sitting in Mrs Walker's class clutching the dog-eared Snoopy card from my dad while the girls in the pretty group paraded their trolley-loads of chocolate, Love Hearts and **I ♥ U** fluffy bears given to them by real boys. I'd thought Valentine's was just an excuse to have a celebration in the boring months between Christmas and Easter. I'd thought it was about making heart-shaped lavender bags for my mum and giving Geronimo my gerbil an extra handful of chocolate treats to show him how much I loved his slightly balding squeaky little self. I didn't realise that, by High School, it would become an all-out war of demonstrative romance.

I pretended not to care. No, in fact, at first I didn't care. So what if Jenny Big-Jugs Juniper got so many Valentine gifts she had to borrow locker space from the plain girls (myself included)? So what if no Secret Admirers could be bothered to declare their intentions towards me on a random day in February named after some saint with a frankly ridiculous name? I didn't care, boys were rubbish anyway and I didn't need some poxy teddy bear with a pained expression to tell me I was worth my place in the world. Until I discovered self-esteem, of course.

By the time I realised I cared about Valentine's Day, it was too late. I could not turn back the clock to January and join the female assault on unsuspecting eligible boys. Besides, I didn't have the assets to compete with Jenny and her friends. Even when I grew them, I didn't know how to use them to get cheap jewellery and giant cards out of the boy I secretly fancied. Every Valentine's Day became the same – a frantic rush to check the post in the morning, rugby-tackling the postman if he dared walk past my house without at least delivering the anonymous card I had cunningly sent to myself (written with my left hand so that my secret admirer unfortunately appeared to be slightly retarded in the handwriting department). Sitting quietly while the pretty girls squealed and aahed and even had the nerve to make comments like 'Gross, why did *he* send me one? Yeah, like, *as if*!' Bloody hell, they had so many admirers, secret and not so, that they could afford to trade and discard them like packs of Panini album stickers. My best friend, Becky, had the usual packet of Rolos from her freaky cousin in Wales. I had the yearly Snoopy card from my now-absent father that only served to highlight how sad I was. I just didn't appear to be the sort of girl Valentine's Day was created for.

Before you go imagining me as some sort of social leper, I must point out that there were many like me at school. If you never realised that, you must have been one of the pretty-girl group. Thankfully, most of us blossomed in our own special ways and were noticed by the time we reached University. I know too, that Emily Pankhurst and her cronies didn't go to all the trouble of chaining themselves to railings just so I could fret about my attractiveness to men for the first two months of the year. But Valentine's Day is not a feminist celebration. Besides, I bet even bra-burning Emily sneakily checked the post on

February 14th to see whether she had attracted enough attention to warrant at least a heart-embroidered lace doily or two.

Anyway it so happened that the day I dreaded like no other became my lucky day the year I met Joe. He was the new guy in the office. Rumours of his mysterious grey-green eyes and his broad shoulders spread like wild fire through the sales manager department via the girls in recruitment. It was February 12th and female hormones were at explosive levels, like pollen at the height of the hayfever season. We finally met at the office Valentine's Party, a painful affair held at Cinderella Rockerfella's where the office geeks invariably chose to cast off their geekyness and reveal the person underneath with the help of several gallons of cheap cocktails. I was the designated driver, hovering in a corner with a lemonade and lime watching people I respected in an office environment throwing themselves at each other like the contestants in *Big Brother*.

"Jaysus, she'll regret that tomorrow," commented a soft Irish voice beside me as Nadia from Business Development began to limbo dance between the MD's legs.

"Probably not," I replied, turning to smile at the man with mysterious eyes. "She does it every year but never believes us when we tell her, she gets fantastic memory loss."

He had a lovely smile. The sort that stops you in your tracks so that you take it in and savour its sincerity. His eyes were everything they had been cracked up to be. Silvery-grey at first glance and almost hollow, pulling me in so deep I felt I could touch his soul. Green and sparkling the next moment as if reacting to our connection. They were breathtaking. He was breathtaking. Not stereotypically Irish at all; there were no freckles, auburn lights or rugged contours. Joe had a boyish face, smooth and dark skinned. His hair was as black as a pint of Guinness and his voice was ten times silkier. He was a designated driver too. Just for himself, as it happens, because he had not made any social connections in the first two frantic days at work. We stood in a corner like a pair of wallflowers, sipping our soft drinks and gradually bending towards each other like sunflowers towards the sun. He had just arrived from a recruitment company in Waterford and had been fast-tracked for management. He played football back in Ireland and was looking to join a team in the area. He liked Chinese food and cheesecake but hated liquorice. His favourite film was *Casablanca* (but I wasn't to spread it around) and his favourite music was 'anything where they play their own instruments and know how to write a riff'. He played the guitar (very well), the banjo (not bad now) and the mandolin (I give it a go). He enjoyed walks in the fresh air and loved being close to the ocean. Why he had ever accepted a job in Reading I will never know. But I will always be glad he did.

Joe said I had gorgeous curly hair that made him want to touch it. I let him. The frizzy mess that I had always prayed would iron itself out one day suddenly became my prize possession. No longer was it the curse of Bonnie Langford, but the 'gorgeous curly hair' that Joe Norton loved to wrap around his smooth hands. He loved the fact I barely reached five-foot-two in heels. I stopped lying about my height. He made me feel so good about myself and I, he said, made him feel 'like the man I am meant to be'. We were so right for each other, everybody thought so. Becky, still my best friend, joked that she would never find a man now because how could she compete with the one I had managed to find? We were a perfect team, Joe and I, and we just knew it.

Our first February 14th, the anniversary of the day we met, we launched into a Valentine's frenzy like lovers possessed. Shares in Clinton's Cards doubled that week as, every lunchtime, I failed to resist the urge to buy him just one more token of my affections. Quite frankly, I was out of control. Cards of all shapes and sizes. Yes, I admit, even the ones the size of a small oak tree that the assistant doesn't have a carrier bag big enough for. I bought mugs with his name on, mugs with rhyming comical sonnets on. I bought cuddly red devils declaring how 'Horny 4 U' they were, and fluffy handcuffs that we would later discover collecting dust under the bed (used once in a slightly self-conscious fashion). I bought funny gifts, cute gifts, sexy gifts, rude gifts. Gifts that in all honesty I would vomit over if anyone suggested I buy at any other point in the year. Yet I was so happy when the gesture was returned. In our first year, Joe was inventive and demonstrative. He made me a card – a collage of hearts and glitter around a picture of us crammed into a photobooth. He baked me a chocolate cake and wrote a message on it in Jelly Tots. He bought me chocolates and teddy bears and the sort of underwear usually only worn by girls with tattoos on their bum cheeks. He even wrote me a song and played it for me on his beloved guitar.

Over the years, the offerings diminished as our lust gave way to something deeper and lucid judgements replaced the February bad-taste madness. Joe would buy me a card, which he displayed on the breakfast table next to a bottle of Sainsbury's bubbly and a box of Roses. We were saving up for our dream home and, anyway, I didn't need extravagance to know he cared. Later, the bubbly became Moet and the chocolates grew into the Belgian variety – more frilly packaging than chocolate, and for three times the price. I was happy. My man loved me, I loved him, and that was the way it was. I knew it every day we were together, not just February 14th.

Then, one Valentine's Day, I sensed something had changed. Joe was anxious for a fortnight before, his gaze distracted by card shops and jewellers every time we were in town, his behaviour secretive and a little suspicious. He booked us a table at the sort of restaurant where the menu may as well be in Hebrew for all the sense I can make of it. You know the kind of place: main courses are confusingly called 'Entrees' and the title of the dish gives absolutely no clue as to whether its contents are animal, vegetable or mineral. The celebrities wear sunglasses, not to hide their identity, but to protect their eyes from the glare off the canteen of highly polished cutlery on every table. I knew something was up and I guessed what it might be, but I didn't want to get my hopes up. But when I saw the diamond glinting at the bottom of my champagne flute, I leapt to my feet and threw my arms around him shrieking, "Yes, I will, yes, yes, YES!" for everyone to hear. The greatest man I had ever (and would ever) meet wanted me to marry him. We cried and laughed; we joked about me choking on the ring and Joe killing me accidentally on a day set aside for romance. But it was February 14th, the day when only good things are allowed to happen and it had become the luckiest day of my life.

I don't know when this started to change, or for what reason. I suppose when I reached my thirties I needed reassurance that he would still choose me as his Valentine if we weren't married and he had to do it all over again. I wanted him to be demonstrative like some of the other husbands. Not just to give me a card with carefully chosen words inside. Not just to write me a song that he sang to me at home; that was too easy for a musical genius like my husband. Listen to me. The man I married wrote me songs and I thought it wasn't good enough. I wanted the stupid teddy bears and the expensive dinners, the diamonds and the little turquoise boxes from Tiffany's. I wanted the extravagant bouquets of flowers delivered to the office by Interflora so that everyone else could see how much he loved me. Other husbands did that, so why couldn't he? Granted, we all knew that the P.A. with the twenty red roses had a husband who couldn't keep his hands off other women, and that the beautiful blonde with the beautiful white lilies could only see her boyfriend when he wasn't with his wife and kids, but at least they had won the Valentine's Day competition. They got to flap around the office looking for a vase-like receptacle, and they could moan about not being able to see over the Amazon rainforest of flowers on their desks. Suddenly I wanted that. Over the years, I had regressed to that girl at High School longing for a Valentine I could show off to the other girls. Longing, I must even admit, for a secret admirer to make my day-to-day life just a little more exciting. If only I had stopped to think just for a moment. Stopped myself that February 14th, when we fought about the size of the card and the lack of effort. When I shouted at him and said I didn't want 'another stupid song', that I wanted what all the other girls had. I still remember what he said: "But I can't give you what all the other girls get, cos you're not all the other girls. You're my girl and this is the only way I know to show you how I feel. I love you every day, I don't need giant bunches of flowers to show you that."

"Well I do!" I yelled, grabbing my car keys and racing off into the night.

Men, I thought, they just don't get it, do they?

I secretly watch him now preparing for Valentine's Day. It is a pained and careful process that begins at least a month before and is never out of his mind. He walks down to the florist shop that Becky opened two years ago, a dream of hers since school. Together, Becky and Joe choose my bouquet. It is big, too big, full of every flower imaginable.

"Except the carnations," Joe smiles.

"Reminds her of old ladies' funeral arrangements," they say in unison.

The sunflowers are perfect, reminding me of how Joe and I were the night we first met. There are Birds of Paradise, orchids, nasturtiums, and hibiscus. Nothing you would find in a £3.99 garage forecourt creation, thank you very much. This is extravagance at its best; all my favourite colours and perfumes, bunched together with a bow big enough to tie around a prize bull at an auction. As Joe lifts the finished masterpiece (I always said Becky had talent), his arms strain under the weight. His face is shielded by foliage so vibrant it could outshine the sun. He thanks Becky and leaves.

I watch him walk down the street and place the flowers so delicately in the car beside the big pink envelope with my name written on the front. He spent so much time choosing the card, nodding or shaking his head as he meticulously read each one in the shop.

"Not funny."

"What a load of shite."

"Call that romantic?"

"That teddy bear looks psychotic."

"Jaysus, she would shove that up me hole if I bought her that one.'

He bought the card and spent hours thinking of the right words to fill it with. No scribbled 'I love you' from my Joe, but a real message straight from the heart telling me exactly how he feels, how sorry he is, asking if I will be his Valentine.

How ironic that now he does everything I wanted him to: now he buys the extravagant bouquet and delivers it in public with the big pink envelope; now he doesn't write the 'stupid song' any more; and that now I know exactly what matters on February 14th.

For as he kneels down, his tears smudging the ink on the envelope, his knees sinking into the soft earth to place the bouquet on my grave, now I know the flowers and chocolates and cuddly toys were not important. Now I would give anything to sit beside him as he reached for his guitar, looking into those mysterious eyes as he sang the song he had written for me. Those mysterious eyes that turned from silver to black the Valentine's Day I ran out of the house and never came back. The day Joe's Valentine's message was delivered by a young policeman with a tear-stained face.

"I'm sorry, Sir, there's been an accident."

I know now that all that matters is that Joe said he loved me and really meant it. He loves me still, even though he has moved on and he and Becky are starting to plan a family. I longed for a secret admirer and now I am one, the secret Valentine watching my lover from a place he cannot reach. I hope he feels my presence now but I don't know if he does. I cannot send him a card or buy him a toy declaring my feelings in the same way as a million other people do. But now I know that that is not the point of it.. You see, Valentine's is just one day. But real love lasts forever.

[illegible]

[illegible]

[illegible]

[illegible]

The Swalec Man

Catherine Merriman

The phone rang at the Little Chef just before 10.00am. Mrs Preece the manager, a pin- legged barrel of a woman, had been having a hellish morning: a succession of customers demanding instant service – as if the place was a bloody McDonalds – the new kitchen boy off, the dishwasher playing up, and all after a night of appalling hormonal sweats. She whipped the receiver to her ear on the tenth ring, snapped, "Yes?" and then, after a moment's stunned pause, whispered, "Not kidding now, are you?" Slowly, breathlessly, she replaced the receiver. Catching the eye of Karen the waitress she mouthed, "The SWALEC man. Here. On his way, now."

Twenty minutes later work had all but come to a standstill. This was not for the practical reason that the man had turned the power off – indeed, he'd assured them there was no need for that – but because the staff, to a woman, were in a quivering tizz. He was here. The SWALEC man. *The* SWALEC man. Finally.

Mrs Preece had just professed a desire to eat him. This was an accolade normally reserved only for exceptionally bonny babies. "Ooh," she sighed in Karen's ear. "Could eat him whole, I could."

Karen didn't hear; her senses were locked on to movements in the storeroom (where the recently-replaced electricity meter and trip-switch were). If she had been listening, she would probably have choked on her chewing gum. Karen was nineteen. 'Eating', to her, as it related to men and women, described an activity with which she would not have associated Mrs Preece. She stood rigid by the clanking dishwasher, staring at the open storeroom door, two forgotten dirty plates in her hand. Her jaws chomped mechanically.

"Didju see 'im?" she demanded in a fierce whisper, as her friend Jody strode in from the public area.

Jody's eyes were wide and she was holding her thin body straight and stiff inside its red-and-white uniform, as if one of the customers had stabbed her between the shoulder blades but she had failed to notice. She nodded mutely.

Their informants had been right. All those gasped reports over the last few months, from the girl at the Shell filling station down the road, friends at Woollies and the Alliance & Leicester in town, and, oh, dozens of other businesses. The female grapevine had not exaggerated. He really existed. No figment. And he was actually *here.*

"Offrim a cup of tea," Karen begged Mrs Preece. "You got to."

Mrs Preece blinked assent. Rank was irrelevant. In an emergency you took vital orders from anyone.

Jody found just enough breath to gasp, "He – is – so – fit."

"You ask him," said Mrs Preece, nudging Karen. Her cheeks had become raspberry pink. 'I'm having a flush.'

"Don't ask him," pleaded Jody. "He might say no. Just tell him it's here."

Karen womanfully accepted the responsibility. She stuck out her small pointed chin and approached the storeroom doorway. She wasn't normally shy with men. Lorry drivers, leather-clad bikers, flirtatious dads, local boys taking the piss, you got them all in here. But this was like having someone from the films in the cafe. Brad Pitt. Or Johnny Depp. Someone with an aura.

He was over in the corner, behind a low wall of boxes, winding electric cable the length of his bare forearm. Like her great-auntie did with knitting wool. Except no great auntie had forearms like his. He glanced over to her – blue-grey eyes, a crinkle of laughter line beneath – and smiled. Her heart convulsed.

"Won't be a tick," he said. "The contractors shouldn't have left this lying around. Can't have you ladies tripping up."

He wasn't a mere electrician. He was the man who checked the work of other, lesser men. When she described him – as she surely would, she was mentally on the phone to friends already – what would she say? What would she focus on, to capture his beauty? His face... Christ. Was it so special? Neat features beneath short brown hair. Ooh, God, though, sexy hair. Short, thick, animal-pelt hair. His body? Not big. But not small either. And fit, yes, fit, like Jody said. Sort of contained. Condensed. That was it. Condensed masculinity. Not flashy, in-your-face, or scary. Just... quietly, confidently, condensed. And those molten, slate-blue eyes...

"Tea," she said. He must think women were zombies. Everywhere he went, women zombified. She tucked the gum to the side of her mouth and made an effort to speak clearly. "Mrs Preece. She's made you a cuppa."

"Be out now." His voice was friendly, easy, as if he was unaware of his effect on her. Unaware of her zombification. Well, he would be. To him it would be normal. God. Imagine being him.

He strapped the bundle of cable with brown sticky-tape. Then squatted to pick up objects from the floor, to stuff them into the canvas bag he had brought with him. Muscles in his forearms moved like snakes under the smooth skin. Deft. Athletic. The top of his head, the way the hair sprang thick at the whorl, then clung to the curve of his skull. Softening to down at his nape. Jesus.

She backed away. A thrill ran through her. How often did you see a man like him? Who looked beautiful inside, as well as out? How a man should be. In real life? Never. Never.

Outside the door Jody grasped her forearm so tightly she said, "Ow!"

"Whaddyou say to him?" Jody hissed. "Izzy comin' out?"

"Course." Karen composed herself. What an idiotic question.

Privileged. That's what they were. They would never be in the presence of such perfection again. A once in a lifetime event. She saw Jody straighten her spine again, dab at her hair above her ears. She smoothed her own uniform. That was how he made you feel. Inspired. Uplifted. Ennobled, almost.

He was at the storeroom door. Out of their league, of course. Anyone's league. Didn't matter. Not at all.

Mrs Preece bustled up, bearing a brimming cup of tea. Her face was scarlet. "There's two waiting out the front, Jody dear," she murmured. She never called Jody 'dear'. And to the SWALEC man, with a little bob – bloody hell, Karen thought, she's curtsying! – she said, "You'll have this out front, now, won't you."

"Very kind," he said, and strolled after her into the public area. Karen followed. Jody, usually an ungracious waitress, was swooping from table to table, radiating goodwill. Mrs Preece sat the SWALEC man down at an empty window table, facing the room and its half dozen customers, as if throning a prince. Giving him pride of place. Their prince, their pride.

Jody returned to Karen. She folded her arms across her chest and gazed dreamily across the room. "God's gift," she murmured. She wasn't sneering.

Karen had just been thinking: he is a gift. This had suddenly become one of those precious, euphoric, so-glad-to-be-alive days. That was what real beauty did, if you let it touch you. And you didn't need to touch it back. In fact, better not. It might burst. Suddenly, for some reason, Karen felt immensely proud of herself. And not just herself. Of Jody too, even Mrs Preece. In fact, proud of all the women who had seen him and admired him, and told their friends, but hadn't let on to him, or made fools of themselves over him, and spoilt it. Kept him an innocent treat, a tonic for everyone. Everyone here looked serene now. Restored. Mrs Preece had returned to her usual colour. She was at the till now, actually smiling at a twittering lady customer.

They had only a few minutes of serenity. But that was right too. Mustn't be greedy. Long enough. Then there was just one more duty to fulfil, and Mrs Preece didn't have to be told. As the SWALEC man rose she joined him, and escorted him to the door. Karen and Jody waited five seconds, then glided over to stand beside her in the doorway. They watched the man climb into his white van. He lifted a hand to them. A beautiful, strong, life-affirming hand. They all waved back.

"Sun Valley factory," Mrs Preece murmured.

"Right," said Karen, and reached out for the wall phone.

Protesting

Angie Quinn

"Remember I'm out late tonight, Geraint." Martha studied the calendar, as she had done every day for weeks. Smiling, she ringed the date in red biro.

"Oh, not that wretched protest thing again?" Geraint grumbled from behind his paper. "Are you sure it really *is* the hotel you're complaining about?"

Martha heard him. She was meant to. Another acrimonious breakfast! Martha couldn't remember the last time she'd sat down with Geraint and enjoyed a meal. Certainly not since the hotel plans had driven a wedge into the local community, and her marriage. Joining the protest group and talking to people who listened to and supported each other had thrown her relationship with Geraint into a harsh light. All those niggles which she had previously ignored were now revealed as huge cracks. She thought of news reports from earthquake zones, and the people who fell in. Was she going to fall in, Martha wondered, or just sink slowly into the coastal marshes? What would be left of them after the hotel complex was finished?

The sun was streaming through the window. Martha cleared the table and decided she wasn't wasting this lovely winter day going round in circles about Geraint.

The work on the Western Winds Hotel and Leisure Centre was starting in the spring. The old hotel needed demolishing, there was no dispute about that. Its cluster of ill-matched buildings with flat roofs, staring plate glass windows and mouldy brown interiors were far too depressing to accommodate the wave of tourists flooding in to this coastal region. But a week after Western Winds Development Company displayed their new plans in the council offices there were mutterings of disapproval and rumours of a protest group. Martha had been horrified by the plans. The new complex was three times the size of the original with a huge car park and new approach road. But it was the fact that they intended to drain the salt marshes behind the dunes for a golf course that really shocked her. Those marshes were an important part of her life story. She'd walked through there with her friends on the way to school. She and Geraint had done some of their courting there. She'd taken her children along the paths when they were small, spied out ducklings swimming on the rush fringed ponds and fed the swans. Her two boys were grown up now and had long since left the area. Nowadays she just had her little terrier, Breezer, for company, but she still walked through the marshes every day and mulled over her hopes and fantasies in the reed-beds.

After a faltering start, the protest group now had over thirty members, mainly women but with a smattering of younger men, which pleased Martha. If her boys had stayed they would definitely have been part of this. When she phoned them they were both impressed at her course of action and reassuringly supportive. It was a pity their Dad couldn't see it that way.

Recently Martha had been out two or three times a week helping to make the banner. This was twenty feet wide with *SAVE OUR MARSHES!* emblazoned across it. Martha's job had been to paint ducks swimming across the bottom. There was a growing argument about where to hang it.

Most people favoured draping it across the main street, but Fiona Lewis and a few vociferous supporters had set their minds on direct action. When this dispute threatened to split the group, Martha's first instinct was to look for a compromise solution. But after a particularly discordant meeting she admitted to a growing admiration for Fiona's determination in the face of so much opposition. Too much of Martha's life had been spent keeping the peace, caught between three male egos. So, finally, she decided to join the rebel camp and come out in full support of Fiona. And that's where she was going tonight. To hang the banner from the crane above the old hotel.

The silhouette of the half-demolished buildings loomed jagged against the frosty sky. The two women stood amongst the rubble with the banner, their enthusiasm shrinking in the cold wind.

"Must make sure this is secure." Fiona's voice was shaky as she tied the banner round her waist. She looked around and shivered. "It's sort of different at night, isn't it?"

"Don't worry," Martha said, reassured that this strong young woman sounded as nervous as she felt. "We'll do it, it'll be fine."

Fiona set off and Martha could hear her metallic clanking growing fainter. The eerie silence on the deserted building site was disturbed only by the sound of waves breaking on the shore and the occasional rattle of falling stones. Feeling very alone, she wondered where Geraint was. The silly old fool was probably in front of the television, snooker most likely. Maybe it was time for her to make a few changes. Fiona's determination had rubbed off on Martha, and the fact that Fiona was married with three small boys didn't seem to hold *her* back.

Fiona was near the top when the scaffolding began to move.

"The thing's moving a bit!" Martha called up. "Be careful!"

A shower of stones and dust rained down around her head, but Fiona didn't answer. Suddenly there was a loud crack.

"Fiona!" Martha shouted urgently. "The scaffolding's shifting! Come down."

Peering up through the shaking structure, Martha could just made out a black-clad shape against the metallic sky. Then there was a second, louder crack and everything juddered violently. Martha watched helplessly as Fiona lost her footing and fell.

There was uneasy tension between the protest group and the hotel owners during the next week. Each was worried that the other was going to sue. Eventually Martha ended the stand-off by arranging a meeting with the director of the company. After an hour they emerged from his office. The director called a press conference and Martha looked quietly pleased. She also felt a twinge of sadness that Geraint was not with her. As she'd talked to the director about one of the bird hides in the marsh, Martha recalled a time when Geraint *had* felt proud of her, when he *had* been interested in her. Behind the clamour of photographers, journalists and well-wishers, Martha didn't notice the stocky man in the tweed jacket carrying orange roses.

An hour later Martha was reading by Fiona's hospital bed. Her friend woke up.

"Martha! Did you survive your brush with Big Business?"

"You can talk! Surviving a thirty foot fall with nothing

worse than concussion and a broken arm."

Fiona struggled to sit upright. "But we got the banner up didn't we?"

Martha smiled. "Yes, you must have just fastened the last tie when the scaffolding went. It looked magnificent there the next day, strung out across the wreckage."

"And the verdict?" Fiona asked.

"At the press conference they'll unveil scaled-down plans for the hotel. They've scrapped the golf course. Instead they're improving the path network in the marshes and re-roofing and extending the bird hides. What about that?"

"Wow! And how are they explaining this loss of face?"

"Well, partly because their visitor survey had showed that tourists came here for a wilder experience and," Martha laughed, "partly in respect of the local community's wishes."

Fiona settled back on her pillows and squeezed Martha's hand. "We did it, Martha, like you said we would."

As Fiona's family appeared on the ward, Martha made her excuses and left. She had her own family problems to sort out.

At her front door a heavy sense of anticlimax engulfed her. Excitement was over, goals achieved, now it was just her and Geraint and their stale marriage. Maybe this was the time for a complete break? But as she walked into the house an unusual smell greeted her. Surely Geraint wasn't cooking! The kitchen was bright and tidy and a vase of orange roses, her favourite, sat on the table.

"Hallo, love." He hugged her. "And before you ask, I had lunch with Nick." Nick was Fiona's husband. "He was badly shaken by her accident and I... Well, I thought it might..." He paused. "Er, anyway, I was looking at the plan for the marshes and I noticed they're going to extend one of the bird hides. Wasn't that the hide where we..?"

Martha smiled. So he'd remembered too. "Yes, on that bitterly cold night."

Geraint opened a bottle of wine and said softly, "Oh, I don't remember the cold. I only remember a beautiful young woman, and how lucky I felt that she'd agreed to come out with me. And then I started thinking that I'd taken her a bit for granted lately. Silly really, I suppose it was jealousy that you'd found something else to do." He passed her a glass and raised his. "To you, Martha, love. I really respect the determination and strength you've shown over these last few weeks."

As Martha tucked into the hot crusty pie she felt a mixture of satisfaction and relief that the bustle of the last few weeks was over. It was only a month now until the *Massage for Couples* weekend. She wondered if this would be a good time to mention it to Geraint...

Before I Loved You

Carolyn Lewis

What do you make of that? That's what I wanted to ask you when I saw two women on the Downs today. Everything they wore was black: their plump legs were squeezed into leggings and they both wore polo-necked sweaters and a tabard tunic. Even their shoes were black. They were throwing chunks of bread to a flock of birds and, as the women threw the bread, the birds jostled and fought, trying to catch each piece before it hit the ground. It looked such an odd picture to me: the sky full of black-winged screaming birds, and the two women dressed in black, silently feeding them.

Where did the women come from? Was that a uniform they wore? One of the women had thick, blonde streaks in her hair and wore a lot of make-up: glittery blue eye shadow, lips glistened with a scarlet gloss. The birds' beaks were wide open, searching for the bread, their raucous shrieks splitting the air and the women's mouth gaped open, mirroring the beaks of the birds as they hurled the bread into the skies.

When all the bread was gone the women walked slowly in silence back to their car. They strapped themselves in, their heads almost touching as they bent over seat belts.

Then they drove off, a dull, grey cloud of exhaust fumes trailing behind, like a tired flag.

What do you make of that? I wanted to ask you, to hear what your answer would be. Then we'd have talked about what the women did and why were they so silent? We'd make up stories about them. Where did they live and in what sort of houses? We'd have fantasised about affairs, joked about steamed-up windows and passionate embraces on the back seats of family saloons. There would be empty Coke cans on the dashboard, crisp packets in the glove compartment. We'd have invented lives for those women, the bird women up on the Downs. That's what we would have done.

I still *talk* to you. Wherever I go the conversations rattle around in my head. You *came* with me on the Downs; we looked at the changing colours of the leaves, we watched the joggers, grinned as they puffed their way past us. I hear your voice in my head the whole time. When I sit in the dentist's chair; are you ok? Did that hurt? You are with me when I go shopping. I can ask you things, things like: what about fish for tea? You are there when I try clothes on in the changing rooms of posh department stores, peering out from behind curtains, the ones with the gaps at the side. What do you think of this? Do I need a bigger size? You are always with me, but only in my head.

It started the first day I met you, when your hand stretched out to touch mine.

"Hello," you said, and then you smiled, the lines around your eyes deepening and hinting at something. Your smile came with me, I took it wherever I went, carrying it in my head, on the bus home, lying in bed, tucking it underneath my pillow.

I imagined you at home at night, living in a flat, drinking beer from cans and never, ever, did I see you with another girl. What do you do on Saturday nights? Where do you go? Can I come with you? Having you inside my head made me brave, bold, asking questions because there was no fear of rejection. I began to tell you all about my life at home, my mum, my dad, the fights I had with my sister. She borrows my clothes and steals my friends. She couldn't steal you, you were mine and nobody knew about you. You always understood, you were my ally, my secret friend.

I spent my days watching you, watching your long strides through the corridors. I heard the creak of your leather jacket as you stretched up to push the hair out of your eyes. Your hair needs cutting, or do you like it that long? All through those long working day at my first job, a newspaper office full of stories of courtroom battles football matches, golden wedding anniversaries and murders, I watched you and told you all about my dreams. Things I had never mentioned to anyone before. You listened to me, listened to all the words I carried with me.

Our working days were frantic, exhilarating and fraught. Working alongside you, phones rang incessantly, shouted arguments ricocheted around the room. Whenever I passed you, rushing from one desk to another, papers flying, my heels clicking on the floor, I wanted your approval, I needed your approval. How am I doing? What do you think of this?

Don't you see, I thought I already knew you.

Then, tentatively, gently, and so softly, you began smiling at me. A look from you across the room made the day sunny. I could smile at you too and then I began to know you. We laughed together, we exchanged glances when a new story broke, we shared confidences and then we really did begin to talk. When you were inside my head my words had bounced, they sparkled, they were light, precise and so clever and I grew afraid that *outside*, away from my secret world, you'd find my words dull, heavy and slow. I wanted to keep you inside. You were safe there, I was safe there, I was strong.

But then, working on a murder story, a front page drama harrowing in every detail, quite suddenly you asked, "Fancy a drink?"

My voice, quiet and hesitant: `Yes, please.' I'd thought my inner conversations with you had taught me all there was to know. But, locked inside my head was only a tiny part of you. We began to discover each other and you talked, really talked, to me. Your words were clear and strong, they encouraged me, taught me to think and argue, they gave me confidence and strength. When you were inside, locked away in my head, all that time I *talked* to you, my words had been sharpened, now they were like swords, shiny, steel-edged. I cut through arguments, slashed away at my fear and nervousness. With you I could shine. My confidence soared.

You spoke to me of travelling. Africa, America, driving through France, the Swiss Alps, and your words brought the world into my head. When you spoke, I could *see* everything, smell the sea, touch the flowers. I could taste the local wine and feel the heat.

"Come with me, I want you to see these places with me." Before you, the world was what I could see or touch. With you I could go anywhere. You said it all the time, "There's nothing to stop you." Nothing did stop me and I moved into your strong, confident world.

"Look at this, look at the view," I said all the time, all the time we travelled together, forgetting that you had seen it before. What I meant to say was, look at it now, with me. You were right, you'd been right all along. I could do it. Travelling the world, sharing the world with you. We talked wherever we went, sitting up late in a smoky French bar, walking back to our hotel through night-dulled skies. Driving over mountain passes, tramping through snow-filled fields. We sailed past the Statue of Liberty, my gaze holding yours as the ferryboat moved alongside.

We invented lives for the people we saw around us: the couples sitting in uneasy silence, the women whose faces were slick with unaccustomed make-up, the solitary man in a busy restaurant, fingers tugging and turning at a worn wedding band. Newly together, happiness freshly minted, arrogance born from our delight, we gave new lives to those around us. We proffered happiness to others, changed lives, giving hope and excitement, making a difference. We were together, invincible, unique. No one had ever felt like this – how could they? We fitted together, two halves of a magical being. We invested some of our magic, we could afford to, we had so much.

Before I loved you, you'd been my ally, my secret friend. Now that I loved you, you gave me even more, more strength, more courage. Working together, our days were heady and full. Our careers grew, my confidence, long lost and stunted, became strong. I was assigned to cover major news stories and my opinion was sought, my views were listened to. I echoed your words, *I can do this.* My name appeared in print, I was praised for my work, my professionalism, my skill.

Watch me! Like a child calling out for parental approval, I still needed your mantle of protection. What do you think of this? Does this work? Tell me! Am I any good?

Your words assured me. They nurtured and strengthened me and then, slowly, for the first time in my life, I began to recognise my own strength. You'd known all the time what I could do. "Just do it," you counselled, "don't ask, just do it." And I did. Weeks travelled so fast, my life changed as fast as I changed. But not you. Why could I not see that you remained the same?

Tell me what to do. My newly honed confidence had been noticed and I was approached. A prominent newspaper, spoken about in reverential whispers, dangled titles and money: features editor, chief reporter, take your pick.

What shall I do? Tell me what to do. You were solid, an island as I began the storm. I moved around you, crashing, whirling, demanding. Tell me!

"Do what you want to do – stay here or go."

"If I go, will you come with me? Come with me!"

You shook your head, your long blond hair tumbling around your face, hiding your eyes. No, you choose. Make your own decisions. I can't help you with this one.

Before I loved you my choices were hollow. My world was small, contained and narrow. But now? Now I wavered, my new strength seeping, leaving me. Help me, tell me what to do. You held me, your arms around my shoulders. I felt your warmth, your love. "Believe in yourself, make this decision on your own. Choose what's right for you."

Whilst you were hidden in my head, locked inside me, you shared my dreams, you'd listened with love and compassion but you didn't listen now. You were tired of my tears and arguments, my sulking silences and demands. I grew angry, stamping like a petulant child, my anger growing in its intensity. You'd let me down, you wouldn't help me any more. I had to do this on my own. I would do it on my own. I didn't need you, they wanted me not you.

"I don't need you." The words hung in the air, they shimmered over our heads like violent heat, warping feelings and what I wanted to say to you. I wanted to whisper, I'm sorry. I needed to retrieve what I'd lost, what had been damaged. You knew that, your face with its lop-sided smile, the long hair flying around, the understanding in your eyes. You knew. All that time that you were locked inside my head, all that time before I loved you, all those times when I talked to you. You were talking to me now. I heard the unspoken dialogue, the silent words. You knew. You knew what I wanted to say, but you wouldn't let me say it. You left me with that.

You left me at the station, a strained goodbye, eyes not meeting, a hurried embrace. We both knew but you wouldn't let me voice it. I'm sorry, let me put it right. Those whispered words were finally drowned by the scream of the train. Leaving you.

My new life was busy, shiny-bright with promises. New friends, new stories, a new life in a world crowding into the spaces where you used to be. I filled those spaces and I was sought after, lauded, I was in demand. Look at me, see what I can do now. But you couldn't see me, you weren't there. You weren't anywhere, not locked inside my head because you'd gone from there too. I couldn't find you.

I don't need you! I'd shouted, yelled those words at you. But I did need you. My new world was brittle, new friendships shallow, glitter blinded me. I didn't see the hollows underneath. Their lights shone, beacons for me to follow. Promises of success, excitement, fast heady lives. Empty lives. There was nothing there, nothing underneath. Where are you?

I tried to reach you, to phone, to talk to you. You'd gone. I'm sorry, please talk to me. I was wrong and I made a mistake. I watched others at parties, in restaurants, smiling when eyes met mine. I sent you messages, secret codes, hidden away again, locked inside my head. You didn't hear me, the words echoed, my new life echoed too.

There were only hollow sounds. I've made a mistake. I'm sorry.

I came back to find you. Where are you? Travelling back, listening to the rhythmic wheels of the train, sitting still, eyes closed, words tumbling in my head. Where are you?

I go to the places we knew. Your flat is empty and cold, the Downs are bleak, dead leaves rattle at my feet. The newsroom is noisy, energetic, desks are crowded and the phones ring out constantly but I can't see you. I don't hear the creak of your leather jacket, I don't see you striding to greet me. I can't see you. Where are you?

I close my eyes again, squeezing the lids tight, banishing light from my inside my head, leaving only room for you. Can you hear me?

I choose words, testing, discarding. I need words that will reach you, find you.

Can you hear me? Where are you?

A Lullaby For Micky Marshmallow

Penelope Alexander

Joe and I used to be lovers.

"Nuala," he'd say, his blue eyes sharp and knowing. "Come here."

Then he'd roll into the cold, naked side of the bed, considerately patting the warmed hollow for me to tumble into. Gentle and unhurried was his style.

"Forget the day," he'd say, kissing my eyes. "This is our time."

It never mattered what had or hadn't happened. There was always time, and if there wasn't, Joe knew how to knit it by the yard. Each morning, I felt like a girl who'd become queen. Joe, grinning, would emerge from our royal divan, stretching his arms to the light till his elbows cracked. No couple could be happier. We should be together forever, despite being more or less penniless. Joe would fix it.

We married and celebrated with a large fruitcake, baked by Ita from the upstairs flat. I had a proper, plain ring.

We still did everything that pleased us, and each other, like lying face to face in bed on a weekend, giggling at our tiny reflections in each others' eyes.

“Looking babies,” Joe told me, tenderly lifting a lock of my hair and curling it twice around my ear.

“Mmmm?”

“That’s what it used to be called, hundreds of years ago. ‘Looking babies.’”

How sweet.

We wanted babies, as soon as possible. We had a wonderful pregnancy. (Joe came to all the classes. He even got the backache instead of me.) And, right on cue, there was our seven pounds of pure joy and dribble. Joseph Michael Ronan. Known as Micky.

“Here’s to the happy parents!” said Ita, raising a glass to wet the baby’s head. “The little fella couldn’t have better! Loving him as they love each other.”

“Do you hear that?” I said softly in the baby’s ear. “How lucky you are?”

Luckier than we were, at any rate. Six weeks since Micky’s birth had already passed, and neither Joe nor I had the stamina for anything more than a kiss. The truth was, if either of us got the chance to lie down our minds grabbed at sleep before our bodies could be aware of it.

We loved our baby, of course we did. We loved the sound when he blew tiny bubbles. Loved his fat cheeks and the wavy line of milk that lay on his lips after a feed. The vanilla smell of him after a bath. But Micky, as Ita agreed, was surely destined to become the next tenor of the High Cs. He cried, without stop, between six at night till six in the morning. Twelve hours, and I counted them most nights like the beat of a funeral drum.

Micky would start with a bagpipe wheeze, and climb the scales from there. If he took a break, it was only to draw breath for the next session. We tried everything, but achieved nothing.

Joe began to look like a marathon runner at the end of his twenty-six mile stint, and I… I don't know what I looked like, as I never dared confront a mirror. A Banshee with a hangover, I would think.

Sometimes, Joe would carry our bundle of joy to our bed first thing in the morning, where he would quieten. But the smaller they are, the more space they fill, so they say. Our baby had the knack of expanding.

"He's puffing up like marshmallow, I swear it," Joe said. "He's practically shoving me out of bed over here."

"Micky Marshmallow," I yawned. The baby chuckled, then sighed. "Look, Joe. I think he's dozing…"

"So he is…" said Joe, raising one dark well-defined eyebrow. "How would it be… if I took him back to his cot..?" He drew a thoughtful line along my arm with his finger, which, despite my tiredness, made me shiver in anticipation. But it was no use. Micky puffed some more, flipped open gig-lamp eyes, chuckled again, and ate the counterpane with his new teeth. We had to admit it, he'd come between us.

Joe won respite when he travelled for work. He was never away for more than a week, but after his first trip since Micky, he returned to find me drunk with sleeplessness while in charge of a kitchen sink.

"Hi." Joe had come into the kitchen that quietly, I hadn't heard him.

I'd planned a welcome. A dab of 'On Impulse' behind the ears for me. (I was feeling hopeful). Candles, a spag bol, and some frankly wicked chocolate mousse for us both.

Joe, it seemed, had other plans. He reached around my waist. Leaving the dishes in the sink, I turned into his arms.

"Come here," he murmured, pulling me forward for his kiss. "Let me seduce you away from those dishes. This is our time, now…"

He carried me upstairs. I swear my eyelids were fast shut by the time he took the top step. He told me afterwards he considered a cold flannel might wake me, but hadn't the heart.

With Joe home, I got to sleep. But never with my husband. Micky made sure of that.

"I'll rock him tonight," Joe said, heading for Micky's room. "Day off tomorrow, so I can sleep in."

Joe always knew when to take charge. I should've felt lucky, but I didn't.

I woke in the small hours to the lilt of a lullaby. I stretched, smoothing deep into the corners of the bed with my toes. I curved one leg over the bedclothes. The cool quilt felt good against my inner thigh, and I was waiting. Every bit of me was suddenly… waiting. Just let that curly-haired Joe roll the long length of him into bed now, beside me. I could *eat* him.

The lullaby stopped. I dozed. After a while, feeling carefully in the gloom, I realised Joe hadn't returned. I lowered my feet to the floor and tiptoed into Micky's room. Joe had sung himself to sleep. Micky, on the other hand, was just tuning up the bagpipes.

At this moment, heaving damp clothes out of the washer for the third time this afternoon, I have only one good thing to say about Micky Marshmallow. He's living proof that once Joe and I were able to spend more than two minutes in the same bed. Together. As man and wife. For long enough to make a baby.

If we get the chance, Joe and I hope to be lovers again. How we're to manage this in the longest sexual drought it's ever been my misfortune to live through, is another matter.

Some women, it says in *Your After-Baby Book,* that I braved a peeved-looking assistant for in the library, do not want sex after the birth. This, it says, is perfectly natural.

The book describes, at length, how to ginger up your AB (After Baby) love-life. Try It, they suggest, in a Different Room. On A Rug, or A Sofa. Possibly Out of Doors (With Discretion). Why should sex become dull and routine, they ask?

There is no mention of the other problem. The one where an expanding baby marshmallow charges a couple's most intimate moments with the allure of a sponge dishmop. For sex to have the chance to become dull and routine needs practice, for goodness' sake. I groan, rocking slightly on my knees before the front-loader.

I find myself whacking wet sheets and towelling babygros and endless Bouncing Bunny baby bibs into the basket, grunting as each blow falls, when Ita knocks on the door.

"Nuala! Are you okay, sweetie?"

I stop, choking only slightly.

"Fine!" I say. "Tea?"

And then I burst into tears.

After Ita's come in and fussed me and pegged my washing and made a pot for two, she offers one simple solution.

"You must get out. The two of you."

"What do we use for money?" I ask. "Buttons?"

"Being cynical doesn't suit you," says Ita, flicking back her bleached bob. "You'll take my old car and go for… a lovely spin."

Ita's car is more like a rocking horse, it has that many blotches painted over the rust. But, as she says, it'll get us from here to Lover's Lane.

"What about Micky?"

For answer, Ita points to herself, and smiles.

"Champion baby's bottleholder, me! Tomorrow, I'll sing the lullaby for Micky Marshmallow."

"Oh Ita, are you sure?"

"Just be certain you tell that man of yours. All that Joe-type gorgeousness going to waste. It's a crime, so it is."

I'm that excited, I confess I don't worry about Micky after that. If he cries tomorrow, Ita will hear him. There is simply nothing, nothing to worry about.

Joe strokes his chin when I tell him. I'm edgy, thinking he won't agree. But he nods, and says yes, a good idea, and trust Ita for the best ones.

"But the car..?" he asks.

"Insured!" I say.

"I wasn't thinking of that," says Joe. "It's just there isn't much room inside a rocking horse, is there?"

"Never stopped us before," I remind him.

"That was then," says Joe. "I don't fancy romancing round the gear stick these days."

"But Joe…"

He says nothing, and I feel ignored. I so want this to work out. I know I'll expire with longing before Micky Marshmallow decides to sleep through the night.

Saturday evening. I've spent all afternoon washing and brushing and buffing. I wear the only one of my non-maternity dresses that fits. I rediscover my fine silver sandals and unkink the battered straps. I turn sideways before the wardrobe mirror, and like myself. Then I turn the other way, and like myself all over again. Six times every hour, I think of Joe. His soft voice. His kind hands. The intense way he looks at me when we love. Sure, he'll take care of everything, as he always has.

And then he's home. Ita arrives, and Micky gets kissed. We leave with Ita's good wishes and the first few notes wheezing from Micky's bagpipes.

Outside, Joe lets in the clutch on the rocking horse.

"How far do you want to go?" he asks.

"Now, there's a question! How far would you like?"

"All the way…" he whispers, making me laugh.

We draw up in the courtyard of a small pub.

"This is it," Joe says, climbing out.

"I thought we were heading for Lover's Lane…" I say.

"Not this time… your four-poster awaits, ma'am."

It's true. Joe has fixed it. Supper in a quiet corner. Soup. Something spicy and melting in puff pastry. A pudding so light you couldn't taste the sharpness of the lemon until the end.

"Coffee?" Joe asks.

"Mmm."

"Got to keep awake, now," he teases, floating cream across the back of a spoon.

We climb the stairs, entwined, and stand beside the draped bed clasped like honeymooners.

"This is wonderful," I say. "All night…"

"Better than inside the rocking horse. Don't say I do nothing for you," Joe grins, unbuttoning. "Here, let me help you… easy, now… that's right…"

The sheets are white and soft with boiling, and we fall into them. Once we've sorted where we fit under all this luscious linen, I stretch beside him. He's warm, and smells cleanly of soap, and if he could gather me any closer in his arms I think he would. He scans my face, eyes half-closed. I watch him from under my lids for as long as I can. I feel the touch of his lips and I'm lost… spiralling into the darkness where there is no sound but a heartbeat…

Then… an unfamiliar nothing. I'm too involved to be worried, exactly, but the atmosphere chills.

After long, tense moments, Joe mutters, "Maybe later," rolls away, and slumps into a large padded chair by the window.

His profile is edged by a faint blue light. This could not, *could not*, be happening. This was Joe, who always knew what to do, and did it.

Furiously, rucking back the sheets, I prop myself on one elbow.

"I'd be glad to sleep any other time. But not now, Joe. Please, not now…"

"Sorry."

"But you've arranged everything…"

"Everything except the vital ingredient." I hear him shift in the chair. He sighs, like the last puff of a storm. Then it strikes me. How he takes charge. How he must've fixed all this, the meal, Ita for the overnight stay, the posh bed…

Suddenly, I'm not grateful, but angry. Angry for him and… burning for him from head to toe, imagining how he must feel and not wanting him to feel that way a moment longer.

"*You* are my vital ingredient," I say, semi-wrapped in a sheet, padding across the bedroom in the dark. I put my arms around his neck, kissing him; I am determined.

Somehow Joe, the sheet, a couple of cushions from the chair, and me, end up not on the bed at all, but beside it.

"I don't care. If we… do nothing more than roll on a… rug, I want you close!"

"But this isn't what I planned, Nuala…"

"You can't control everything," I murmur, quieter now, rocking him in my arms and kissing his eyes back and forth. It's so good to hold him, to smell him, to be warmed by the length of his body.

"Come here… and forget the day. This is our time," I say, remembering.

I tell him about rugs, and advice from *Your After-Baby Book*, and later, giggling, we can agree there's definitely something about Doing It Somewhere Else.

I shoot bolt upright in bed and look for the clock, panic rising in waves when I can't see it.

"Micky!" I say, and then remember where Joe must've lifted me after last night. He turns sleepily.

"'S'okay," he says.

"But Ita has to get to work…"

"Sunday…" Joe slurs. "Calm down…"

But the thought that Micky might be howling for his mum and dad while they are far off in some strange frilly bedroom, means I can't. Joe finds his mobile.

"Ring," he says, falling back on the pillows, watching me. Ita answers.

"Everything all right?" I say.

"Fine, sweetie. How're you, then?"

Joe has roused himself and is trailing small kisses up my nearest arm.

"Great," I say.

Joe has reached my neck…

"He drank all his milk, too," says Ita.

..and my unoccupied ear…and he knows where I'm most ticklish…

"Good, Ita. Thanks. For everything. OK," I gasp. "Bye!"

Joe's kiss slides warm against my throat and I drop the mobile beside the bed.

"So, how's Micky Marshmallow?" Joe asks, cradling my shoulders as we slide down the bed together. I smile.

“Ita says she doesn’t know why we worry. Little man slept all night without so much as a burp.”

“Let’s hope,” murmurs Joe, against my lips, “he’s getting practice at what he ought to do best. Like his dad…”

Yin and Yang
Jill Steeples

The celestial alignment was all wrong, according to my best friend Zoë. Mars was in retrograde, the Moon was in Capricorn and what had happened to Uranus just didn't bear thinking about. Which meant, as any heavenly creature worth her salt would know, things were doomed from the start. I happened to mention this to Mark, as we lingered over linguini in our favourite Italian restaurant.

"You don't really believe all that mumbo jumbo, do you?" he said, looking at me sceptically.

"No, but Zoë said …"

"Oh well, I might have known she'd have something to do with it. She's a fruitcake, Jen, spouting all that new-age stuff and feng-shuiing everything in sight. She should get a life!"

Mark had never quite bonded with Zoë in the way I'd hoped. She, in turn, had taken a pathological dislike to my new boyfriend on account of his riverside apartment, the Armani suits and his red convertible sports car. Funnily enough, those sorts of things don't bother me.

But had it not been for Zoë, I don't think I'd ever have met Mark in the first place. For ten long months, my love life had been a barren patch of wasteland. Not a single eligible man nor even, come to that, an ineligible man, had shown the slightest interest in me. I was beginning to think I was destined for a life in the spinsterhood. Over a bottle of Chardonnay on yet another Saturday night spent at home, I remember bemoaning the fact to Zoë.

"Well, is it any wonder," she'd said, grabbing me by the arm, flinging open my bedroom door, and confronting me with the mess inside.

"Um, yuk," I said, surveying the battleground that doubled as my sleeping place. Discarded underwear in various hues of grey adorned every surface, dust motes danced in the air and the bed looked decidedly crumpled and uninviting. "Okay, it's a mess," I admitted, sheepishly, "but what on earth has that got to do with my love life?"

"Feng Shui," she said, by way of explanation. "All that clutter in the west corner is sapping energy from your relationship zone. Your bed's pointing in the wrong direction. And those mirrors will have to go, too."

Well, I reckoned a little re-organisation in the bedroom department was way overdue and to be honest I was that desperate to improve my romantic prospects, I would've danced naked round the shopping centre if I'd thought it might have helped. Thankfully it didn't come to that, but under Zoë's expert guidance I got to work putting a pair of pink scented candles in the newly uncluttered west corner, a bowl of water in the south-east corner and a yellow-flowered plant in the south-west corner. Oh, and just to be on the safe side, I threw out all that grotty old underwear and splashed out on some new, lacy, black and red combinations. I'll admit all those colours clashed a bit, but if it was going to turn my love life round, who was I to care?

Well, no-one was more surprised than I, when two weeks later, Mark walked into my office and into my life. It's funny the things that first attract you to someone, but, with Mark, it was the delectable sight of his long, bronzed neck, against the stiff whiteness of his starched collar. Eminently kissable. We made an immediate connection, his dark eyes locking with mine over the new laptop he'd come to install. We didn't look back and, six months down the line, our relationship just kept on getting better.

Now, as I watched him from across the table, the heady aroma of garlic, tomatoes and wine wafting, with a subtle hint of lemon-scented aftershave, in the air, my stomach performed one of those startling topsy-turvy manoeuvres.

"Zoë just wants the best for me," I said.

"And you think I don't?" He dipped a finger into his wine and traced its seductive wetness over my lips. "Besides, this has nothing to do with Zoë," he said, his voice heavy with intent. "You don't have to consult her or the runes or whatever the latest new-age thing is, before deciding what you want from life."

I laughed. I hadn't stopped laughing since I'd met Mark. But this? This was something altogether more serious. Looking into Mark's reassuring, twinkling eyes, I knew that beneath that jovial exterior, he'd never been more sincere about anything in his life.

"The thing is," I ventured, giving voice to Zoë's cautionary words, "you're an Aries and …"

"Oh, here we go," said Mark, banging his hands exaggeratedly on the table. "So let's get this right. I'm Aries. You're Scorpio." He stood up from his chair, flung his arms wide open and broke into his best Doris Day impression. "The future's not ours to see. Que Sera, Sera?"

All the other diners turned and swivelled their heads as one to view the impromptu performance. Embarrassed, I made a futile attempt to blend into the red-checked tablecloth. Whatever else could be said about Mark, life certainly wasn't dull in his company.

"No, but I just think it's worth considering these things," I said, quietly, twirling a strand of pasta around my fork.

Mark snorted derisively, took a swig of champagne and sat back in his chair, folding his arms in front of him. He was enjoying every minute of this, I could tell. Under the scrutiny of his burning gaze, I felt my cheeks redden. My head was telling me one thing, my body something entirely different. Determined not to be put off, I continued.

"It's all to do with our elements, apparently."

"Is it now?" he said, leaning across the table, his eyes crackling mischievously. "And what would they be?"

"Well you're fire and I'm water."

"Yes,"said Mark, throwing his hands up theatrically. "Sounds good to me. You light my fire every time, sweetheart."

"I'm just saying," I continued valiantly, "it might not be the best combination."

"You have the most beautiful eyes," he said, taking me off balance again. "Like deep, rich aquamarine pools. That would be the water in you, I suppose."

"Mark, stop making fun of me. I'm trying to make a serious point. You might not believe in astrology, but all sorts of people use it to help them make the right decisions in life."

"I know, I know," he said, stroking the length of my fingers, "but what about trusting your own instinct? Following your heart? Yin and Yang?"

"Yin and Yang?" I asked, incredulous.

"Don't tell me you haven't heard of Yin and Yang," he said, the barest hint of a smile reaching his lips. "You represent Yin, being all things feminine, receptive and dark. I'm Yang, which represents the masculine, fire and movement. Two poles of existence that are opposite but complementary. Like you and me."

I raised a querying eyebrow.

"I'm not just a pretty face, you know," he said, teasingly, dazzling me with that megawatt smile of his. "Trust me, I know more than you realise."

You see, that's another thing I love about Mark. He's full of surprises. And, come to think of it, what did Zoë really know about these things anyway?

"So?" Mark said, expectantly, perhaps sensing the subtle shift in my attitude.

"So?" I said, in reply, my turn to do the teasing.

"Come on, Jenny, put a guy out of his misery. What's it to be, yes or no?"

Sneaking a furtive glance around the room, I realised all eyes were cast upon me, a sea of expectant faces anticipating my next move.

But what was there to think about? Yin and Yang just about covered it all. My heart heavy with desire, I looked into his imploring eyes.

"Yes," I said breathlessly, as a huge wave of applause erupted around me. "Of course I'll marry you."

Fish in the Sea

Lynne Barrett-Lee

Holiday romances are a little like Christmas – the anticipation, the excitement, the heightened emotions, and the sense that everything is slightly unreal. The sky's a little bluer, the sun's a little hotter, the place where your heart normally goes about its business just a little more vulnerable to a stray cupid's dart. And also like Christmas, it's over too soon. All glitz and sparkle for as long as it lasts and the doldrums as soon as the whirlwind's passed by. I'm forty two, so I know all about it. My daughter, Kate, being sixteen, doesn't.

Not yet. And I don't think she's ready for the telling.

"Have some toast," I urge instead. "It'll be a long morning. You can't go off to school on an empty stomach. You'll be –"

"Mum, I'm not *hungry*. Okay?" Her answer is short. Snatched away by her sigh. Like a sad little rag that's caught up in a breeze.

Her first day back at school. And she's looking so, well, droopy. Her shoulders droop. Her hair droops. Her clothes – now she no longer has to wear uniform – are a positive rhapsody of droopiness, from the hang of the battered old jacket she won't part with, to the fall of the voluminous jeans they all wear.

“Then take something with you,” I tell her, more sternly, proffering a banana like a relay race baton, while she gathers her things up and prepares to leave.

She takes it, along with her lunch money and backpack, but I know it’ll be coming back with her at teatime, all blackened and weepy. And, well, droopy. But it makes me feel better. It’s something, at least.

We’d talked, Jack and I, about holiday romances. Sitting on the low wall that snaked down to the harbour, on a morning three weeks back that was blinding with sunshine. A day so unlike today and yet I can almost still taste it. Boats bobbed in the bay, diamonds danced on the water, and trippers – so many of them – thronged the tiny quayside, all eager and smiling and unshackled from their cares. We smiled and reminisced and drank Diet Cokes from dusty bottles. He had a crate of them slung in the corner of his hut. Jack ran the boat trips. In the summer, at any rate. In the winter, he told me, he worked at his “day job”. Which was boat building. I’d never met a boat builder before. My ex-husband was – is – a chartered accountant. No holiday romance component to my marriage. We’d met in the real world. Parted there too.

Jack and I had smiled as we recalled our own teenage escapades. My anguish when I’d said goodbye to the boy in the next caravan but one in Tenby, Jack’s terrible yearning for a ginger-haired girl who’d broken his frisbee, then gone back to Hull and broken his heart. Oh, yes, we agreed, we’d both certainly been there. That oh-so-brief but terrifically intense journey that Kate had tentatively embarked on that day. The day that Gareth – for that was his name – first approached her, as she sat reading her book on the sand.

She’d not been thrilled with the idea of a holiday, of course. Being sixteen was all about hanging out with your mates, not being holed up in a holiday flat with your mother on a fishing village quayside. And without the umbilical cord of your CD player. But I'd insisted, being all too aware that the time when I'd no longer be able to do so was approaching fast. And though a part of her, I knew, felt an obligation to keep me company, the main thing to tip the scales was that it was late August, and a lot of her friends had already left town themselves. To the Costas, Greek Islands or Florida, with their families. No such luxury for us two. This flat, which I'd rented through a friend at work, was the best I could afford, so would just have to do.

And it was, as it turned out, both pretty and practical. The top floor of one of five narrow houses that gave straight onto the quayside, it had a giant sash window that looked out over the harbour and the sea. It was mere yards from the beach, mere lanes from the shops, and mere minutes, it turned out, from the posh end of the bay, where Gareth and his sisters were staying, in a geranium-flanked cottage that was owned by his Gran. Another lonely young soul set adrift in a comatose village. Not surprising, therefore, that they two should meet.

It's been going like this. The postman comes, there's a thunk on the doormat, then a minor stampede as Kate rattles down the stairs. Then silence. Then more silence. Then the slow thump-thump-thump of her boots on the stair treads as she stomps back upstairs. I'm not sure what to do. What *is* there to do? He either will or he won't and that's all there is to it. I want to say "plenty more fish in the sea". But I don't of course. It wouldn't be helpful right now.

Or it goes like this. The tinkling tone of her mobile starts up. The tootle-toot-tootle than means there's a message. Then a flurry as she ploughs though her back pack to find it and the anxious scrolling to read what it says. Then another stab, perhaps an exhalation of breath. Then it's back in the bag and the scowl's back in place. I'm tempted to say "plenty more pebbles on the beach". But I don't say that either. I stay silent. Wouldn't you?

Through the kitchen window, I watch her leave now, her shoulders straining against the heavy bag as she heads off to the bus stop. Now she's back at school she leaves before the postman, and I find myself almost as anxious to hear him as she is. Hoping he'll arrive with good news before I leave. Perhaps today it'll happen. Perhaps he'll write, or he'll text, and she'll be happy again. Then again – now I'm late, so I skip clearing breakfast – perhaps he won't. He's back in the real world. As is Kate. As am I. That's what a holiday romance is like. She'll get over it. Get over *him*. And so she should. She's young still. She has her whole life ahead of her. All the time in the world to find love.

The second day of the holiday, I embarked on a plan. Nothing too ambitious, this was a holiday after all, but a plan to photograph some of the boats in the harbour, with their gay colours, their fluttering flags, their tarry underbellies, both gouged and smoothed by the sea. Taking pictures is what I do for a living, but mainly, which is why it can get a little samey, of school children, toddlers, family groups. I like taking pictures of seasidey things. And the village, huddled so prettily in the crook of a craggy rock elbow, was picture-book perfect.

I met Jack that morning, as well. He was difficult to miss, what with his battered little hut and his placards advertising trips round the bay. Perhaps Kate and I would like to try one? I'd shaken my head. Kate gets terribly seasick. Perhaps *I'd* like to try one, then. I returned his bright smile and said I'd see.

Kate had a plan too, but hers was of a teenage, and therefore largely sedentary, persuasion. She would lie on the beach. Just that. Every day. And read heaps of books. She's a great reader, Kate, more adventurous than I am, and had bought enough volumes to furnish a small library. Everything from weighty biographies of pioneering women to densely packed narratives by literary greats. She's doing A' level English. She wants to be a writer. And she'd make a good one. Where I record real life with my trusty camera, Kate can paint beautiful pictures with words.

"Would you believe," she announced breathlessly, as I came down to join her on the beach for some lunch. "That I met a boy this morning who's actually read *Far From The Madding Crowd*?"

My pictures taken, I'd popped up to the bakery and grabbed baguettes for us. I slipped off my sandals and sat down beside her, stretching my legs out and digging my feet in, the sand cool and pleasingly damp between my toes. In the distance I could see Jack's boat chugging out of the bay, a knot of waving day trippers bunched at the prow. I handed Kate her baguette and smiled. At the notion that such a thing would so impress her. But then this is, after all, a computer-led age.

"It's been known," I laughed, before biting into my baguette. The boat disappeared around the headland, leaving a faint creamy stripe in its wake. "But it's still nice, isn't it? When you read something special and find someone else you can share it with." Especially when that someone's a boy, I thought. But didn't say so, of course. "Who is he?"

"His name's Gareth," she told me. And even then, as she sank her teeth carefully into the end of her baguette, I could see a spark of something had come alight in her eyes.

That had been the Monday, and by Wednesday, in that speeded-up way such things happen, they were already an item. A fixture on the beach. And, as I said, Jack and I had laughed about it.

"He's my nephew," he'd confided as we watched them on the beach below us. It was lunchtime, the sun pansy-yellow above us. As I'd taken to, I stopped to chat for a moment before popping into the flat to drop off my gear. I might, I thought, spend the afternoon on the beach myself. Have a swim, maybe. The sea looked beguilingly blue. I'd spent the early part of the morning up at the other end of the harbour, taking pictures of such fishing fleet as still existed here these days as they landed their catch and sold their slippery wares. And on my way back, I'd spotted Jack talking to Kate and Gareth, before they headed off with ice creams back down to the sand.

"Really?" I accepted the coke he was proffering. He pushed a hand through his dusty blonde curls. "My sister's eldest. Down for a couple of weeks with his Gran while she's at work. He's a nice lad. Though not too thrilled to be stuck here, I can tell you. But that's hardly surprising, is it? The nearest we get to action down here is if the bulb blows in the lighthouse."

Which was exactly why I was loving it so much. I stretched my legs out in front of me and let the sun warm my skin. "They certainly seem smitten," I observed as I watched them, Kate's hair brushing Gareth's wide brown shoulders as they sat, both engrossed in the book in his lap.

Jack nodded, then upturned the coke to his lips.

"Nice, isn't it?" he said as he finished it and grinned at me. "To be sixteen again, eh? Living in the moment. In love."

And now it's a wet Monday morning and those sultry days suddenly seem a long, long way away. I wonder what Gareth's up to now. Probably on his way to school, just like Kate. He doesn't live so very far away, as it turns out. An hour down the motorway, no more than that. I wonder what'll happen if he does get in touch. Taxi time, I muse, as I back out of the driveway. The poor car, as if listening and registering its protest, splutters and wheezes its way down the road.

"A proper photographer, eh?" Jack remarked, late that second Tuesday. He was taking his boards down, shutting up shop for the day. It had become a pleasant routine, sitting on the wall with him, chatting. His little shed – where the tickets were advertised and sold – was literally just under the window of our flat. It had been a good day, he'd said, non-stop business, but now he had to go back down to the boat and make a few repairs. He was standing a little further along the wall, unfastening bunting that had been up all summer and that had now become more than a little tangled and forlorn. His big hands coped easily with the knots and the ravels, the muscles in them sinewy under his nut-brown skin. "I thought that camera of yours looked impressive. What sort of photographer?"

"Just for a studio," I said, feeling a small stab of melancholy as I watched him work. It was almost the end of August. He wouldn't bother replacing it, he'd told me. The first sign that summer was coming to a close. "You know, portraits and so on. Plus schools. We do lots of school photos. I'll be pretty busy right through next month."

He paused to gaze out along the skyline. "And I'll be off for a couple of weeks on *my* holiday." His mouth curled in a smile as he turned back towards me. "I'm going to sail around – hang on!" He put a finger to his lips. "Quick! Come over here!"

I got off the wall and went over to join him at the far side of the hut. He silently pointed to the beach down below.

Kate and Gareth, hand in hand, were headed towards the steps down below us, a watermelon sun slinking towards the horizon behind. Their heads were close together, their fingers entwined.

"You want to get a picture of that, "Jack whispered, grinning. He curled his own fingers around mine to help me climb up. And it sent electricity through me.

It's a lovely picture. A little dark on account of the setting sun, but nevertheless a fine composition, even if I do say so myself. I haven't given it to Kate, of course, what with Gareth not getting in touch. I don't want to make her any worse than she is.

She's already home when I get back from work, the kitchen table covered with books and files.

"Well?" I ask. "Good day? How does it feel to be a sixth former at last?"

"Okay," she replies, carrying on sorting her files out. "Mandy Smith's away. Broke her leg water skiing, apparently. But apart from that nothing much to report." She shrugs. Then turns to face me. "I don't suppose –"

I shake my head. "Nothing today, I'm afraid. Kate, look –" I sit down beside her. "Have you thought about writing to *him*, maybe?"

She shakes her head firmly. "Absolutely not," she says indignantly. "Mum, I'm not going to chase him, you know!"

"It would hardly be chasing him, Kate. Just a short letter, you know, asking him how he is and so on. You wouldn't need to make a big deal of it, or anything –"

She plonks down a file and looks at me as if I recently beamed in from Mars.

"Mum, don't you know anything? You just don't *do* that, okay." Then she considers. "*I* don't, at any rate. The arrangement was that *he* was going to get in touch. That *he* was going to get in touch with *me*. And if he's decided he's –" She has to stop because her chin is wobbling.

I hurry to fill the silence. "Perhaps he lost your address. Perhaps he hasn't had a chance yet. Perhaps –" I tail off. Perhaps nothing. She's right. If he'd wanted to he would have. No sense in prolonging the agony by hoping. The best thing's to move on. Consign the holiday to memory. A few weeks and she'll be over it, for sure. I hug her instead.

"It's tough, love. I know that. But –"

"Mum, you don't know. You *don't!"* I watch helplessly as a single tear tracks down her cheek. I *do* know, of course. Doesn't every woman? I go and grab her some kitchen roll to blow her nose with.

In amongst the mess of papers on the table there's a small furry bug in a lurid shade of green.

"What's this?" I ask, picking it up to inspect it. It has a ribbon of tail which says 'Missed you!' in pink. She glances up, sniffing.

"Oh, it's just something Liam gave me."

"Liam?"

"Liam Bennett. You know. Lower sixth. Actually, no." She shrugs. "He's in the upper sixth now."

She sounds totally disinterested. She *is* totally disinterested. Her mind – her whole world – is still on summer holiday. Hand in hand, on a beach, with her first summer love.

I look out. It's still raining. Will it always be raining? "How about we go out for supper?" I try.

Kate shakes her head. "I'm really not hungry," she says.

Fish. There were certainly plenty of them down on the quay that Thursday morning. A bumper night's work, glistening and glaring from their nests of crushed ice. I was up as the boats came in, snapping them in the pearly dawn mist. Curious how early I was rising on this holiday. My normal morning mode (sluggish, bordering on comatose shuffling) had been replaced with an energy I'd forgotten I possessed. Jack was down there too, helping out. It was very much a family business. His father, as weathered and craggy as the cliff face, was still out every night and bringing in his haul.

"Coffee?" Jack suggested, as he lifted his last crate. "And a bun, perhaps? They do a fine currant bun at the bakery in Quay street. Still warm at this time." He wiped his hands. "Fancy that?"

It wasn't yet nine. I'd had no breakfast. I was hungry. Yes, I said. I did. We headed up the steps.

He stopped at the top and turned round to grin at me. "So," he said. Reading the flush in my cheeks? "How about this boat trip of ours?"

The end of the week. I've got two big school jobs to get through today, so I leave before the postman. But when I pop home to grab a bite of lunch between them, I flick through what's come. There's nothing, again.

The sea, at night, is as deep and dark and unfathomable as it is gay and bright and sparkling by day. The boat, this large workaday cruiser than I'd watched plough the bay almost every day for two weeks now, had become charmed by the moonlight, a shy Cinderella dressed up for the ball. It trailed a phosphorescent light that made the surface gleam lemon. The cooling evening air rippled though my hair, and the tang of seaweed was sharp in my nostrils. The bay was now no more than a scatter of distant diamonds in the blackness. Everything felt slightly unreal.

"Strictly speaking," said Jack, "I don't drink when I'm sailing, but one half glass won't hurt, will it?" I shook my head. No, it wouldn't. He dipped his arm, grabbed a rope, pulled a bottle from the water. Then had me go fetch two cups from a cupboard below.

When I returned, the bottle was open, and Jack's lean form was silhouetted in the wheelhouse.

And something had happened. Something had changed. The air was now charged, and it stirred as I approached him. Stirred as I took in the slope of his shoulders. Stirred as my bare feet traversed the small distance that would take us from new friends enjoying a boat trip to a place I hadn't visited in a very long time.

He smiled at me then. And beckoned me closer. Poured wine into our mugs, which we sipped with locked eyes. Then he put down his mug and lifted one finger, which he wordlessly traced down the side of my cheek.

"I love it out here," he said. "Thank you for coming." His eyes held my gaze and I suddenly felt reckless. Sixteen again. Ready to live in the moment. Ready to surrender myself to *this* moment. This time and this place and this man.

We embraced then, the dark water lapping beneath us. And we kissed our way down to the velvety deck and we said nothing more for some time.

When I get home the following Friday, Kate's handbag is in the hallway and she herself is tripping, all dressed up, down the stairs.

"Oh, you're back, Mum. Good day? Can I ask a *huge* favour?"

She shrugs on her jacket as I take off my coat.

And she's smiling. "Can you give me a lift into town?"

I put my coat back on.

"Off out somewhere, are you?"

She nods. "But I'm late. And I think I've missed the bus."

I hand her her bag. "No problem," I tell her. We step back outside. "Anywhere nice?"

"We're off to see a movie. And then going for a pizza."

"That's nice. So… *with* anyone nice?"

I catch her blush from the corner of my eye. "With Liam."

"Liam Bennett?"

She nods again. "And some others as well."

But her smile says the others really don't matter *that* much. Chapter closed. Kate's holiday romance is behind her. I smile to myself as we climb into the car.

"Two weeks," Jack said. "Two glorious weeks." He looped the end of the mooring line round the bollard on the jetty. The sky was impossibly crowded with stars now. He straightened and smiled at me. "Then it's back to reality, of course."

"Sounds wonderful," I said, wishing reality away as we made our slow way hand in hand along the dockside and back to its chilly embrace.

"It will be. You know, you should try it some time, maybe."

"Oh, I'm no sailor."

"You don't know until you try. Besides, I'd be captain. You could try it for...well, for a weekend sometime, maybe?" He squeezed my hand. Pulled me towards him as we walked.

"I don't think so. I don't know a hull from a halyard."

Not true. But almost. He pulled me a little closer.

Then he stopped and said quietly, "But you don't get seasick."

Which *is*, of course, true. I don't.

The house seems very quiet tonight. I make myself some supper and try to watch the TV, but what with the rain hammering against the windows, and the relentless ticking of the clock on the fireplace, I can't seem to settle at all.

I pull my purse from my bag and riffle through the receipts, cleaning tickets, odd bits of paper, all of which were probably important at some point, but which now have no meaning at all. Except one. And it's still there, where I put it, so carefully folded. I open it up and read the phone number on it. Then read it again and consider for a while.

"Well?" he had asked me. "Sometime? Are you game?"

I'd shaken my head. "I don't think so," I'd said. The thing about holiday romances, of course, is that they're best left where they belong. Like the crabs in a bucket you spent the day catching, which are best put back when the day's done. Except, well, I'm *not* sixteen, am I? So I don't have all the time in the world any more. And, sure, there are plenty more fish in the sea, but if there's one thing a little maturity gives you it's the wisdom to know, if belatedly, when you've found one you very much want.

We'd parted – one last electrifying kiss – on the quay. And that, I had thought, had been that. The moment done. The note I had found the next day, with my name on. Sitting on the mat just inside the front door.

'No problem,' he'd written, 'if you don't ring, of course. No pressure. The ball's in your court.'

The fishing boats were in when we'd left that morning. The hut all shut up. The signs all taken down.

I look up at the clock. Kate will be home soon. Kate will come in and the moment might pass. Good sense might prevail, as it often does with mothers. Especially mothers as grounded and sensible as me.

But he was absolutely right. I *don't* get seasick.

I'm a little giddy, nevertheless, as I pick up the phone.

A Racy Little Number

Carole Matthews

Some women seem to spend their lives being lavished with gifts – diamonds, weekends in country manors, plane tickets to St Tropez, etc, etc. Whereas I, Lucy Harris, do not.

Every year, when Valentine's Day looms large on the calendar, I have to start dropping hints the size of boulders to my long-time, dearly beloved, Alex.

He has many charms but he could never be called one of life's natural present-buyers. As soon as New Year is over and all my resolutions about not cajoling Alex into reluctant gift purchases have been forgotten, I start making comments about the sort of romantic item that might add joy to my life on this February the 14th, the day for lovers. I usually precede the statement by a few well-aimed coughs and then go on to mention bouquets of fragrant flowers, luscious chocolates, romantic weekends in Paris, expensive lingerie and all the other things my heart desires. They normally, without exception, fall on deaf ears. But I wouldn't have thought it was too much trouble for him to splash out on some expensive undies – though preferably not of the red, peephole variety which most men seem to favour. Wouldn't all of our lives be improved by a racy little number?

Alex says that he shows me that he loves me every day of the year and doesn't want to be forced into overt displays of commercialism just because the retail trade have decreed it. I think this is man-speak for 'I am a cheapskate'. Last year I got nothing and he, in turn, got me sporting a sulky lip for three days.

This year the lack of a glossily-wrapped gift is the least of my worries. I run a small print shop which sounds a lot more glamorous than it is. In reality my debts are escalating at an alarming rate, my business is in trouble and it's not down to my own mismanagement, but one of my biggest customers bouncing a rather large cheque on me, leaving a gaping hole in my accounts. Such are the risks of having your own company. I'm struggling along manfully, but I'm going to have to make some serious cutbacks to keep my head above water.

I look out of the window of the shop and eye my lovely Ford Fiesta, Roxanne, with something approaching misery. Last year was a different story, business was booming and I splashed out on my first ever new car. Brand spanking new, complete with enough gadgets to keep even Alex amused. She's red, raunchy and drives like a dream. And now she's got to go.

Believe me, it will be like cutting off one of my own arms. Frankly, I'd rather sell my house and sleep in the car, but I'm erring on the side of sense for once. Sell the car and I can clear my debts. Simple as that. But I will admit to shedding a tear over my decision. Just as Alex isn't a natural shopper, I'm not a natural taker of public transport. I like having my own wheels. It gives me a sense of independence and achievement. Plus I don't want to get mugged while I'm waiting for a bus.

I cry again when I drive Roxanne to her fate. The garage has given me a very good price for her and this should make me happy, but I still feel I'm betraying her. As I walk away she looks so forlorn, sitting in the forecourt.

That night, when Alex and I have dinner together, I'm inconsolable.

"It's the right thing to do," he says.

"Yes," I answer without enthusiasm. But I can't begin to explain to him how it's not just handing back a car – Roxanne was an intrinsic part of my success and now I feel like a failure.

"It's only a car."

Typical man. I give him a black look. She and I were a team. We took on the world and serious traffic congestion together. How can he not know this?

Alex takes my hand. "If I'd known that you'd feel so bad, I would have lent you the money."

"But you didn't," I say and burst into tears all over again.

Fate, fickle thing that it is, brings a huge new contract into my little print shop just one week later. I am ecstatic with joy! Not only have I cleared my debts, but I have enough to go and buy back Roxanne. Hurrah! I can't wait to rush to the garage but, of course, the phone doesn't stop ringing all day and I can't get away. When I finally bowl up there, the space where last week Roxanne was displayed in all her glory is standing empty. I rush into the salesroom. "Gone," the salesman informs me. "Straight away. A lovely little car." As if I didn't know that. "Can I interest you in another?"

No, is my answer. I don't want another car. Not yet. I have to grieve for Roxanne.

So Valentine's day rolls around again – unmarked, as usual, in my household. No card, no flowers, no ostentatious declaration of love. Nothing to adorn, or increase the size of, my hips. I am still catching buses everywhere and I'm still not happy. In fact, I'm barely talking to Alex. I haven't even arranged to see him tonight. My plans involve curling up on the sofa with *Bridget Jones' Diary,* a bottle of cheap wine and box of Dairy Milk – bought by myself.

Just as Hugh Grant makes his first appearance on the screen and I'm half-way through my chocolates, my door bell rings. I pad out to the door and Alex is standing there, looking rather cute, I have to admit. He hands me a small box.

"Open it now," he instructs me.

I do as I'm told and peel off the wrapping paper which reveals a small model of a red Ford Fiesta. "It's just like Roxanne," I gasp. Inside, on the little passenger seat, is a key attached to a fluffy red heart.

"Happy Valentine's Day, darling," Alex says as he stands to one side.

My lovely car is parked on the street outside, large as life. "Oh," I say. Tears fills my eyes. "It really *is* Roxanne." There's a single red rose under one of her windscreen wipers.

"I had to go and buy her back," my lovely, lovely boyfriend admits. "You'd missed her so much."

"Thank you." I wind my arms round his neck.

"I love you," he says.

"I love you too."

Alex opens Roxanne's door and I slide in. My baby's home! "So," he says, "'If I forget to buy you a card next year will I get away with it?'"

“Yes.” I settle into the driver’s seat and pat her steering wheel contentedly. “And probably the year after too…”

February Blossoms

Josephine Hammond

Juliette looked at her watch again. It was only 10 o'clock. With a sigh she got up and re-arranged flowers in her shop for the umpteenth time. She always felt that customers would be more likely to come in if she looked busy. It was a dank, drizzly day. The passers-by were sunk into their overcoats hurrying from their comfortable cars to the bright warmth of offices and shops.

"Everybody warned me that it was a bad time of year to start a business," she castigated herself, "but I wouldn't listen. December wasn't too bad. I sold a nice lot of holly and pot plants. Not enough to pay the bills, but enough to be hopeful. January, oh God, January! All those flowers I had to throw away."

She shivered with both distress and cold. She had no heating on in her shop. It made the flowers last longer and saved money.

In her head she could hear her mother's scolding voice. "Why do you do it to yourself? Up all hours to fetch flowers from that freezing cold market, worrying yourself awake all night. Why don't you get a normal job and settle down like your sister? She's doing so nicely now."

"Shut up, Mother," she said aloud to dispel this inner nagging. "I must make sacrifices if I'm going to succeed."

She wasn't sure which nagged more, her flesh and blood mother or the image of her that she carried in her head.

If I can just hold out till the spring, she thought, things will get better. Today at least should bring some custom. Not everyone sees Valentine's Day cynically. There must still be some romance out there.

Romance made her think about Jack. She had met him just before Christmas. She smiled as she pictured his handsome face and tall frame. They had first met only a couple of weeks after she had opened the shop. At six o'clock in the morning she'd taken her van down to the market to collect her stock.

She had been standing by the flower suppliers waiting her turn to load up. It was one of those damp and misty mornings and of course still dark since it was early and it was December. The lights of the vans and lorries reflected off the shiny, wet tarmac and fog was blowing around like steam. He seemed to appear from nowhere, tall and slim in suit and tie and one of those very elegant camel overcoats flowing behind him. He walked towards her across the wet road, the lights shining behind like a halo.

She had suddenly felt warm all over and found herself unable to hold his gaze. Their eyes had met briefly and then she had had to look away, afraid of the power of the emotions sweeping through her. He had suggested a cup of coffee and they had stood by the van drinking the hot steamy brew. His piercing blue eyes seemed to see straight through her as he asked all about her business.

Jack had been coming to the market for years. He had started with a fruit and veg stall in Brick Lane. He now had a chain of exclusive groceries-come-delicatessens. He knew everyone in the market place.

She knew she wasn't his type. He always had girlfriends who were of the chirpy buxom blonde sort. She was thin and with her hair tied back, no make-up and jeans and baggy pullover. She could hardly be said to be glamorous. But then he asked her out – to the cinema.

The invitation took Juliette by surprise. She had been wanting this since the first moment she saw him but hadn't dared hope. When she was with him, every nerve in her body thrilled to him. When his hand lightly brushed against hers as he passed her a cup of coffee at the mobile van, the shiver of pleasure that ran through her was so powerful that it once elicited concern from Jack that she might be cold. He had taken off his coat and put it round her shoulders. The warmth of it and the smell of him enveloped her in an aura of total bliss. But she couldn't bring herself to show how she felt. She had noticed his accent when they first met and they way he flirted with all the bimbos working in the market. He wasn't interested in her in that way and she knew what her mother and oh-so-successful sister would say about him: "So common." But she didn't care. She had come to love his voice and longed to hear him whisper words of love in her ear and feel him gently nuzzle her neck with his soft warm lips.

So she accepted his invitation – the first of many. But nothing had happened. Perhaps they were just too different.

Now it was Valentine's Day. A day Juliette had always disliked. The day when for most of her life her hopes had been dashed as postmen laden with huge bundles of cards rushed past her door to someone else's. Now she had another reason to dislike it. Business was not coming up to expectations.

Her thoughts went to Jack once more.

He's successful at everything he does, she thought bitterly. But I just can't make him out. All those wonderful evenings together and he has never shown any more inclination towards romance than a brotherly goodnight kiss. I'm sure he enjoys my company as much as I do his. So what's wrong? Perhaps I am too thin, as Mother says.

Just then a man came in and asked for a bunch of carnations.

"Is it for a Valentine?" Juliette asked with a smile, as she wrapped the flowers.

"Good gracious, no," came the reply. "I don't have anything to do with that tomfoolery. They are for my mother. She's in hospital."

So much for romance, even today, she thought as she watched him disappear into the scurrying crowds outside.

The day wore on. Only two more customers came into the shop. Juliette was beginning to despair. If she couldn't sell flowers on Valentine's Day of all days, she might as well give up. She began to worry about her finances again. Her thoughts chased each other round and round her head. She longed for someone to come into the shop, even if they didn't buy anything, just to put a stop to the downward spiral of her thoughts. At about three o'clock the door opened again.

"Hello, what a lovely surprise!" she cried.

"I was just passing," said Jack, "and I thought I would buy some flowers. After all, it is Valentine's Day." He smiled apologetically. "Are you keeping well?" He looked into her large dark eyes.

"I'm fine. Business is none too brisk but it'll probably pick up when everyone is on their way home tonight. What was it you wanted to buy?"

"Everything."

"Everything?"

"Yes, everything. I want to buy every flower in your shop. You needn't wrap them. Just help me load them into my car."

"Goodness!" said Juliette. "She must be a very special lady." She struggled to keep the shock and disappointment out of her voice.

"She is. She really is," replied Jack.

She pursed her lips and totted up how much he owed her. Then she helped him to fill his car with her entire stock of blooms. He paid, and with one of his maddeningly fraternal kisses was gone.

Juliette sat in her bare shop. It seemed even more silent and lonely without all the flowers. Why did he come here? she asked herself. He could have gone to any shop in town to buy flowers. Why taunt me by flaunting his romance under my nose? Then another terrible thought struck her. He did it out of pity. He feels sorry for me because he knows my business isn't doing too well. Damn him, I don't want his pity or his money.

For the first time in weeks she had a till full of money and she could not bear to look at it. She knew she could ill-afford the impulse to give it all back. Wearily she looked round her little shop. She was cold, tired and miserable.

"Well, I've nothing left to sell so I may as well shut up shop. So much for Valentine's Day."

The tiny cottage that Juliette rented was mercifully warm and cosy. She made herself a pot of tea and sank down into her favourite chair by the Rayburn. She soon warmed up, enjoying the luxury of heat and a rest until well after dark. Then she got up, switched on the lights and drew the curtains. She suddenly thought of Jack again and wondered what he was doing tonight. A vision of him declaring his love to his unknown lady came into her mind, engulfing her in misery. She heard her mother's voice telling her to "brace up. It's not worth crying over. Go and have a hot bath. Nothing like a nice hot bath when you're down". Of course mother's right as usual, she thought as she went to run her bath. Afterwards she did indeed feel better and was just going to the kitchen to rustle up some scrambled eggs when there was a knock at the door.

She opened it to find Jack standing there with an armful of flowers – her flowers. For a minute she thought he was bringing them back because he wasn't pleased with them. Then she saw his smile. He said, "For a very special lady," and held the flowers out to her.

"Why thank you, Jack," she gasped, taking them from him. "Come in."

"Just a minute," he said, disappearing into the darkness. He came back wheeling the rest of the flowers in a shining new wheelbarrow. He pushed it into the sitting room and set it down. "Happy Valentine's Day," he said, and started to fill the room with blooms from the wheelbarrow. When he had finished, the room was full of the colour and scent of a thousand blossoms. He turned to Juliette, lifted her in his arms and carried her over to the sofa where he gently laid her down. He knelt beside her.

"I have something to tell you," he said. "You are *very* special to me." His voice was deep with emotion. He bent to kiss her passionately for the first time. Juliette closed her eyes as she matched him kiss for kiss.

The Guitar Man

Della Galton

I remember the first time we met. You were playing your guitar on the beach, close to my parents' home, sitting on the rocks, one evening just before sunset. The tide was out and I was walking on the hard damp sand. It was a beautiful evening and I was so deep in thought that at first I didn't notice the music, drifting on the faint breeze. And then, when I did, I thought I must have imagined it. For a fleeting moment, I thought of the tales of the sea Dad used to tell me when I was small. Tales of sirens singing sweetly to lure sailors to their deaths on the rocks.

I stood still and listened. I didn't remember there ever being any male sirens and this was a man's voice, clear and earthy. No, the music was definitely real, but where was it coming from?

As I rounded the next little inlet, I saw. You were sitting on a rock, high up on the beach, the guitar resting across denim-clad knees, your head bowed and your fingers plucking away at the strings. I paused, feeling suddenly like an intruder, but drawn. And then you looked up and saw me, and you smiled, and it would have been rude to have carried on walking, so I went shyly up the beach to you.

You didn't stop playing until you got to the end of the song and then you looked up again and I saw that your eyes were as black as the rocks you sat on and that your hair, also dark, was what my mother would have called an indecent length for a man. You were wearing a brightly-coloured short-sleeved shirt over your jeans; your feet were bare. Your arms tanned and muscled, your fingers long. You gave me a look, the kind of look I would grow to know meant that you were feeling a little pensive and had come down here to escape. But I didn't know any of this then. I was escaping too.

I sat on the rock next to you.

"Am I interrupting? Is it all right if I stay and listen?"

That smile again. "Feel free."

So I did. I stayed where I was, listening to you play. Sometimes the music was gentle, sometimes fast, your fingers moving so quickly I couldn't see how you didn't make a mistake, but you never did. I found that I was tapping my fingers against my leg, and my toe on the soft sand at the base of the rock. In the distance the sun began to sink slowly towards the navy sea and the air grew cooler around us. I closed my eyes, lost in the music, and I didn't open them again, even when you stopped, until you said softly:

"Any requests?"

Then I did look up and found that you were studying me, your eyes quizzical.

"Something by Brian Adams?"

And you smiled and nodded and began to play 'Summer of 69', but you sang '89' instead, which was the year it was, throwing back your head and laughing and I found myself singing along with you. Until eventually you stopped and I clapped and then you put your guitar down, leaning it against a rock.

"So what's your name?"

"Ginny."

"I'm Ross." And the way you said it reminded me of waves washing over rocks. Musical. Somehow not quite of this earth. But later, when you took my hand and we sat watching the sunset paint the sea orange and gold, there was nothing unearthly about you. I leaned against your shoulder and you put your arm around me. It was as though we'd always been together. Even then.

We weren't alike. I could see that straight away. Maybe it was part of the attraction. But your music had opened a door between us and we talked a lot that night. I was escaping from a broken love affair. I can't even remember his name now, some lad I'd met at a barn dance. You were trying to escape too, not from love, but from the staleness of living in a remote part of Devon. While I found the restrictions of village life comforting, you found them oppressive. You told me about the band you'd set up. How you were tired of playing small gigs, how you wanted to get away to a city somewhere, or at least a big town. I remember saying, with all the flippancy of being seventeen, that not all city streets were paved with gold. Not like our beach, with the sand glowing gold beneath the moonlight as we walked along it. Later we kissed and I ran my fingers over the strong lines of your face and shivered. It's odd, but when I think back, I can't ever remember not loving you.

It's hard to believe that evening was thirteen years ago. We spent a lot of time on the beach that summer. We could always find a deserted stretch to walk on, to play music, and to talk. We shared each other's dreams. Yours were simple. You wanted to be famous. Mine were more difficult, and as time went on, I realised, impossible. I wanted you to stay with me, get married, have children and settle into the life my parents had.

I thought, sometimes, that I was like the sand, content to stay more or less in one place, and you were like the sea, forever restless, being tugged this way and that by forces too powerful to resist. I knew, even in those heady days, that you'd go some time and that going with you would probably break my heart more than if I stayed where I was.

"Living in a city wouldn't be that bad, Ginny, would it? Why don't you come? Try it for a while."

But while I could see the attraction city life held for you – bigger venues, lots of work – I knew I wouldn't have fitted in there. The dry city air would have suffocated me. So I let you go alone.

To be fair, you did try and stay in touch. Was it bitterness that made me return your letters unopened? Bitterness because you'd put your dreams ahead of our love? Or deep down, was I ashamed because I hadn't had the courage to go with you?

It was easy for me to keep track of what you were up to anyway. Write-ups in the music press, ecstatic reviews and once I found an article in our newspaper. *Local Musician On His Way To Stardom.* When I saw your face in a woman's magazine I knew you'd made it. That dark hair, fashionably long suddenly, the angular lines of your jaw, the mesmerising blackness of your eyes.

You made your dreams into reality, Ross, and I stayed here and tried to find new ones.

In 1995 I married Alan Jacobs. It was a different love to what we'd had. Not a passionate, heady thing, but a sensible love, based on friendship. Alan could give me what you hadn't been able to. A steady life, with kids, and he had a job that would never take him that far away from me. He was a landscape gardener. A job that was as down to earth as he was. I told myself that I was happy. Glad to have swapped a man who made music for a man who laid patio slabs and lawns. I'm not sure if I ever really believed it. When things started to go wrong, I kept asking myself that if Alan and I had truly loved each other, would we have let our marriage slide through our fingers so easily? After all, having kids wasn't the be all and end all. Having each other should have been enough. But, somehow, it wasn't.

We got divorced a year ago. Around the same time that you reached your peak in the music business. You'd never quite made the glittering heights but you were famous in Cornwall and Devon. You'd achieved what you'd always wanted. You were making money from playing music full time. I often wondered if you were happy.

The posters announcing that you were coming to Taunton, to play an open-air concert, started to go up a couple of months ago.

"Will you go?" Mum asked me one evening, as we sat in her kitchen sipping tea.

"I don't know. I doubt it."

She looked at me thoughtfully. "Maybe you ought to. Get him out of your system, once and for all."

"What do you mean?"

"Well, you never really have, have you, Ginny? You've been carrying a torch for him all these years. Poor Alan never stood a chance against such a glittering memory, did he?"

I stared at her in shock. Mum never said stuff like this. It had been Dad who'd been a bit of a dreamer, like me. Mum was strictly of the oak tree brigade. Firmly rooted and content to stand in the same corner of the forest all her life.

I was about to deny her words, but she put a finger to her lips. “Think about it. If you go and listen to him play, you might finally see him for what he is. An ageing rock star, who would never have made you happy. I bet he’ll have dyed hair and wrinkles.”

“I doubt it,” I said, smiling despite myself. “He’s only thirty five, Mum. Hardly over the hill, just yet.”

“You just go and see for yourself,” she said huffily. “I bet I’m right.”

So, that’s how I came to be here. Sitting on a blanket in a field, with a load of ageing hippies and a whole new generation of young groupies, about the same age as I was when we first met. I’m quite near the front, sitting on the grass, with my knees tucked up and a strange, fluttery feeling in my stomach, at the thought of actually seeing you in the flesh again. Because, even though you’ve toured this way a couple of time over the years, I’ve never had the courage to come before.

The lights dim on the stage and there is an expectant hush as the musicians start to take their places at keyboards, bass guitar and drums. And then finally you appear and lope across the stage with that same careless walk I remember. You reach your microphone, pick up your guitar and smile. Your smile hasn’t changed either. All around me, people are on their feet, cheering. The noise is deafening and I stand up too because if I don’t I’ll be crushed in the crowd. As you start to play, your fingers plucking out the same magic, the same rhythm, there is a tight ache of pain in my throat, because Mum was wrong. You don’t look any different to me than you did thirteen years ago. Your face is still as strong, your eyes as vibrant.

And I realise what, perhaps, I've always known: I've never stopped loving you.

The concert is an exquisite mix of ecstasy and agony. I can't bear to leave and I can't bear to stay. On the practical side it would be pretty hard to leave anyway, because I'm hemmed in on all sides by frantic dancers. You play for three hours and when the crowd encore you back for what turns out to be third and final time, you play 'Summer of 69' and once again you change the year to '89' and I wonder if you ever remember that year. That time when you had an audience of one.

I feel old and slightly foolish as I queue up with girls half my age, to try to catch a glimpse of you afterwards. Several people are clearing the stage and I'm just beginning to think that you must have been spirited off somewhere when I see you. I'm not the only one; you are instantly surrounded by autograph hunters, chattering females. You don't seem to mind too much. You laugh, sign their books, and pose for someone to take a snapshot. Jealousy twists inside me, but still I wait. I just want to say hello. Nothing more, nothing less. See your reaction. But when finally it's my turn, the words dry up in my throat.

As I take a step forward, you glance up. And then your face goes still. Neither of us speaks, and all I can think is that you're just as gorgeous close up as you ever were. Mum was wrong about that too.

"Long time, no see," you say at last and I smile.

"Thirteen years to be precise. And you don't look any different."

"Neither do you."

It's odd, but I don't feel at all uncomfortable talking to you, despite the fact that we're surrounded by people. We might as well be alone again.

"We've got some catching up to do, Ginny. Want to go somewhere a bit quieter?"

I nod and you reach for my hand. And I feel a jolt as your strong, clever fingers close around mine.

We end up driving to the beach where we first met. I only live a pebble's throw away, but I can't bear to take you home, because once I have a memory of you in my house, I know I'll never get it out again. So we walk instead, and we talk, and at four a.m. we end up sitting on the rocks, because neither of us is tired and there still seems so much more to say.

"No regrets?" I ask you now. "Are you happy, Ross?"

You nod, slowly, your eyes as soft as the velvet night. "Yes, I'm happy, but everyone has a few regrets. I should have tried harder to make you come with me."

"It wouldn't have worked. I had to stay here as badly as you had to go. We were different people then."

"So, where do we go from here?" You take my hand and kiss the fingers one by one.

And every bit of logic I have is urging me to say 'Our separate ways, I guess'. But I don't say it because I know I can't bear to let you go again. Whatever it takes. I was just as selfish as you in those long ago days. I pursued my dreams as relentlessly as you pursued yours and none of them meant anything without you. Perhaps neither of us really knew what love meant then.

"I'm not letting you go again," you say quietly, echoing my thoughts. "We've got to work something out, Ginny. Whatever it takes."

And I know we will. Because one thing has changed over the last thirteen years. I think we both know a bit more about love these days. And the compromises that we need to make to let it grow.

The tide is coming in, as we walk back along the shore. And I can’t help thinking, as I thought one long ago evening, that the sea and the sand might be different elements, but in the end they are as intrinsic to each other as the night is to the day. And as inseparable.

The Better Player

Linda Povey

I'd always thought there was something sexy about women playing pool. I watched the two girls as I waited for my beer. One was fair-haired, the other dark.

"Those two come here a lot, do they?" I asked the bartender.

"No, never seen them before," he said.

"Lookers, the pair of them, don't you think?"

The bartender finished pulling my pint. He leaned towards me and lowered his voice. "Can't play, though, can they?"

I winked. "Wouldn't mind giving them a few lessons."

It was true that they were both playing pretty badly. Neither had potted a single ball yet. All the reds and yellows still sat clustered together around the middle of the table.

I'd just taken my first gulp of beer when the dark-haired one potted the white ball.

"Foul!" cried the blonde. "That's two for me." With a couple of shots at a red ball that was now fairly close to a pocket, she was in with a chance. Sure enough, it slipped into the hole on the second aim.

I clapped and shouted, "Well done!"

The blonde turned and grinned at me. "I'm good at this,

aren't I?" she said.

I laughed. "Sure are."

"Like to play the winner when we've finished this game?" she asked.

One of them against me? It would be the quickest game of pool ever. "If you like," I said.

I was on my third pint before it ended, and I'm not a fast drinker. The blonde won, I was rather pleased to note. Every time she'd potted a ball, she'd turned towards me as if to register my approval. Definitely a come-on.

When her friend went to the bar to get a drink, she came up to me. "I'm Katie," she said.

"Jake," I told her. "Like a game, then?" I picked up a cue. With my fancy waistcoat, I thought I looked quite the part. I've always been a snappy dresser. I rolled up my sleeves to reveal the Rolex watch I'd bought on holiday last year.

"Ready and willing," she replied.

"Do you want to break?" I asked.

Her lips curled into a seductive smile and she put her head on one side. "I think I'd like you to do it," she said.

I hit the white ball and the reds and yellows flew in all directions. A yellow one fell into a pocket.

"Say, how about making it a bit more interesting?" Katie suggested.

I looked at her. "In what way?"

"We'll have a little bet," she said.

"Okay, say a fiver?" I thought perhaps I'd let her win. It wouldn't be fair to take her money. I smiled to myself

"Mm, something more interesting." Katie grinned cheekily at me. "Say, if you win, you can come back to my place for a coffee later on.".

I swallowed hard and re-thought the situation. I'd win, but not too easily. Make one or two silly mistakes, miss the odd ball. Yes, I could do it.

"What happens if she beats you?" I turned towards the sound of the voice. It was the dark-haired friend. She was standing behind me, holding two bottles of those alcopop things.

"She comes back to my place?" I laughed.

"I think you should let her have that watch." The friend pointed to my Rolex.

Nothing to lose in agreeing, I thought. "It's a deal," I said.

The friend shouted to the bartender, who was listening with interest. "You heard that, didn't you?"

"I did!" he called back.

Katie held out her hand. "May the better player win," she said.

"The better player," I repeated, and we shook on it. I looked her up and down. She really was a cute little thing.

I potted two more yellows with ease, then missed a third, deliberately.

"My turn!" Katie cried. She leaned over the table, head low down. Funny, she hadn't played like that before. She'd hit the ball from her hip, like a lot of woman do when they don't know how to play properly. Still, I wasn't complaining.

A red ball whizzed straight into a pocket.

"Good shot!" I called out in surprise.

When she managed to place a second, third and fourth, I wasn't so happy. She missed the next by a fraction and I took up my position. I glanced in her direction. She was standing in a provocative pose, with a very smug look on her face.

It put me off and I missed.

"Bad luck," she said. And went on to pot another two.

I got one more in, but I was so nervous by now I

misjudged the angle of the next. I knew it was all over.

Before long, she'd pocketed the black with ease. She came over to me and shook my hand for a second time. "Good game," she said.

I smiled wryly. "You played very well," I told her.

At that point the friend walked up. "So, don't you owe her something?" she said.

I stopped smiling. "What's that?" I asked.

"Rolex." I noticed Katie's expression had become intense all of a sudden.

"Surely you weren't being serious?" I said.

"Absolutely. Barman!" Katie called. "You remember the deal, don't you?"

"Certainly do," he said. "Hand the watch over, chum. A deal's a deal. I don't want any trouble here."

I took the Rolex from my wrist and gave it to Katie. I narrowed my eyes. "You girls have done this before, haven't you?"

Katie laughed. She didn't seem nearly as attractive now. "They're not all as easy as you," she said.

The girls walked out the door, giggling together. I shrugged my shoulders in resignation. They'd taught me a lesson I wouldn't forget.

I just thanked my lucky stars that Rolex was a fake.

Rendezvous
Jackie Winter

An owl hooted in the eerie darkness and Polly shivered. Where on earth was Ned? They'd said 9 o'clock and he knew how difficult it was for her to get away from home. Adam was definitely getting suspicious and Polly was fast running out of excuses. And it had been a mistake to say she was nipping out to the chippy. Now she'd lumbered herself with stopping off on the way back to buy a pickled egg, three pea fritters and a bucket of chips.

She was longing for Ned's arms around her, the heat of his body, hearing him say she was the only woman he wanted. The only one who drove him wild with lust. She felt desperate to see him. Had been dreaming about this moment ever since the last time. All too long ago…

Polly undid a few buttons on her skimpy top. They wouldn't have long. They never did. But it all added to the excitement. She heard a rustle in the bushes and gasped. Warm hands slid around her waist.

"Only me." Ned chuckled. "Sorry I'm late. Did Adam give you a hard time?"

"Plenty of awkward questions so I'd better not be too long. And it's really spooky hanging around in the park this time of night."

But Polly couldn't stay cross with him for long. Not while his hands were searching underneath her jacket, his breath hot on her neck. It didn't take him long to undo the rest of the buttons.

"You're gorgeous, Poll," he murmured. "Got any more surprises for me?"

"Well, if you hang around long enough, there might be a spare pea fritter," Polly giggled.

Ned pushed her back against a tree and began kissing her passionately. All this certainly added spice to her dreary, predictable life, Polly thought. She was glad she'd worn his favourite black stockings. Ned was showing his appreciation in some very imaginative ways. Not that she'd ever be able to wear them again, one being wrapped across a holly bush and the other hanging out of Ned's trouser pocket. Removing it, she dangled the black silk under his nose.

"How would you have explained that when you got home?" she asked and he paled.

"The evenings will soon be too chilly for this sort of carry-on." Polly shivered, wincing as she stabbed her naked foot on some holly. "We're going to have to find somewhere else to meet. How about your car?"

"You unromantic trollop." Ned twisted a silk stocking around her wrists, just a little too tightly.

"Ouch! That hurts." She struggled, unconvincingly.

"You love it. But this holly is a bit of a turn off. Did you bring a rug?"

"You must be joking! How many people wander down to the chippy with a rug under their arm? Sort out something soft to lie on while I remove the rest of my kit."

Polly slipped off her few remaining clothes, slowly and provocatively. "How do I look?" she purred, sinking onto Ned's fleece, laid on a pile of rustling beech leaves.

"Wonderful," said Ned, huskily. "All pale and mysterious in the moonlight."

Pulling off his jeans, he lay down beside her.

"Come on, sweetheart. We've been planning this for days," he muttered.

Ned was the best. He didn't try to rush her. Gave her all the time she needed.

"Nice?" Ned kissed her throat.

"You're fantastic and I adore you." Polly sighed then suddenly sat up. "What was that noise?"

"You were being pretty noisy yourself," Ned grinned.

"Sshh! I can hear something." Polly peered through the bushes. "It's a man, walking his dog," she hissed. "He's coming this way. What shall we do?"

"Lie low and keep quiet," Ned whispered. "We're well away from the main path. He'll never see us."

Like a couple of kids, they held hands and tried not to giggle. The man was walking towards them, his dog straining at the lead.

"Hold on, Prince! What have you found? Well, I never!"

Curiosity overcoming caution, Polly wriggled into a better position. Oh no! The dog was dragging her stocking out of the holly bush! Now he was wagging his tail and offering the tattered bit of black silk to his master for approval.

"Takes me back forty years, that does," the man said. "I had some fun on this heath when I was a lad too."

Polly gasped and Ned smothered a hoot of laughter.

"Those were the days." The man sighed, wistfully. "Now the only exercise I get is walking you. Down, Prince. Leave it be."

As his footsteps disappeared into the distance, Polly breathed a sigh of relief.

"Whew! That was close." She shivered. "I don't fancy getting caught."

"You weren't so timid five minutes ago." Ned said. "Come here."

Fifteen minutes later, outside the chippy, they shared a large portion of haddock.

"We can't keep on meeting like this." Ned licked his fingers. "Adam's going to follow you one of these days."

Instinctively, Polly glanced over her shoulder. But their teenage son was nowhere to be seen. Still baby-sitting his little sisters. Hopefully.

"I had to resort to bribery this time but it was worth it. Well worth it." She cuddled up. "Let's start on the chips."

"Better leave some for the rabble." Ned put his arm around her. "What sort of parents are we, gobbling up their supper?"

"The sort who want some time to themselves, occasionally," said Polly. "Three nosy kids and no lock on the bedroom door. Who needs it?"

I'm Not Your P.A. And I'll Cry If I Want To

Phil Trenfield

"Good morning, KRM Marketing Department, how may I help you?" Jane sang into her headset. "Oh Mr Jones – hi." Trying to sound professional she continued, "Of course, I'm on my way." Her colleagues glanced at her as though she was making her way along death row. Jane knocked nervously on the door.

"Ah, Julia," he said.

"It's Jane, sir," she replied. She had worked for the company for nearly four years and the man had not got her name right once.

"Jane?" he replied, surprised. "Can you get me a drink, please? Rather a lot of paperwork to do, I'll have the usual." He waved his hand in the air without looking up, to usher her out of the door as quickly as possible.

What an idiot, she thought. I'm a marketing assistant not a bloody tea lady. Just because his P.A. is off on vacation doesn't mean he can call on me every few minutes. "Anyone else want a drink whilst I'm going anyway?" she called. Predictably half a dozen answers came back at her. She mumbled obscenities to herself and stomped off.

At the Maxpax machine she looked at the tray that she had balanced on top of the water cooler, trying to recall all the orders. What am I missing? she wondered? Oh, of course, Chicken soup for Baldly Locks and the Three Hairs, I don't know how he can drink that stuff – it looks and smells like something my cat would bring up.

The Maxpax machine whirred into action making sounds that reminded her of the cat bringing something up. She gingerly put the last cup on the tray and walked back to her section on the busy 14th floor.

"Right, here we are, who had the orange squash?" She handed out the drinks out and then knocked on the office door again and the usual grunt followed. "Mr Jones here's your…" she stopped mid sentence as her brain was uttering the words 'cat sick'.

"Chicken soup?" He looked at her suspiciously.

"Yes, that's right, your chicken soup." Jane avoided eye contact.

She felt herself retch as she focused on the floating bits of whatever the hell it was they put in that putrid drink. She returned to her desk and cradled her cup of tea, watching the steam wisp upwards. Ah ha, two e-mails! The first was from Maria who sat just two desks away. 'Thanks for the coffee' and a smiley face. The second message was from Jenny, in the call centre: 'OH MY GOD!!!!! We have a new temp that started today who is absolutely gorgeous. You just wait until you see him. Gotta go as we have thirty-two calls waiting in a queue. Love J xxxx.'

"Hey, Maria, have you seen this new guy who started today in the call centre? Jenny has just e-mailed me and said they have this stunning bloke working there."

"I haven't seen anyone in that call centre who doesn't resemble a troll, so no in answer to your question," Maria replied, without looking up from her copy of *Hello*.

"I might venture down there later. I could do with a bit of eye candy."

"Why do you need eye candy? I thought you were dating some new chap?" Jane asked.

"Had to end that, he started to get some weird obsession thing with my feet. I came home early and found him in my wardrobe with my new strappy sandals."

Jane nearly spat out her tea as the giggle made its way up from her stomach.

"It's not funny, those sandals cost me £95 and I didn't spend all that money so some bloke could come round and paw them. So, Missy, I'm back on the market, looking for a normal guy."

"Well, if you do go down there let me know what he's like. You're not the only one on the market, you know." Jane had a hopeful look on her face.

On her way out Jane considered having a peek out onto the 9th floor, just in case this god was hanging about. But when she got into the lift and the American-voiced recording asked her to choose a floor, she resisted and pushed the silver 'G' button. The doors closed and another day came to an end.

The next morning Jane spun through the revolving doors at 8.35am. She said her usual hello to the security guard, who was as usual drooling over the model on page three of his paper, and then got in to the lift. She pushed the button for the 9th floor; it couldn't hurt to have a look around and she could always raid their stationary cupboard. The doors opened on the ninth floor and Jane immediately spotted Jenny on the phone.

"I understand that Mrs Thomas but your no claims bonus can only be used if you haven't made a claim in the past year, and you have." Jenny yawned and rolled her eyes.

Jane had got to the stationary cupboard and hadn't yet seen the sexy new guy. She could still hear Jenny who was becoming more insistent "...Mrs Thomas, I'm not being patronising I'm trying to explain it to you so you'll understand."

Jane started to pile up her booty as though she was some sort of pirate pillaging a merchant ship of its cargo. She turned around, satisfied she had enough, and bumped into someone, sending everything in her arms flying left, right and centre.

"I'm so sorry, I didn't see you there." She looked up, and there stood one gorgeous hunk of a man. Looks- wise he resembled Colin Farrell, she thought. It was like opening a page of a glossy magazine and having the star of the article staring back at her.

"Here, let me help you." He bent down and began to pick everything up.

Jane's eyes were travelling over his body watching his muscles ripple under his fitted black top. She was hoping he would just drop everything and sweep her into his arms, but alas it didn't happen.

He stood up and handed it all back and gave her a grin. Her hand gently brushed against his, and the hairs on her arms stood up with excitement. "You must work in a busy department – you've wiped us out. Jane smiled; if only he knew, she thought.

"I'm Sam, I've just started here," he said, holding out his hand, and, realising her arms were full, quickly retracting it.

"I'm Jane," she replied, blushing, "I work in the marketing department on the 14th. We never have any of this stuff so I came down here to get some." She could feel herself staring but wanted to soak up every detail of his face.

"Well, I'd better get back to my section. They'll be crying out for these, nice to have met you, Sam. Hope to see you again soon." Jane watched as Sam walked away, his jeans cradled around his sexy, firm bottom. She let out a sigh and walked towards the lift.

Back at her desk Jane picked up a pack of Post-its and hit herself on the head. "Stupid, stupid, could I have acted anymore like an idiot, he must think I'm a right loony." Her phone started to ring. "Yes, Mr Jones. No this is not Julia, this is Jane. The usual drink, no problem, I'll bring it to you in a few minutes." Jane put the phone down. "What an idiot," she said out loud. "Why can't he get his own bloody cat sick in a cup?" She got out of her chair and stormed off towards the Maxpax machine.

Over the week Jane and Sam kept bumping into each other, in the staff restaurant, in the call centre, in the lobby. They said their hellos to each other and there was a bit of flirting, mostly on Jane's part but nothing came of it.

"Why hasn't he asked me out!" Jane cried at her desk, after she had bumped into Sam again in the lobby.

"Gay," said Maria. "He has to be gay. Look at you, Jane, you are stunning. I would kill for your hair, and your figure, and your boobs. I mean look at mine, two aspirins on an ironing board."

"There is no way he is gay," Jane replied, shocked. "I reckon he has a girlfriend or something."

"Jane, take it from someone with first hand experience of the carnal appetites of a homosexual. I dated a guy for three months and he turned out to be gay."

"Are you sure you didn't turn him that way, Maria?"

"No, I bloody didn't, you cheeky mare. I should have guessed he was, though, he collected early Victorian china and worked for Royalty magazine. He actually got paid to follow the Queen around the country. And I mean the woman who sits on the throne with a crown on her head, before you come out with any smart lines, Missy!" She looked at Jane with one eyebrow raised.

Jane's stomach was aching she was laughing so much. "Well, I still think he's straight," she said. "But I'll probably never find out as our conversations only consist of 'hi' or 'hello' or 'need any more stationary?' Speaking of which I'm so bored I'm going to the stationary cupboard to see if there is anything I didn't swipe, then I'll go and get drinks for everyone."

Jane walked into the stationary cupboard to find Sam in there looking for paper clips.

"Hi Sam, how are you?" she said, surprised to see him.

"Jane, hi, I'm good thanks."

God, he's gorgeous, she thought. I wish I had bigger boobs, despite what Maria thinks, and I shouldn't have worn this lipstick. She reached past him to get a box of rubber bands and then stepped back. "Well, mission accomplished," she said. Sam leaned in and brushed his hand over her cheek. Jane's brain couldn't get her words out. "Wha, wha, what did you do that for?"

"You had an eye lash on your cheek."

"Oh, an eye lash, thanks."

Sam did it again.

"Another eye lash?"

"No, not that time," he said.

She moved closer to him. She could smell his cologne and feel his breath on her face. She looked into his beautiful brown eyes and they kissed. Sam moaned with satisfaction. His hands on her back skilfully slid up to her hair. Jane couldn't resist squeezing his bottom to see if it was as firm as it looked and she wasn't disappointed. They kissed passionately for what seemed like a few minutes but was actually only about 30 seconds before releasing each other. Jane took her thumb and wiped it across Sam's perfect lips, removing the lipstick she had left behind.

"I can't believe we just did that," she said. "I mean, the stationary cupboard. It's the sort of thing you read about in cheap magazines. I slept with office junior in stationary cupboard on pile of manilla envelopes, admitted Sue, 49, from Solihull."

Sam laughed and pecked her on the cheek. "I've wanted to ask you out since the first time you bumped into me but haven't had the courage. So now's my big chance." He swallowed hard. "Would you like to come round to my place tomorrow and I can cook us a meal."

Jane looked into his hopeful eyes. This is too much to be true, she thought. Great kisser, gorgeous and he cooks. "That would be lovely," she said. "I'll bring a nice bottle of wine. Speaking of drinks I'd better go and get them for my section. They will be wondering where I've got to."

"I'll come with you," he said. "I need a drink."

"Ladies first," Sam said, as they reached the Maxpax machine. Jane started pushing buttons and putting the drinks on to a tray. After she had made her selections, she looked up at him. He pushed the button for his drink. Jane could feel that this was the beginning of something amazing. Thank you KRM, she thought, for bringing this hunk into my life… As the machine started to make a very familiar and stomach-churning sound Jane was wrenched from her daydream. Sam pulled his drink out of the machine, took a sip and then saw the disgusted look on her face.

"Jane what on earth's the matter?" Sam asked.

"URGH you don't drink that chicken soup do you?" she cried.

That Old Magic

Rachel Sargeant

Some wedding anniversary this was turning out to be. Ursula was never going to kiss another frog as long as she lived. The result was terminal celibacy. It was alright for princesses. They had to pucker up to a pond full of toads before one turned tall, dark and human. But witches like Ursula could conjure up a coach load of charmers with a single peck on a slimy cheek.

No reason for celibacy so far, you might think. Certainly not for a saucy sorceress, in it for the once-upon-a-time night of passion. But it was different for Ursula, romantic, naive, stupid Ursula, with her bizarre preference for the relationship to outlive the hangover. The first time she'd locked lips lizardstyle, she'd bagged a prince, fallen in love and headed off for the happy ever after.

Fairytale wedding, action-packed honeymoon, grand coronation, even more action-packed marriage, beautiful children and then… And then, welcome to the monastery. It was their wedding anniversary and how were they spending it? Cocooned under the counterpane? Leisurely lunch? Candle-lit dinner? Early night? No, he was out saving the world and she was in minding the kids. He was obsessed with his latest campaign of restricting wolves to damsel-free zones, while she was valiantly toddler-taming instead of practising her ancient craft. The King was spending more and more time with his colleague, that Red Riding Hood woman. It was Red this, Red that. Anyone would think he'd fallen under *her* spell. Come to think of it, he hadn't mentioned Red so much lately. Guilty silence perhaps? But, of course, that wasn't possible when he had his very own sex-hex at home. Many a time she'd concocted for him a love potion hot enough to stoke a furnace. Trouble was nowadays he seemed to think she'd swapped burning lust for blocks of Lego.

In a last-ditch attempt at conventional childcare, Ursula placed a Jack and the Beanstalk sticker book in her son's line of fire. The decoy worked. The three-year-old released his hostage, the Baby Princess, declared a ceasefire and scrambled up to join his mother on her throne. They were grappling with the tricky fourth leg of Daisy the Cow when they heard the familiar cranking of the portcullis.

"Daddy! Daddy!" The Little Prince bounded to the castle door in an instant. Flicking through the abandoned book, Ursula listened to the Prince's delighted squeals as the King bounced him up and down in his arms. Time to bath the baby, she mused, and scooped up the Little Princess. She slipped past her husband, engrossed in his lavish male-bonding display, and noted how quickly she reached the spiral staircase. There was no squeeze of her waist, no playful pat on the posterior, no wait-til-I-get-you-alone smile to delay her. She'd become invisible, without uttering a single charm.

Tetchily, she splashed water over the baby's tummy. Above her startled shrieks, she heard father and son head for the kitchen. The Prince would soon be on Daddy's knee, eating up his tea. Daddy would only have to wave a fork in the vague direction of the boy's mouth and he'd devour the burnt offering in an instant. It would be the same tea that he'd refused to take from her earlier after she'd lovingly created it. She hurled the soap into the tub. It wasn't for her own amusement that she'd spent hours slaving over a hot cauldron while, at the same time, she'd made the Prince a scale model of the house of straw and posted slices of enormous turnip into a loud and hungry Princess. She bet Red couldn't multi-task. That woman had a one-track mind…

"Can you get the Prince some pudding!" shouted the King through her disturbing thoughts. "You know what he's allowed." Ursula trudged downstairs carrying a freshly bathed Princess wrapped in a towel. One-handed she reached for the fruit bowl.

"Not one of your apples," wailed the Prince. "I know what they did to Snow White." He sank his head into the King's shining armour and howled.

"Can't he have a gingerbread man, just this once?" asked the King, as he did every evening. Ursula pulled out the biscuit tin. Time was when the King's knowledge of desserts hadn't extended beyond lashings of whipped cream, and no spoon.

She returned to her exile upstairs. Somewhere along the line she'd traded in her handsome hunk for a fairy godfather. She heard the King and the Little Prince move back to the great hall to act out the Little Prince's favourite tale. She braced herself for the loud splintering of wood, which duly came as King Goldilocks sat in Baby Bear's chair. As she laid out the Prince's pyjamas, a tight knot formed in her stomach. She wasn't just angry about losing even more of their best Chippendale. (She could always wave her wand on that one.) She found herself brooding over when exactly she'd changed from raven-haired sex siren into mousy mother-of-two. It seemed only yesterday that *her* role-play games had had the King swinging from the balustrades. These days she made the dinner while the Little Prince ripped up her charm books. She dusted the dados while he threw darts at her magic mirror. She cleaned the garderobe while he took her black cat for a swim in it. And she'd lost count of the number of times she'd told him to keep off her spinning wheel but he never listened. How often had she patched up his finger and then forced him whimpering on to the back of her broomstick for the urgent dash to casualty, all the time slapping him to stay awake?

It wasn't that she didn't love her children. She adored them and motherhood brought its own rewards, but there never seemed to be any time left over for her to be even a little bit, well, wicked. The worst part about it was that the King didn't even seem to notice. He was happy playing Daddy – on all fours chasing round the banqueting hall, launching an inflatable elf at the ceiling, building a life-size beanstalk which threatened to poke through the mezzanine floor. Tonight (after she'd pointed at the hour-glass) they'd play ugly ducklings in the wooden tub by the fire. Later tonight (after the sand had long since run through and she'd delivered another dire warning, "You'll turn into a pumpkin if you don't soon get a shift on"), they'd share noisy jokes over several bedtime tales. By the time she'd intervened and grappled the wide-awake child into bed, they'd be too exhausted to do anything except collapse comatose into their own bedchamber.

Still, tomorrow was Saturday. No office, no Red. A belated anniversary treat wouldn't go a miss. Fat chance. The King would be helping the Little Prince to ride his winged horse, play trolls under the drawbridge and feed the golden geese. Ursula would do the ironing and make the swan and pickle sandwiches.

She headed for the scullery to clear up the Prince's empty dish. She could hear him in his room plucking out a noisy caterwaul on his harp with the King on backing vocals. They could always wait until Sunday and have an anniversary lie-in of *lurve*. But only after the early morning trumpet recital and the weekly pillow throwing competition. And before they were unceremoniously dragged out of bed to push the children around the courtyard on an ancient toy dragon with muddy water slopping over the tops of their wellies. She tried to remember life before green Wellingtons, when patent leather thigh boots had been her usual footwear. She bet Red wore thigh boots. Crimson, with four-inch heels.

The overhead concert had gone suspiciously quiet. Ursula stuck her head round the bedroom door, expecting to find father and son engaged in some minor misdemeanour. "What the..?"

"I'm packing, Mum. We're going to Red's tomorrow," said the Prince, excitedly forcing toys into a holdall. "Daddy says it's her way of saying thank you."

Thank you for what? Ursula wasn't waiting to find out. Now, to turn scarlet women and wayward kings back into pond life. Ready, aim, f…

"I've been covering Red's work while she's been on honeymoon," said the King.

Honeymoon? Ursula lowered her wand.

"She thought we might like to go out on our own but…" continued the King in a deep voice, taking her hand, "…as it's our anniversary, I thought we might prefer to stay in."

She'd used no magic but suddenly he spoke less like a Daddy and more like a husband. He stopped talking but his eyes had more to say. Ursula could swear it was something they hadn't said for a long time. She was sure it was something really, really wicked.

[illegible]

Memories
Gemma Forbes

"Daydreaming, Mum?"

I jumped as the door opened and Melanie's voice brought me back from the lavender scented hills and white stone villages of Provence.

"Mmm. Lovely to see you, pet. Thanks for coming. I need to talk some things over with you but first, what on earth am I going to do with all this." I pointed to all the boxes stacked everywhere.

"Well, that's up to you. I can store some of it," she said. "How much do you have to keep?"

I shrugged my shoulders and spread out my hands in an unconscious Gallic gesture. "I don't know. Trouble is I can't seem to throw anything away."

Melanie laughed. "I'll help you sort it out. Fancy a cup of tea?"

As she left the room I looked out of the window at the 'Sold' sign leaning at a crazy angle over the rose hedge, then I turned back to stare at the chaos in my living room. Those boxes contained my life. Filling each one had taken ages. Drawers and cupboards filled with memories.

Just before Melanie had arrived I'd taken an old patchwork bag out of a drawer. Its squares of multicoloured velvet were faded with age but not the memories it held. Now I smiled as I tugged open its drawstring and tipped out seven leather juggling balls, one of each colour of the rainbow. I lifted the red ball and it lay soft and heavy in my hand. I took up two more and juggled them, clumsily at first, then throwing them higher and higher. I added more, one at a time, until as I tried to add the seventh they all dropped at my feet. I retrieved them and gathered them in my lap, remembering.

I'd met him after a disastrous love affair. I'd been jilted and almost had a break-down. In a mad moment I'd quit my job, let my flat, packed a rucksack and gone travelling.

One evening, weeks later, I was sitting on a beach of soft sand in Provence watching the sun turn the sea to beaten gold. A shadow fell across me. Then the man sat down beside me, and changed my life. He said his name was Jacques and he chatted and flirted with me in a mixture of French and heavily accented English. He seemed a little crazy but in the best possible way. He laughed at life and made me laugh too. When I smiled at him that first evening I felt all the muscles in my face, every one, and they ached from lack of use. We went to a bar on the beach and he bought me a drink, rich red wine that warmed me through. We sat holding hands and I felt his strength enter me. We stayed in there until the sun had long gone and the sky was filled with stars. The bar closed and we strolled down to the sea, arms entwined. As the warm waves caressed our feet he drew me closer and kissed me. I felt all my tension finally go.I leaned into him and returned the kiss.

I went back with him to his psychedelic-painted camper van and we made love. I was nervous, clumsy. He was caring, tender. Afterwards I wept for lives lost, times wasted, and he held me close. He didn't question my tears, he just kissed them away and said we should live for the present. So we did.

He taught me to juggle, how to work a crowd, how to live on little but love and those were my richest times. Even now I found it hard to say his name, Jacques. I said it softly, with a French accent, Jacques, and heard his voice. He always called me Libby. He said my real name, Elizabeth, was too formal for the me that he loved. I still remembered the feel of his silky brown skin, the white laughter lines at the corner of his dark brown eyes, how there was always a smile on his lips.

We travelled the dusty roads into the white villages in the hills above the coast. Lavender fields stretched into the distance and the air was warm and scented. I remembered siestas when dappled sunlight played upon his chest and I leaned over him and let the curtain of my dark hair shut out the world. When we were apart, even for an hour, my heart ached. Oh how I loved him.

As autumn approached and the tourists deserted the beaches we travelled up to the Lot region. There we took a house in a hilltop village and Jacques and I found work in the vineyards picking the late grapes for the heavy sweet golden wine. Sunshine in a bottle.

We came home in the dusk touching, our hands sticky and sweet smelling from the grapes. Every evening we cooked together: duck breasts in red wine, rich fish stews, prunes simmered in Armagnac. We lay together in the light of the fire and talked softly in French, the language of love. We made love, familiar with each other's needs, then slept arms and legs entwined. I grew plump and rosy, blossoming in the warmth of his love. By November when the grapes were safely in I knew that I had a harvest of my own, for I carried his child.

Melanie came back into the room and brought me back to the present. I took the tea and cradled the hot beaker in my hands as if trying to recapture the warmth of those long gone days. I smiled at her and reached out to touch her hand.

"Remember how I told you that you were the reason I came back to England?"

She laughed. "Of course I do, Mum, but I'll indulge you if you want to tell me again."

I waited a moment before I spoke, looking at my lovely daughter, the last gift Jacques gave to me. She was so pretty with her glossy dark hair gathered at the nape of her neck, her golden skin and dark brown eyes, so like him.

I sighed. "I haven't been completely honest with you. Jacques didn't leave me. I left him."

"Yes Mum. You always said he went to Spain to find work and you wouldn't go with him."

"I know, but it wasn't quite like that. There was a restlessness in him. He was at heart a traveller, always wanting to move on, to see what lay beyond another horizon."

Melanie interrupted me. "So why didn't you go with him, what stopped you?"

"Why? You of course. When I felt you stir inside me, as I grew heavier, I had this nesting instinct, an overpowering urge to settle, to make a home for you. I couldn't ask Jacques to give up his life. I couldn't tie him down, make him take a regular job. I'd have watched the light fade in his eyes, his skin would have lost its golden sheen. I loved him too much to let that happen, so I lied to him. I said I didn't love him enough to wander forever. I told him that when you were older we'd find him. I made him go but I gave him my address, and he said he would write. We cried a lot but I went."

"And did he? Did he write?" Melanie asked, her voice tight.

"Yes, he did." I reached again into the faded velvet bag that had held the juggling balls and took out a thick bundle of letters and postcards. I held them out to her. "They came every few months over the years but then they stopped. I've been so wrong to keep them from you. Forgive me?"

She didn't answer me. She couldn't, because as she read the first card tears spilled from her eyes. I moved to sit beside her. I held her to me and we read them together.

At last she spoke. "How could you keep these from me? These are part of my life, too."

"I'm sorry. My only excuse is that I was afraid I'd lose you, that you'd want to go to him as soon as you were old enough. When they stopped I tried to put them out of my mind. Can you see that? Please speak to me, forgive me."

"I don't know if I can, Mum. Give me some time."

I sighed. "Time may be a luxury we can't afford."

I stood and walked to the table and brought back another letter. "This came last week. Jacques is back in Provence. He's not too well and he hopes the warmth will make him feel better. He wants to see you, he wants to see us both. Now I've sold up there's nothing to keep me here, except you, of course."

At last Melanie spoke. "So is that where you're going, back to Jacques?"

"Yes, love, I am. I've decided that anything else can wait. I need to see him again to tell him how I've missed him over the years. Do you want to be a little bit crazy and come with me?"

She frowned. "I'll think about it."

"Melanie, don't think, just do it. You'll love it down there and you'll love Jacques. Surely there's some of him in you. Can't you just up and away?"

"What, like you, Mum? You two were more alike than you know."

"Do you think I'm being stupid leaving here, going away from everything, everyone?"

"Come on, Mum, don't be silly. You'll love to see Jacques again and if it doesn't work out, what have you always said? New faces, new places?" At last Melanie smiled.

"Yes, but I'm older now. It's not so easy." I sighed.

She snorted. "You'll never be old, Mum, sometimes I think I'm older than you."

"I know what you mean and it worries me. You've got to move on, put all that business with Paul behind you." I reached out and touched her face, looked into her eyes. She, like me so long ago, had been let down by her man.

"Leave it, Mum, I'm OK."

There was a silence, each of us lost in our thoughts. The silence dragged on then we both said together, "Oh for goodness sake!" and dissolved into laughter.

We were always doing that, saying things at the same time. So alike, yet so different. Was she right or was I about to do the stupidest thing in my life?

"They'll just have to go into store," Melanie said, nodding towards the chaos in the room.

"What, all the boxes?" I asked.

"Yes, all of them," she said, "I can't have them, I'm coming with you."

"You are? When?" The words tumbled from me.

"When you go. I've just decided. I'll find Jacques with you and then I'm going to follow in your footsteps and travel. I need what you've got. I need to make memories." Melanie's face lit up.

"And I'm going to find an old lover," I laughed. "At my age!"

Then it was my turn to be quiet as once again Jacques filled my mind. I felt that familiar warmth. I was sure I would know him when we met. One glance and the years would fall away.

"New places, old faces!" we said together, and hugged each other.

Games People Play

Zoë Harcombe

No. No. No. Not even if world peace depended on it. Maybe if I were really drunk…

Emma was playing her usual game to relieve the drudgery of travelling on the tube each day. The rules were simple – you had to check out all the men in the carriage and decide if you would sleep with them, under any circumstances. It was a good barometer of her self esteem too, as there were some days when Robbie Williams wouldn't have got a look in, and others when the grumpy ticket inspector looked like marriage material.

Today Emma was feeling pretty good, so far more men than usual were being rejected with little more than a cursory glance. Her hair had decided to behave for a change. She was as close to her dream weight as she was ever likely to get (give or take half a stone). She had on a new wrap-over top and for once her costume-drama curves and healthy glowing cheeks didn't seem too hateful. Play on…

No. No. No. Excuse me, but did you dress in the dark? No. On principle – reading the *Telegraph.*

And then suddenly she saw him.

Well, hello!

She wondered for a horrific moment if she had said it out loud but life carried on as normal so she decided that she must have got away with it.

Well, hello again!

Emma suddenly believed in Greek mythology – one of its gods had come to life in front of her eyes. He was chatting to another man who looked nice but dull. Emma couldn't help thinking that, if she were out with her stunning friend Laura, the Greek god would go for the luscious Laura and Emma would be left with Nice But Dull. It was always the way. Why couldn't she have the one with the infectious energy and the grin that was so disarming? She decided that it was time for the game to move to the next level….

Level two was a fantasy about the mystery stranger. The objective of level two was to get from first base to home run all in her head. In the game, Emma could have the Adonis, and Laura could have NBD, even if it would never happen in real life. Adonis: the name was tailor made. Adonis, with the floppy fringe, that gorgeous smile and the cutest bum on the planet (as observed when he got off at Shepherd's Bush.) And he was there the next day, and the next…

People called fantasising 'day dreaming' but this was not strictly accurate as the 'day dreaming' could become 'every-waking-hour-dreaming', 'week dreaming' and all other sorts. The fantasy started and got embellished every time it was revisited. The detail was incredible. What she wore (took ages), what they wore (no time at all), what she said (always witty, sexy and leading somewhere), where it all took place (somewhat academic), how she flirted (effortlessly and seductively) and then that magical moment when the line was crossed from stranger to lover.

Wow, she thought, if men had even the slightest idea about what goes on in our heads when we fancy them they would do more than blush! Oh, the joys of being a woman.

So, on the morning after selecting Adonis as the object of her desires, Emma spent the time between Ealing Broadway and Oxford Circus working out what to wear right down to the detail of the irresistible lingerie and the lace-top stockings. The stockings were critical, as the best moment of her fantasy was always the little gasp from Adonis when he realised that she was wearing them.

She loved to take the story as far as she dared. They always ended up in bed but the best bit was how they got there. Some days they had a tantalising dinner first and other days they ripped each other's clothes off on the tube during the rush hour. The first electric touch, the first kiss, the way he held her – she could melt just thinking about it.

The fantasies occasionally went further – some days they were ecstatically happily married and living in a trendy flat in Kensington with two Fairy Liquid advert children and a chocolate Labrador puppy. Adonis was the perfect husband. He could cook, make love and clear the bathroom of spiders – all before breakfast. But generally, Emma considered this line of thought a tad 'forward' so she stuck to thinking about the 'honeymoon' rather than the marriage.

The days went by and Adonis continued to make the same journey as Emma. Some days their timing was out and she had to go a day without seeing him. But she was often quite glad about this as it was difficult to concentrate on the fantasies when the subject of them was sitting opposite! If only he knew. Sometimes she thought about this again – yes – if only he did know. They were hardly going to have either a delicious dinner or sensational sex if they never actually spoke to each other, but level two tended to overlook this kind of detail.

As best friends do, Emma confided in Laura – though not the gory detail, of course. (We share the blow-by-blow account when we get lucky but not the fantasies beforehand.) But Laura was left in no doubt that Emma had a crush on Adonis of school girl proportions. Laura wanted to reach out and hug her lovely friend. Poor Emma had no idea just how gorgeous she was. Men didn't see the pounds that Emma was always trying to diet away. They just saw the mass of curly dark hair, huge brown eyes and a friendly face that a kitten would have been proud of. She was the sexy, funny woman that Laura longed to be and yet Emma had no idea that men would fall at her feet, if only she would let them near her.

On a glorious Sunday morning in Covent Garden, after their third skinny latté in Starbucks, Laura picked the moment to give her buddy the advice that she really needed. It was this advice that consumed Emma for the rest of the day and kept her awake all night long. It was still all she could think about as she made her way to the station on Monday morning.

She could hardly wait until Acton Town to see if she had timed it right to catch Adonis on this momentous day. When the doors opened, without even looking up, she knew that she had. When he stepped into the carriage her heart skipped a beat but she just stared at the floor as if she had been asked to guard it with her life. How could she make the first move? "Just get him talking," Laura had said. Well, that was easier said than done. How on earth could she start a conversation with the man who had occupied her every waking thought for the past few weeks?

"If you are half as good in bed as I think you are, we are going to be great together," didn't quite seem right as an opener somehow! But then nor did, "What do you think of Emily if it's a girl?"

Just as she was starting to think that Nice But Dull might not be so bad after all, the impossible happened. She dared to glance up and, in that moment, Adonis caught her eye. She looked at him and he looked back and, incredibly, they both held the gaze for that split second too long. Polite strangers would have looked away by now but neither had. Her whole world seemed to stand still. As she continued to stare deep into his eyes, the grin started to break out and Adonis actually spoke. "*Hi*" he said.

To this day she does not know how but, from somewhere, two words emerged with the sexiest voice ever heard on the Central Line. "Well, hello," she found herself saying.

Second-Hand Rosie

Christina Jones

"Look, Rosie!" Sal waved something excitedly under my sleepy nose. 'You know what this is, don't you?'

"An envelope?" I hazarded dozily, just managing to open one eye. "A bill? A final demand? An eviction notice?"

I'm not at my best in the mornings. I was at the breakfast table, but still virtually asleep.

"Ten out of ten for envelope." Sal continued to wave it around. "And now guess what's in it?"

"I've already – "

Sal perched on the edge of the table, all fizzing energy. Sometimes it's very wearing sharing a flat with a lark. I don't even become human until lunch time.

She ripped the envelope open and proceeded to flap the contents irritatingly in front of me.

"Tell me about it this evening…"

As usual, Sal ignored me. "It's the invitation I was telling you about! For Valentine's Day! And get this – there's posh – it's at Barton Hall! *Mr and Mrs Howard request the pleasure of the company…*"

"Who?" My second cup of coffee was just starting to have some effect. "Mr and Mrs who?"

“Howard!” Sal stood up and sort of danced round the kitchen. I say sort of, because, to be honest, the kitchen’s too small to walk in comfortably, let alone dance. Her eyes shone with fanatical fervour. “Mr and Mrs Howard! Matt’s parents!”

Matt? Matt Howard? The name didn't even begin to penetrate the outer layers of my brain. “No, sorry. Still no idea what you’re talking about...”

“I told you about Matt, Rosie! I met him last week at that sales conference. Tall, dark and gorgeous, with a smile that could melt granite, and eyes like –”

I sank further into my coffee cup. Sal fell in love on a regular basis. At least twice a week. I, being what Sal called picky when it came to men, could never keep up.

However, for the sake of good flat-sharing relations, I tried to show some enthusiam. “So, this wonderful Matt Howard – who you met last week, just once – has invited you to Barton Hall which is as close as we get to a stately home round here. Why?”

“He hasn’t.” Sal looked appalled at my early-morning lack of understanding. “His parents have. The invitation’s from them. They organise this huge Valentine’s Day ball for charity every year, and Matt mentioned it while we were having coffee and biscuits at the sales conference, and I said we’d love to go…”

“We?” I was wide awake now. “*We*?”

“Of course. The invite is for both of us. I wouldn’t go without you, would I? Just imagine it. A ball! Not a disco or a club or anything – a proper ball – with proper frocks and proper dances, and…”

“Stop right there.” I staggered to my feet and reached for the coffee jar again. “I can’t do proper dances and my wardrobe doesn't stretch to ball gowns.”

Sal clicked her tongue in irritation. “Anyone can waltz, Rosie. Anyone. You just shuffle round to the music and let the man worry about the technical stuff – and I’m going to wear my bridesmaid’s dress, so you could…” Our eyes met. We both knew I couldn't wear the only bridesmaid’s dress I’d ever had. My sister was a huge fan of the Rocky Horror Show and had had a themed wedding. My bridesmaid’s frock would scare Trick or Treaters.

“Well, okay, how about hiring?”

“Too much money,” I sighed. “The overdraft is on meltdown. And I’m still paying off my car loan, and my credit card for last year’s holiday, and…”

“You’ll just have to improvise, then.” Sal danced away into the living room. “Use your imagination – but you’ve got to be there, Rosie. Somewhere swish like that, even you should be able to meet a man you actually like enough to see twice. Oh, and if you don't want to be late, you really should get a move on...”

I glanced up at the clock and yelped in terror. Matt Howard’s stately-home-owning parents and ball gowns and suitable men were the last thing on my mind as I belted around getting ready for work. The impending wrath of Fergal Nixon, my boss, was far more immediate.

I sighed happily as I wandered back to the flat late that afternoon. This was my time of day. Work had been okay for a Monday, and even Fergal Nixon had been in a good mood. He’d casually mentioned that he and his wife had received an invitation to the Howard’s Valentine's Day bash at Barton Hall. As did everyone else I’d bumped into all day. It seemed as though Sal’s gorgeous Matt had invited the entire world.

Sal had her off-the-shoulder pale green chiffon bridesmaid’s dress that would make her look like Scarlett

O'Hara, Fergal Nixon's wife bought her clothes in Milan each year, and everyone else said they were going to hire something – and hang the expense. It really looked as though I'd be the only person stumbling round Barton Hall's parquet dance floor to the strains of Strauss in combat trousers and a cut-off vest.

That's when I saw it.

Tucked in between the pizza delivery place and the newsagents was a charity shop where I quite often eked out my salary when I needed new clothes – much to Sal's disgust. The long elegant strappy evening dress in pale blue silk cascaded across the window display. It was love at first sight.

The shop was still open and I stuck my head round the door. "Hi, Dot. That blue dress in the window? Has anyone put their name down for it yet?"

Dot, kindly and grey-haired, was used to selecting things for my wardrobe. She shook her head. "Not yet, Rosie, love. We only put it in this morning. Gorgeous, isn't it?"

I agreed. "It's just what I need because…"

And I went on to tell her about Sal's drop dead gorgeous New Man, and his imposing stately-home-owning parents, and the Valentine's ball at said stately home. Dot lapped it up.

"That blue would look fabulous with your hair, Rosie," she said. "Shall we have a little try-on session? See if it fits?"

I swirled around the tiny shop, sashaying between the crowded clothes racks, feeling like a million dollars. The frock fitted as though it had been made for me, and even had an effect on my feet. I was sure I'd be able to waltz until dawn.

Dot's eyes shone with maternal pride. "Beautiful. You'll be the belle of the ball. Shall I hold it until Friday for you?"

"Yes, please." I let the folds of silk slither through my fingers, not wanting to take it off. Friday was pay day. "I'll collect it on my way home."

Barton Hall glimmered beneath the diamond-drop glow of chandeliers. Tall pink candles and scarlet sequins shimmered on the tables. Glamorous men in dinner jackets and bow ties laughed with even more glamorous women in jewel-bright gowns. My blue silk dress – which had brought admiring gasps from the ever-critical Sal, so I knew it looked great – was equal to any of the frocks on display.

I gazed at the red-rose-and-pink-heart-strewn ballroom in awed silence. It was like stepping back in time, or on to a film set, or, oh, just into a dream. The band was playing on a balcony as couples dipped and swirled round the floor, and everywhere and everything glittered. I was utterly seduced.

Sal grabbed my arm. "Look – over there. Talking to that sparkly woman in the white dress. That's him – Matt Howard."

I squinted through the sea of impossibly elegant people and blinked. Matt Howard was everything Sal had said – and more. Much, much more. She had a habit of talking-up her current fancies, but not this time. Tall, dark and gorgeous he definitely was. And he was walking towards us.

"Hi, Matt." Sal beamed.

I beamed as well. Matt grinned at both of us, which was nice of him, I thought.

"Hi, Sal – and..." His eyes rested on me for a moment with a flicker of recognition. "I'm sorry – have we met before?"

My high estimation of him deflated like a pricked balloon. I mean, you'd expect someone as landed-gentry as him to have more original lines than that, wouldn't you?

"No, I'm sure we haven't."

Sal carried on beaming like her face was going into overdrive. "Matt, this is Rosie, my flatmate."

He nodded in a polite way, but still looked puzzled. I probably just looked disappointed. Anyway, the delectable Matt asked Sal to dance, and I watched as they wove their way through the gliding couples. I reckoned that with someone as lovely as him, she'd probably make allowances for his lack of wit and scintillating small talk.

"Rosie!"

I groaned as Fergal Nixon, my boss, homed in on me.

"Hello, Mr Nixon – oh, and Mrs Nixon..."

Fergal's wife stood quivering like a greyhound beside him. Stick thin, she was wearing a tight dress made out of something green and shiny, with a yellow pashmina bunched round her bony shoulders. It made her look like a daffodil.

Fergal, for once in party-mood, was full of scary bonhomie. "I don't think I've ever seen you in a frock before, Rosie. You look like a female for once – ha-ha! It's very pretty."

"Oh... er... thank you. It's – um – new."

"And Designer, if I'm not mistaken..." Fergal Nixon's wife said icily. "You must be paying her too much, darling."

I laughed, then stopped. Mrs N wasn't joking. And I was damned if I was going to tell her the dress had cost me a tenner from the charity shop. Amazingly, at that point, Matt Howard reappeared at my elbow.

"Sorry to interrupt, but I wondered if I could have the next dance?"

I stood back, wondering what Fergal Nixon's wife would do with the pashmina while they were gavotting and decided she'd have to tuck it under her arm.

"Rosie?" Matt Howard spoke a little louder. "I – er – wondered if you'd dance with me?"

"Me?" I squeaked. "*Me*? Oh, no. I don't think so. I don't... Can't..."

Matt Howard, obviously used to ordering hordes of flunkies around the battlements or whatever he did in his spare time, wasn't taking no for an answer. Much to Fergal and Mrs N's amusement, he led me through the hundreds of couples into a space on the dance floor.

"It's easy. Just go with the music. I'll lead the way..."

I tentatively let my hands rest loosely in his, fighting the urge to grab them. I mean, despite his lack of original chat-up lines, Matt Howard was, without doubt, the most gorgeous man I'd ever set eyes on.

"I – er – thought you were with Sal?"

"Dancing with her, yes," Matt smiled down at me. The smile was even more giddy-making at close quarters. "But we're not an item. Just mates. In fact, she got snaffled by our MD's son three quicksteps ago. Love at first sight she says it was. And, after all, we lowly reps know our place."

I nodded. I thought it was very New Peerage for Matt to be working at all, let alone some way down the rung of the corporate ladder.

Then the music started, and Matt swept me into the throng. I hadn't got a clue whether it was a waltz or a polka, but it was great. Matt held me and we whizzed round and round and at some point I felt as though my feet had left the ground. I wondered dizzily if dancing lessons were part of the nobility's extra curriculars. Whatever, they had certainly paid off. I felt as light as thistledown in his arms as the pale blue silk dress shimmied and floated with me.

"I thought you said you couldn't dance," Matt said, as the music ended.

"Oh, you know..." I tried to look nonchalant. "I don't like to brag."

"Let's see what you're like on the fox-trot, then." Matt grinned as the music started up again. 'This one took me ages to learn..."

About six dances later, when all I'd done was simply float round in his arms – and it was all a million times better than anything Sal and I had ever done at any night-club – we'd talked and laughed and I was more than a little bit hooked on Matt Howard. The warm glow of well-being increased as we gazed at one another, and then the bubble burst.

Matt suddenly grinned. "I know why you seemed so familiar when Sal introduced us! We haven't met before – it's that dress!"

"Dress?" I yelped. "What about the dress?"

"My mother had one exactly the same... Exactly. In fact, I could swear it was the same one."

I wanted the highly-polished floor to open up beneath my feet. I was happily falling for my hostess's son, soaking up her stately-home hospitality, and preening myself in one of her cast-offs!

"Really?" I tried to smile through rigid lips. "No, I don't think so. I mean, I'm sure this was a – er – one-off. Oh, look... sorry..." I scoured the ballroom for Sal and couldn't see her, then with zonking relief, spotted the friendly and familiar face of Dot from the charity shop. “Would you excuse me? There’s someone I really must speak to.”

And leaving Matt alone in a sea of dancers, I belted across the floor towards Dot.

“Rosie!” Her smile was radiant. “Didn’t I tell you that dress was made for you? You look so beautiful, love.”

I groaned, and because Dot was motherly and knew all my secrets, I poured out the whole sorry story. “And it had to be his mother’s dress!” I finished. “Oh, I don't mind him knowing I buy second-hand clothes – we can’t all be as fabulously wealthy as the Howards, after all. But why, oh, why did it have to belong to his *mother*?”

“Rosie...” Dot was laughing. “Calm down, love. Have you thought that Matt might have thought you’d look gorgeous even if you’d been dressed in a third-hand bin liner? Have you thought that Matt’s mother may be delighted that the dress now belongs to someone who can more than do it justice? Someone whose figure is – well – a fair bit trimmer than mine, shall we say? And if I’m not mistaken I think your young man is coming over to find you...”

“Oh, no!” I yelped, watching as Matt skilfully negotiated the dance floor towards us. “It’s too embarrassing.”

“Hi.” He reached us before I’d had time to hide. “I didn’t know you two knew each other.”

And to my amazement, he kissed Dot on the cheek.

“Rosie, I was going to introduce you, but you obviously already know my mum...”

“Your *mum*?”

Dot nodded, smiling serenely. “That was my dress, Rosie. My one and only dance frock. I haven’t been able to fit into it for years and it seemed such a shame to let it end its life at the back of my wardrobe. That's why I was so pleased when you chose it. It was meant for you, love..."

"But – ooooh no!" I remembered all the things I'd confided to Dot in the charity shop. "But this house, and the Valentine's ball, and the nobility bit and…"

"This isn't our house, Rosie, love." Dot grinned. "We live in a semi like everyone else. Lady Barton is the patron of our charity and lets us have the ballroom for the Valentine's Day fund-raising function every year, that's all."

I gulped. "So why didn't you tell me about it – and you – and him...?" I flicked an embarrassed glance towards Matt, then looked at Dot again. "When I told you about the ball? And Sal? When I bought the dress?"

Dot didn't look even slightly abashed. "Well, you didn't name names, did you, love? It could have been any Valentine's charity do, couldn't it? And I just so wanted you to have the frock."

Matt held out his hand to me. "I think this – er – misunderstanding will take ages to sort out. Ages and ages – probably years... And in the meantime, I think you should show off some of that fancy footwork again."

Dot was grinning in a very smug fashion as, still mightily embarrassed, I sort of melted into Matt's arms. This time, though, he didn't do his Ernie and Dilys Truelove School of Dancing bit. This time he pulled me closely against him and smooched. Happily, now on familiar territory, I wriggled even closer and smooched back.

And as I fell head over heels in love with Matt Howard, on Valentine's Day, wearing his mum's best dress, the band was playing 'Second-hand Rose'.

Adonis

Dawn Hudd

Serena coiled her long fair hair into a loose bun and secured it with a gold clip. She placed her towel on the poolside recliner and gracefully sat down. It was early, not yet seven, but he was there, as she knew he would be.

They were alone. The other hotel guests slept on, or took breakfast in the distant dining room. It would be at least another hour before the families would make their appearances and disturb them; lunchtime at least before the groups of partying twenty-somethings would emerge.

She watched the young man making elegant arcs in the pool, droplets streaming like sweat from his back as he rose from the water with each stroke. She shivered as she gazed at his olive skin, darkened even more by the Spanish sun; she trembled as she took in every strand of the black hair that clung damply to his head. He, as every day, took no notice of her, but continued his progress from one end of the pool to the other.

At 7.45 he swam to the side, directly opposite Serena. She watched as he pulled himself from the water, and turned just for one second towards her. She looked down, unwilling to look into his green eyes. She knew they were green. It was the only colour. As he turned his back to her and walked away, she raised her eyes again. He disappeared into the trees that lined the perimeter of the complex and Serena stood, picked up her towel, and returned to her room.

The next day she was almost late. She had only four days left of her holiday. Four days more to watch her Adonis. Today she had brought a book. Over the pages she observed his change from butterfly to breaststroke, and back again. She saw him pause, only briefly, for breath. Today – for her, she was sure – he swam on his back also. His muscular body slid effortlessly through the water.

At 7.40 he stopped. He trod water and stared at Serena. She put her head down, and studied her book without reading the words. At 7.45, as usual, he pulled himself from the water and left the complex.

The following day Serena arrived early, to see where he came from. But he was there already, as if he had been there all night. Waiting for her. She took her place on the recliner, and placed her book by her side. Today she made no pretence of reading. This time she watched openly. He performed for her, dancing in the water, turning and pirouetting, spinning until she was breathless. Then he pulled himself once again from the pool and walked away. Serena knew the time. It was 7.45. She left.

With only two more days to go, Serena arrived at 7.00. For three quarters of an hour he swam for her. This time she smiled at him. As he swam, she dared to hope that what she saw was a flicker of a smile, just a chance that he felt the same. At a quarter to eight he disappeared.

Today would be her last day at the pool. The next morning she would be packing her bag, preparing for her flight home. Alone. Back to work, back to her flat, back to her cat and away from the little piece of paradise that for ten days she'd had here. Today she would just enjoy him, watch him in his natural environment. At 6.55 she drew near to the pool.

She gasped slightly when she saw the woman sitting on the recliner next to the one she always chose. She looked into the depths of the clear blue water. She couldn't see him. The woman had broken the spell. She would never see him again. As a tear began to slide down her cheek a ripple broke the surface of the water. Olive skin and dark green eyes rose above the side of the pool. The woman looked from Serena to her Adonis, silently retrieved her belongings, and left.

Serena placed her towel on the recliner and took her place. The young man resumed his swim, moving from end to end of the pool without changing his pace. Until. Until he turned and faced Serena. They said nothing. It was time. Serena stood and removed her wrap, revealing a simple black bikini vivid against her pale skin. He held his hand out to her and she took a graceful dive into the water, to her rightful place beside him.

To silent music they danced together. They waltzed in the water, anticipating each other's moves. They performed together as if it had always been so. The music moved Serena to heights she had never reached before. Alone, they swam. Together, they moved.

The music stopped. Serena took a breath. Her Adonis put a finger to his mouth, then placed it on hers, denying her speech, daring her to snap the fragile thread between them with sound. She watched as he moved gracefully to the poolside and pulled himself from the water. She cried as he took his towel and, for the last time, walked into the trees and away from her. It was over.

The next day she packed her bags and her souvenirs, threw away her sun cream and her black bikini, and flew home – alone.

Though the years were kind to her, Serena never forgot that brief summer of love. Every time she swam in crystal waters, or felt the sun on her bare back, she remembered. And every time she took the hand of her own Adonis, with his green eyes and his olive skin, every time she gently caressed his black hair, still damp from bath time, every time she looked at the boy walking beside her, she whispered, "My son," and remembered.

Breaking The Chain

Rachel Loosmore

"How do I get on such ridiculous mailing lists?" I asked through a mouthful of cornflakes.

"Why, what's that?" Izzy, my flat-mate, splashed soya milk over her organic muesli.

"It's a chain letter," I ranted. "Some imbecile, who is obviously aware enough of their pathetic inability to contribute to society to withhold their name but not enough to cease such ludicrous activities, feels the need to con me out of five first-class stamps at the risk of being cursed for life!"

"Ooh, I love chain letters – such an interesting modern response to age-old voodoo activities. You are going to obey it, aren't you?" Izzy suddenly looked serious.

"Of course not. I can't afford to obey the Inland Revenue this month, let alone some crank with nothing better to do." I defiantly ripped up the letter. Hearing my final-word-on-the-matter tone, Izzy said nothing, but rolled her eyes in a 'you're gonna be sorry' manner. I rinsed my bowl under the tap, grabbed the rubbish bag from under the sink and headed for work. "See you tonight, Izzy," I called.

"If you make it through your cursed day you will, yeah!"

As I galloped down the front steps the first incident occurred. The bin bag split, dumping milk cartons and dead teabags all over the pavement. "Damn it!" I cried. "I'm gonna be late." The whole clean-up operation took a good ten minutes.

At 9.15am I burst through the doors of the office and ran straight into Mr Robinson, my boss. "Good *afternoon,* Miss Wilkinson, shame you chose today of all days to be unpunctual. I was going to ask you to represent HR and be my escort to the company ball, a week Friday. But in your untimely absence I've asked Fiona instead." He turned on his heels and minced out. Fiona shot me a 'thanks for nothing' look as I headed for my desk.

"Thank God for split bin bags," I muttered as I turned on my PC. I could think of nothing worse than a night escorting 'Boring Banks' to a boring ball. Cursed indeed, I thought.

At lunchtime I worked an extra five minutes to make up for my lateness and then popped out to town. As I turned out of the car park the steering wheel shifted, the whole panel came loose and I found myself struggling to keep control of the car. "Damn it! Damn it! Damn it!" I swore, emphasising the last cuss by slapping my palms against the offending equipment. I reluctantly pulled over into the garage, my knuckles turning white as I struggled to control the turn.

I must have reached at least six 'damn its!' by the time I left the garage to walk back to the office. I was not amused by the sixty quid estimate the mechanic had quoted. But I was determined not to let the chain letter theory win, so decided to get the bus to the gym after work regardless.

Once I finished my workout I went for a shower. I flung my towel over the door of the stall and turned the shower tap. A sudden clunk followed by a hissing spray noise caught me off guard. My feet shot from beneath me and I landed in a heap on the wet tiles. It took a couple of seconds before I realized that the spout of water surging from the broken pipe was scalding hot. I scrambled about on all fours, screeching in pain as I tried to get up and escape the burning geyser. My screams caused all those in the immediate vicinity to come running. As I burst through the stall door red-raw and naked I was greeted by a crowd of concerned on-lookers. Claudia, the disturbingly large self-defence instructor, came to my aid. That's about right, I thought. It couldn't have been one of the half-a-dozen lush hunks that work here could it?

Holding a antiseptic pad smeared with burn cream over my forearm I thanked the taxi driver and tried to juggle closing the cab door, nursing my wound and finding my ringing mobile phone in the depths of my handbag. I muttered a few more 'damn its'. Flipping the phone open I demanded, "YES?" into the phone.

"Miss Wilkinson?" a male voice asked. "It's Gary from the garage. I found another problem. It's your brakes. There must have been a leak for ages. You've virtually no brake fluid left in the pipes. Damn lucky really, a few more miles and you would have had complete break failure. I'd say your steering column fault might have just saved your life."

"Oh, OK, Gary, thanks for letting me know," I stammered soberly as I closed the phone and walked through the automatic doors into A&E. My momentary relief was snuffed out as I read the red light message board: 'Your waiting time for non-emergencies is approx three and a half hours. The NHS would like to apologize for any inconvenience. Patients will be seen in order of priority.' I didn't bother with 'damn its' as I registered with reception and took my place amongst the waiting patients. I had finally accepted the power of the chain letter. I was just resolving to Sellotape it back together and send it on when an unfamiliar male voice broke into my thoughts.

"Is anyone sitting here?" he asked. I stared into the most perfectly-perfect face I'd ever seen set off by a mud-covered, shorts-wearing, rugged, manly, god-like rugby-playing body. "Is yours a priority case?" he asked, nodding at my arm.

"Um, no afraid not. Looks like I'm in for the full three-and-a-half hour wait," I replied, trying to raise a smile without dribbling.

"Me neither, just a sprain I think, should have passed the ball a little sooner! Still it looks like we're just have to keep each other company doesn't it? No so bad after all."

"I guess so," I replied and silently uttered a million 'thank yous' to that blessed chain letter.

A Foreign Affair

Kate Roberts

At 10.15pm last Sunday evening my life as I knew it ended. In one single minute I was thrown into a world of emotional somersaults and on to a roller coaster ride that I didn't want to end.

My cousin, Jude, had persuaded me to go for a drink with her at a local wine bar. Up to that point my social life had been virtually non-existent. My husband, Jerry, had walked out just before Christmas, claiming he was going in search of a 'younger model'. Having celebrated my thirty-sixth birthday a month earlier and he being six years older than me, I thought this a bit of a cheek! Ten years of what I'd thought was a good, sound marriage had been torn away leaving me broken. It was now April and my self-esteem was at an all-time low. When Jude asked me if I fancied a night out, I was reluctant to say the least.

The bar was crowded. It was hot and smoky. I felt pangs of envy and sadness as I watched couples chatting, holding hands and smiling at each other. Jude was doing her best to cheer me up.

"Sorry Jude, I'm just not ready for this," I moaned.

"Don't worry about it, Sue" she said. "It'll take ages for you to get over Jerry. Try to smile and look as though you're enjoying yourself. You never know who might be looking your way. Jerry was mad to leave you. You are a lovely person. You're beautiful, clever and funny. He probably thought you were too good for him. Forget him. Move on."

"Flatterer!" I laughed. Easier said than done though, I thought.

It was nearly the end of the evening. I had enjoyed chatting to Jude but was ready for home. Jude had just nipped to the loo and I was staring into space, when something made me look towards the bar. A man standing at the bar was looking straight at me and we made very definite eye contact. I couldn't believe the intensity of his stare. I looked away quickly, embarrassed. In that brief moment, I'd noticed he had piercing blue eyes and the faint hint of a smile on his lips. I felt his eyes still boring into me and I had an overwhelming urge to look at him again. I stole a glance and, sure enough, his startling blue eyes immediately locked onto mine. This time I held his gaze, unable to pull away. There was intensity and fire in his eyes. Unmistakable passion.

I blushed and continued to look at him, despite my heart pounding against my rib cage. It was impossible to feel like this after looking at a man for just one minute. Someone touched my arm and woke me from my trance. It was Jude.

"Are you OK? You look as if you're going to faint."

"Mmmm. Yeah… yes," I stammered, unable to utter an intelligent word. Suddenly I felt reckless, like a wicked, mischievous teenager. Impulsively I searched in my bag for a bit of paper and a pen.

"What are you doing?" said Jude, pulling my arm. "I thought we were going. Come on!"

"Hang on. Give me a minute," I replied, quickly writing a note on the back of an old receipt. Before she and I knew it I had walked straight up to Mr Cobalt Blue, put the note in his hand and muttered, "Call me!" He looked as stunned as I felt but took the note and stared at it, then stared back at me. Thinking Oh my God what have I done! I turned on my heel and pulled an equally stunned Jude towards the door.

"Don't ask. Just keep on walking," I hissed, through gritted teeth.

"What the hell did you write?" Jude insisted, once we were outside heading for her car.

"Only my phone number and first name! And I asked him to call me!" I was high on adrenaline. I'd never done anything as crazy as that before. Not to mention potentially dangerous. He was a complete stranger and I've given him *my* phone number!

"You are definitely MAD!" said Jude, "but I like your style. Oh my God! There he is, leaving the bar with another bloke. He's not bad either! I haven't seen either of them around here before."

Mystery man and his mate sauntered over to a very smart sports car. As we passed them in the car he looked straight at me again with those piercing blue eyes. It was as though he could see into my very soul. I blushed madly, my heart beating like a kettledrum, and squeezed Jude's hand hard. "He'll *definitely* call!" she laughed.

I couldn't sleep for thinking about my recklessness. I was almost regretting it. What if he was some kind of psycho, a madman, a lunatic stalker!? Calm down, I reasoned with myself, I hadn't given him my address and there was no way he could find out where I lived. He probably thought we were just two crazy women having a laugh. He'd just bin the receipt and forget about it. Secretly, though, a little butterfly in my stomach hoped that he wouldn't.

The next morning I woke to a bright, sunny spring day. A delicious spark, like electricity, shot through my body as the vision of the stranger ran through my mind. All day I pottered around, my heart beating madly every time the phone rang. I ran to it only to find my mother wanting to discuss, in minute detail, Auntie Jean's daughter's wedding arrangements or Jude, for the sixth time, to see if 'mystery man' had rung. By the evening, just as I had begun to think it had all been a vivid dream, the phone suddenly blurted out its high-pitched tone.

"Hello!" I snapped.

"Hello," a hesitant, male voice replied.

"Hello. Who is this?" I asked.

"Jean-Claude," came back the reply, in a foreign accent. Somebody is messing about, I thought. Probably Jude's boyfriend joking around.

"I see you in bar last night. I am French. You give me note," he continued in delightfully broken English. This was no joke. It was real! Out of all the people in the bar he had smiled at *me*. My mind was racing. French? What was a Frenchman doing in our small town? Who was he? I was intrigued.

He went on to explain beautifully in broken English that he was working in town for a while. He told me he was staying at a hotel, which I eventually understood to be 'The Merryfield'. He also thought I had a lovely smile. "Would you like to meet?" he said, in his lovely accent. All thoughts of Jerry and the heartache he had caused were pushed out of my mind for a moment, and I threw caution to the wind. Without hesitation I replied, "Yes, where?"

"In the hotel. At the bar?" he suggested. It was madness, meeting a complete stranger in a hotel bar. Then I reasoned that people go on blind dates all the time. I knew the hotel.

It was a public place and I would tell Jude where I would be. Besides, I deserved a little adventure.

"*Oui! Oui!* Yes, yes! That would be lovely," I said, my heart beating wildly. My God I thought, I don't even speak French!

"OK. Seven-thirty is OK?" he suggested.

"Yes, yes! I will be there. Bye."

"*Au revoir.*"

Looking at my watch I saw it was nearly ten past seven! Less than fifteen minutes to make myself presentable! Not before telling Jude the news. After all she had been the one who had persuaded me to go out for a drink. My hands were shaking so much that I could hardly dial her number. It took me three attempts before I finally got through. I heard the dial tone. "Come on, Jude, pick up," I muttered to myself. After what seemed like an eternity she eventually did. She sounded breathless.

"Hello".

"Jude?"

"Yes. Sue. Sorry I was in the bath. He's rung?"

"Yes, yes. Just now."

"Tell me! Quick! I'm dying to know."

"He's French!"

"No! You're joking! What's he doing over here?"

"Working at the power station. On a contract. At least that's what I think he said. His English is like my French, limited. But a bit of my school French came back to me."

"Fantastic! What else? Are you going to meet up."

"Yes!"

"Aaaggghhh! When? Where?"

"Tonight. In ten minutes to be exact!"

Jude screamed again, even louder.

"Where are you meeting him?"

"At his hotel. You know it, The Merryfield, where Diane had her fortieth?"

"Oh yeah, I know it. On Park Road."

"That's the one. Look I'll have to go, I've only got seven minutes to make myself presentable."

"Listen, Sue."

"Tell me."

"Have a great time but be… "

"I know. I'll be careful. I've got my mobile. Bye. I'll let you know how it goes!

"OK. Have fun!"

Click. She had hung up. I took a deep breath and placed the receiver slowly in its cradle. This was it. A chance to forget Jerry, if only for one evening. I had to take it. After a quick make-up and hair check, I was ready.

Ten minutes later I bundled into the hotel foyer, almost tripping on the carpet and hurtling myself into the arms of the porter. Apologising profusely, I propelled myself into the bar and was brought up short by Jean-Claude smiling warmly at me. In that moment I knew this was the right thing to do. He walked directly up to me and kissed me twice, once on my left cheek and one on my right, the French way. The details of the room faded into a fuzzy obscurity as he took my arm, and masterfully guided me to the bar. He had that wonderful charisma and panache I'm sure all Frenchmen possess. Even the way he addressed the barman and ordered us fine red wine with such ease, despite his limited knowledge of the English language, was intoxicating. I was walking on air as he led me toward a large, comfortable sofa in a quiet area of the bar.

Jean Claude was fabulous company. Witty, charming, a perfect gentleman. His English was limited, but miraculously, from nowhere, the French I had learned at school came back to me. So, we chattered away in French *and* English! He told me he was a contract worker at the local power station, and would be in the area for a little while. We had a wonderful evening and arranged to meet again the following day.

Jean-Claude, being a true gentlemen, walked me to my car. It was a beautiful clear moonlit night. The stars twinkled brightly for us and the whole world seemed vital and alive. To be escorted to my car by this handsome man was a thrill in itself. He had, in very simple ways, made me feel special and sexy. That was something I hadn't felt for a long time.

He touched my arm gently and I turned to him to say goodnight. I looked up into his beautiful eyes and felt a tingling all over my body, inside and out! Then he kissed me, his sweet lips on mine. It was the most exquisite kiss I'd ever had. Not tonight though, I needed to wait for him. And I needed to make him wait for me. But it was proving difficult. He stroked my hair, showering my face with tender kisses. Then he pulled away, whispering, "Bon nuit, sweet dreams. Until tomorrow."

I floated to my car, pinching my arm to check if I was really there and it was really happening. My arm hurt like hell!

The next evening, true to his word, we met at the bar. Confident, suave, handsome, he took me in his arms and swept me away. We spent a fabulous evening in a great music bar, dancing close, drinking a little wine. Later, when he dropped me off at home, I invited him in for coffee, and I meant *only* coffee. I wanted to wait.

"Tomorrow. We shall meet tomorrow," I managed to murmur.

"Yes, of course… but I want you very much," he replied, huskily.

"Mmmmmm… yes… I know. Waiting is good," I insisted.

The wait would be worth it. My God! I was turning into a minx extraordinaire! I released myself from his steamy embrace and reluctantly pushed him towards the door.

"Until tomorrow then… mademoiselle..," he smouldered, blowing me a kiss, through the half-closed front door.

"Goodnight… monsieur… " I took myself off to bed with a wonderfully warm feeling in my heart.

Dinner the following evening was a splendid affair, despite the fact that we didn't eat a single morsel. Our meals went cold as we simply held hands over the table and spoke in our own unique blend of French and English. From somewhere we found a common language, a meeting of hearts and soul. There was marvellous intensity between us. Deep inside I knew that we only had a short time together. His contract ended at the end of the week and I knew I would probably never see him again. It didn't matter in the slightest. Jean-Claude had given me so much in those few days, and yet hadn't expected anything, especially physically. He had been the perfect gentleman, undemanding and tender, allowing me to set the pace. That night I invited him in for more than coffee. He was wonderful. Gentle, yet passionate. Masterful and caring at the same time.

During those few days with Jean-Claude, I regained my confidence. He gave me courage and a small glimmer of hope that it *was* possible to have a passionate and loving relationship after Jerry.

Last night was our last together. Just before dawn, I drove him back to his hotel. It was snowing, which I thought was strange for April. I parked the car outside the hotel and he looked into my eyes and said he would call.

"No," I said, "don't. Just remember."

He took my hand, brought it to his lips and kissed it tenderly. With one last look into my eyes, he smiled, opened the car door and got out. I swung the car around in the car park and blinked away tears of joy and sadness. It had been wonderful, but I would never see him again. I glanced in my rear view mirror and saw him, his arm raised in a salute to goodbye.

The memory of that wave has filled me with confidence and hope. The time spent with Jean-Claude has enabled me to look forward. I know what it is to love and to be loved, again. And, most importantly, 'je ne regrette rien'.

Magnetic Attraction

Ginny Swart

"Would you like to try a sample of our latest perfume?"

Without waiting for Tessa's answer, a tall, well-groomed sales lady stepped forward from the cosmetic counter and sprayed her liberally with something heady and exotic, almost choking her with the sickly fumes.

"It's called 'Magnetique,'" she added confidently. "It comes in a carved crystal flagon…"

"It's *horrible*," replied Tessa tartly. " I could knock down a horse at twenty paces with that stuff. I prefer something a bit more subtle, thanks."

As she walked to the restaurant to meet Mark she was aware of the heavy, musky smell which clung to her. This will probably give me a headache, she thought crossly – but then spotted her brother at a corner table and forgot about it.

"Tess, meet Jeremy Woolf, he joined our office this week."

Tessa offered her hand to the dark, good looking man standing next to Mark and as she did so, her stomach gave a little lurch of pleasure. He's *very* cute, she thought, but automatically checked for the tell-tale gold band. Good, no wedding ring.

"So, Jeremy, what are you doing at McKinley Techtronics?" She patted the seat next to her and he slid into it, smiling.

"I'm in Sales. I've just come down from Brisbane and Mark's been showing me the ropes."

There was an instant electricity between them. Tessa could feel it and she knew Jeremy could too. I'm not rushing into anything here, she thought, this time I'm being very careful. He's too gorgeous to lose. But she replied calmly enough, her heart thumping.

"Lucky you, being transferred to Sydney. Have you found somewhere for your family to stay?" Checking, but not too obvious, she thought.

"I've found a bachelor pad up in Queens Cross. Luckily I don't have any family to worry about. One room and somewhere for my baby is all I need."

"Your *baby*?"

"A Morgan two- seater."

"Oh, a sports car." Phew.

"Not just any sports car, sis." Mark sounded envious. "Jeremy's car is a hand-made work of art. Each one takes six months to make, leather seats, walnut dashboard and all. They're imported and there's only a handful of them in the country."

She looked at Jeremy from under her eyelashes. "D'you like driving fast?"

"Sure. Don't you?"

"I like doing most things fast," she said evenly. "But sometimes it's more enjoyable to take things slowly. Very slowly."

"I couldn't agree more," he murmured.

For the rest of the evening, conversation flowed easily between the three of them although she was aware of Jeremy's burning gaze on her all the time. Her brother must have sensed the undercurrents, because he made an excuse to leave before coffee was served.

As Mark kissed her goodnight he whispered, "Be good, little sister, or be careful."

"I will!" she grinned, and leaned back to find Jeremy's arm across the back of her chair, his face close to hers.

"Mmm, you smell wonderful, " he murmured into her neck, his eyes closed. "I've been wanting to tell you that all evening. I'm a sucker for beautiful women who wear perfume, I just go weak at the knees."

"If you're weak at the knees it sounds as though it's time for your bed. It's definitely time for mine," she said, standing up decisively.

"I have a lovely new bed at my flat. A king-size one," he said softly. "It's a pity to waste all that empty space."

"It won't disappear, will it?" She smiled teasingly at him over her shoulder as they left the restaurant. "Call me next week."

She was going to take this affair slowly and enjoy every tantalising minute until they finally ended up where they both knew they would – in Jeremy's king- sized bed.

But to think he liked that awful perfume! There was no accounting for taste. I'll buy a bottle tomorrow, she decided. 'Magnetique' certainly lives up to its name.

If Annabelle the sales girl was surprised to see her back the following day, she was too tactful to show it.

"I'll take the larger size, please," said Tessa. There goes my rent money, she thought, but worth every smelly drop.

As she walked to her office, her cell-phone beeped.

'MEET ME MARIOS LUNCHTIME GREAT NEWS Y X'

Tessa realised guiltily that she hadn't seen her old college friend Yvonne for nearly three months. A small salad was about all she could afford after splashing out on the perfume, but it would be fun to catch up with things.

'C U THERE' she replied.

"So, Vonnie, what's your news? You're looking really good!"

Yvonne was radiant, a huge smile on her face and a big diamond ring on her finger, which she waggled triumphantly in front of Tessa.

"Ta-da!"

"Hey, fantastic! Congratulations!" Tessa felt doubly guilty. She hadn't even known Yvonne was in a serious relationship with anyone and here she was, engaged to be married. "Who's the lucky guy?"

"Tess, you will not believe this, but I met Spike on holiday three weeks ago and we just clicked. We both knew the minute we met that this was *it.* For keeps. I was planning to move up to Brisbane to be near him but he's wangled a transfer to Sydney. And when we met for lunch yesterday he produced this! Stunning, eh?"

"It certainly is."

Tessa held her friend's hand and admired the gem sparkling and flashing in the sunlight. She couldn't help a small stab of envy at the size of the diamond and the fact that it was on Yvonne's plump finger. Tessa, twice voted Beach Babe of the Year, had always assumed she'd be the first to get married, but it looked as though dumpy, plain little Yvonne was going to be first in the marriage stakes. Ah well.

"Have you set a date?"

"Not yet, but Spike wants us to have a big engagement party soon, so he can meet all my friends. We'll worry about the wedding later. Maybe next year."

"That's sensible. You have to admit, this was a holiday romance and you don't know if it will last."

"Yes, I do," said Yvonne firmly. "And when you meet Spike, you'll know why. Our party's a fortnight on Saturday, be there!"

"I wouldn't miss it for the world." Tessa got up and gave Yvonne a big hug. "I'm madly jealous and very happy for you."

"Don't forget, you promised to be my bridesmaid ages ago. I'm going to hold you to that."

"I haven't forgotten." Although she had, actually. "Just tell me your colour scheme and I'll be there, boots and all."

On Tuesday evening, her phone was ringing as she opened the door of her flat.

"Tessa? Jeremy. Remember me?"

"Sort of. That short blond guy with freckles?"

They both laughed.

"What are your plans for this evening?"

"Mmm… a boiled egg in front of *Survivor*, I think."

"I've got a better idea…"

Dinner at El Greco was an intimate three-hour affair, each course accompanied by glasses of red wine, and a delicious curtain-raiser for the rest of the evening.

"Coffee at my place?"

Tessa nodded dreamily and held Jeremy's hand tightly as they left the restaurant. She nestled into the deep leather seat of the racy little sports car, watching the city lights flash by and enjoying the wind in her hair until he braked sharply outside his flat. Then he turned and folded her in his arms.

"That heavenly perfume…god, woman, how I want you…" Jeremy was peppering her neck with rough, demanding kisses, and he didn't notice the gear stick jabbing uncomfortably into Tessa's thigh.

"Ouch… let's go somewhere more comfortable," she gasped. The bucket seats were not designed for seduction.

Once inside his flat, Tessa sank onto the sofa, glad to let him make some coffee while she caught her breath.

Typical bachelor, she thought. A big, bare room with only the sofa, some bean bags and an expensive music system. Wait till Jeremy sees what a woman's touch will do. A few pictures, some fresh flowers and some decent curtains would make all the difference.

Then she noticed a small silver-framed photo on the cupboard and got up to examine it.

It was Yvonne, her hair tumbling about her shoulders, laughing into the camera. Tessa was stunned. *Yvonne?*

She turned speechlessly to Jeremy who came into the room balancing two steaming mugs of coffee.

He laughed awkwardly. "That's my little sister," he said, and laid the photograph flat. "Um…we've always been close. Come on, sit down.."

"No – I don't think so." Her voice was shaky and she hoped she wasn't going to cry in front of him. "I think I'll call a cab…Spike."

His head jerked up. "What did you call me?"

"What your fiancée calls you. Spike. You two-timing pig."

She snatched up her coat and bag and ran blindly for the stairs. Jeremy, or Spike, didn't follow her.

To tell her, or not?

Yvonne was so happy, and so sure of her love for Spike a.k.a Jeremy that she didn't have the heart to confront her friend.

Give him the benefit of the doubt – maybe he'd turn out to be a devoted husband, although Tessa didn't think this was likely. She just hoped that before the wedding, Yvonne would find out for herself what sort of rat her fiancé was.

She invented some excuse not to attend Yvonne and Spike's engagement party, but much as she wanted to, she couldn't avoid the wedding.

"We've decided not to wait," burbled Yvonne happily over a cappuccino at Mario's. "How do you feel about a cream silk sheath dress with coffee accessories? With your red hair, that would look stunning. And I'll be in cream shantung and Spike's wearing a cream suit…"

Oh great. The colour-coded wedding she'd hoped would never happen. She must have looked a bit odd because Yvonne stopped in mid-flow and asked, "Is something wrong? I know we always planned on turquoise but that's so dated…"

"No, it's nothing." Tessa still couldn't bring herself to mention her encounters with Spike. It had been six months ago and who knows, he might have changed.

But when the wedding came, she walked down the aisle behind a glowing Yvonne, sick with anxiety. Would 'Jeremy' acknowledge their previous meeting? And how would she deal with her own overwhelming desire for her friend's new husband?

Jeremy was standing with his back to her in a dress suit. Yvonne's father kissed his daughter and gave her hand to a shortish, blond man standing next to Jeremy.

The next twenty minutes were a confused blur for Tessa. Spike *wasn't* Jeremy! Then Jeremy really *was* Yvonne's brother! What fool she'd been! The minute they walked back down the aisle together, as best man and bridesmaid, she'd speak to Jeremy, apologise and explain.

She knew he'd laugh, and forgive her. The attraction between them had been so strong, surely he wouldn't hold a silly mistake against her, and this wedding was a marvellous occasion to rekindle the flame.

Pity I threw away that bottle of 'Magnetique', she reflected, as the organist struck up the familiar chords and she took her place next to Jeremy to walk out of the church.

"Hello, Jeremy," she whispered, smiling up at him, "We meet again. Remember me?"

"Yes, you're that short girl with freckles." He grinned. He hadn't forgotten! Just walking next to him without touching sent delicious shivers of anticipation down her spine.

As they reached the church steps, Jeremy turned to her with that look of smouldering passion she remembered so well. But he was looking past her, at a tall, well-groomed girl who emerged from the crowd of excited guests and gave Jeremy a resounding kiss.

"Clever boy, you didn't drop the ring after all," she said.

"Tessa, meet my fiancée, Annabelle," he smiled.

Tessa became aware of a strong, rather unpleasant, musky smell. It was the saleslady from the cosmetic counter. And Jeremy had that familiar, weak-at-the-knees expression he got when in close contact with 'Magnetique'.

Dancers
Dawn Wingfield

After making love they would lie sealed together, watching the rain pulse in waves down the skylight over his bed. She remembers it rained often when they were together. But as they lay breathless they had also seen stars blooming. The skylight was in the middle of the room, a square of light in the ceiling, spilling silver downward. He'd arranged his bed beneath it, an island marooned in a sea of books, papers, bottles and strewn clothes. The air was always tinged warmly with the smells of coffee and incense. The bed was soft, and smelled of them.

These are the thoughts in Carrie's head when she sees Ned in the supermarket. It's nine o'clock and customers are sparse, looking dazed and exhausted as they roam around picking up bread and pints of milk. Muzak floats meaningless through aisles of jam and cereal and meat. Ned is looking at cheeses. He is as she remembers him, tall, with receding black hair and a mouth that smiles easily.

Carrie is shocked into stillness for a moment, before the memories start to come at her, stinging like little nicks and cuts. Dry-mouthed, she skulks over to a display of baked beans. He mustn't see her. She feels vulnerable tonight, plump and swollen in a pair of jeans and a baggy T-shirt, face bare, hair dragged into a stringy ponytail. The lights in the store are brutally neon. And there is Ned, just feet away, placing a scarlet disc of Edam into his cart, alongside a bottle of wine, some crackers and a bag of apples. Easy foods that don't need cooking, the kind you eat in bed. He likes things easy, Carrie remembers. Her legs feel weak. She wants to walk away but she can't seem to move.

As if she's called his name, he looks up, straight at her. His eyebrows rise in surprise, then he shrugs and comes over. "Carrie – how the hell are you?" he demands with a smile.

She goes for a bemused look. "Fine – how're you?" Asked as if she doesn't care that much.

They only lasted a year. Carrie fell in love, deeper and deeper, as Ned gradually lost interest. However, to make things easier, he continued to smile and make love to her, even as his silences deepened and his absences were more and more frequent. And Carrie danced, faster and faster, trying to interest Ned, trying to seduce and fascinate him, trying to make him love her again.

His eyes move over her. She wonders if he ever thinks of that holiday they spent together, a week in Cornwall, drunk on love and apple cider. They bicycled all over the countryside, searching for secret places to make love in.

"Well…" he murmurs, already looking a bit bored, wondering how he can tie this up.

She wanted to die when it ended – she actually thought she might die, was amazed that her body kept drawing breath and moving through the days, in spite of the fact that her heart was cracked wide open.

For the first time Carrie notices a long-fingered hand on his arm, attached to an anxious-looking girl with long pale hair. "Oh, hello," she says, with a sad smile of recognition, as she sees this girl is dancing too, a fast, desperate dance of longing. She has to stay thin enough, interesting enough, sexy enough. Inevitably though, one day soon, she will collapse in a broken, bloody heap of pain while Ned walks off with an apologetic smile.

"You're a bit out of your way, aren't you?" Carrie suddenly feels elated.

"Oh, I gave the flat up about a year ago," he says and she feels a pang. Someone else lives there now, furniture arranged sensibly, the skylight shining its patch of brightness on to a hard-wearing carpet. Then something in Ned's face flickers. He does remember: the sex, the holiday, the way they bickered over the names of their someday children. He remembers, but what's the point of dwelling on the past?

"This is Sarah," he says, and the blonde woman clutches at his arm and gives Carrie a wary smile.

"Well," Carrie smiles. "It was nice bumping into you."

She pays for her milk, frozen pizza and infant painkiller and exits into a cool evening lit faintly by the moon. No one can see her face, so she smiles as she walks back to the house.

Ray has left a light on in the kitchen. This is Carrie's life now: a house with a floral sofa in front of a television, a kitchen with wedding-gift non-stick pans and brown tiles they will change one day, a husband, a baby named Leo. There is no Carrie and Ned. She stopped dancing years ago.

Carrie dumps the food on the counter, puts the kettle on and shoves the milk in the fridge and the pizza in the freezer. Ray is upstairs. She opens the bedroom door carefully and he looks up and smiles. He is holding Leo's tiny, slumbering body against his broad chest, one large hand tenderly supporting his son's back.

"How is he?" She can hear Leo snoring; he's still congested.

"Dozed off about ten minutes ago." Ray looks exhausted. Neither of them has managed much sleep since their eight week old came down with a cold.

"Fancy some tea?" Carrie whispers.

"Sounds lovely."

On impulse, she leans forward and gives him a kiss, because Carrie has just realised something. She wants exactly what she has: this man, this baby, this life.

The Green Man

Rosemary Laurey

“Josie, Michael arrived early.”

Josie’s knuckles whitened on the steering wheel, hearing her sister-in-law’s voice. “What happened, Sally?” Her hand holding her mobile shook.

“He upset Dad by bitching about the funeral arrangements, and nagged about us ordering sherry that was too cheap – but never offered to go out and buy better. He’s now drinking coffee in the dining room, and griping because I made instant.” Sally paused. “So far, no one’s told him you’re coming.”

“Perhaps I’d better not.”

“Yes, you will! Dad’s counting on it and you promised Mum before she died!” This was the main reason Josie had agreed to go in the first place. “Arrive tomorrow morning. That way Dad will see you, and even Michael won’t make a scene in front of all the friends and relations.”

True enough. Josie’s ex-husband charmed everyone except his ex-wife and close family. Just hearing his name gave her goosebumps. Her ribs had mended and the bruises had faded – but only on the outside. She was truly dreading seeing him again, but she’d promised her dying mother-in-law to look him in the eye, and then get on with her life.

Josie wished she possessed Margaret Malone's courage. She'd been an inspiration and support to Josie when she needed it.

"Stay at the Green Man," Sally said. "I called them. They're expecting you."

Sally's directions, to a village pub a few miles from the Malone's house, were easy to follow. She was expected, welcomed, and shown into a large high-ceiling room with two small windows looking down on the painted Green Man pub sign, and the car park opposite. At the other end of the room, a wide balcony covered with climbing roses in bloom opened to the gardens and a view of the Downs. With beamed ceiling, carved four poster, and luxurious bathroom, it seemed more like a honeymoon suite than the spare room of a country pub.

"We don't often rent it out," the landlord's wife said as she showed Josie the room. "Just once in a while when a friend of a friend needs it. We call it the Green Man room." She walked over to the window. "On account of being so close to The Man himself."

The man himself hung from a wrought iron bracket. Josie looked down. He had an arrogant, almost lascivious, look about him. A glint in his eye that was downright sexy.

She had been alone too long if she was having wild thoughts about a pub sign! She needed a good night's sleep to face the morning – and Michael.

Not feeling up to a bar of jovial strangers, Josie took a ham ploughman's and a Guinness to her room, flicked on the TV and tried to settle for the evening.

It wasn't easy. Despite her ex-father-in-law's insistence, and Sally's urgings, Josie was dreading tomorrow. But Margaret Malone had welcomed Josie into her family as a daughter, apologised through her tears when she learned the details of Michael's abuse, even lent Josie money after the divorce. She owed Margaret and would go to her funeral, even if it meant facing Michael.

She just hoped she was strong enough to indeed look him the eye and wish him in to perdition. Trouble was, she was scared she'd start shaking and throwing up when she set eyes on him.

Originally Michael had said he wasn't arriving until the morning of the funeral, which was why Josie had agreed to come the night before to spend time with Sally and her father. Trust Michael to wreck her plans.

Irritated at the mindless cheerfulness of the TV, Josie flicked it off, showered and decided to turn in early. A good night's rest might help her face her ex. She knew in her heart that if she could only, just once, look him in the eye, without fear, she'd be free of him. Unfortunately, she suspected she needed some sort of divine assistance to get the courage and confidence.

She showered, using the expensive lavender shower gel – impressive country pub this was turning out to be – slathered herself with the matching body lotion, and eased herself between crisp, linen sheets that smelled of sunshine and clean air. The pillows and duvet were real down, sheer luxury, and just what she needed for a good night's rest.

Except it wouldn't come. Between the talk from the bar below, engine noise, and headlights from departing cars, Josie tossed and turned. Finally she got up, and made herself a cup of herbal tea, from the supply provided with the coffee and tea bags.

She went back to bed, and sipped the aromatic, and vaguely sweet brew. Eventually the noises below eased and the last car revved out of the car park. Lulled by the scent of roses, Josie dozed. The last sound she heard was the old inn sign outside her window, swinging on its rusty hinges…

Her dreams came wild and jumbled: dark images from her marriage, mixed with kindnesses from her friends. The Old Green Man creaked, and a dark shadow drifted into the room.

Josie murmured in her sleep, but now the images of hurt and loss faded into a welcoming tunnel redolent of lavender, rose petals, and moonlight. She dreamt of loving, of gentle touches. As she turned in her sleep, a whisper of a breeze caressed her back. She threw off the duvet to feel the touch of summer on her skin, and to soak the life around her into her wounded spirit.

Towards dawn, and long after her sighs faded in the dim room, a breeze ruffled the discarded sheets, bringing night scents into the room. As the first streaks of light washed across the sky, the dark shadows over the bed drifted out the window and the old painted inn sign creaked again.

Josie sank into a deep sleep, missed the rooster crowing in a nearby garden, and the rattle of a milk crate landing on the stone steps. It was the bright light of morning that finally woke her. As she sat up, refreshed and renewed, and ready to face the day, she realised just how weary she'd been the night before.

Later that morning, Josie parked on the drive that led up to the crematorium, and walked to the chapel, her feet crunching on the gravel.

John Malone nodded at Josie as he passed her on his way to the family pew. Sally smiled, and Michael glowered. With a courage she never imagined she possessed, Josie returned his glare with a formal nod. Later, in the crush of friends and relatives at her in-laws' house, he cornered her. "What the hell are you doing here?"

His hands gripped her arms. She twisted her shoulders and moved sideways, breaking his grip. “Your mother invited me!”

“She couldn‘t...” he began.

“She did, and I promised her I’d be here! Now if you will excuse me.“ Josie pushed past him, and crossed the room. She never looked back at him, and knew she never would.

The Spice Of Life

Diana Appleyard

"When was the last time you made love outside?"

"I beg your pardon?" Carole's hand was half way to the kettle. She paused, turned, and looked searchingly at Rachel, who was sitting drawing dreamy lines in some milk spilt from Ben's morning Special K. "That's a very personal question."

"No, it isn't. I need to know that I'm not the only one with a sex life less exciting than that of inert gas. It's just that Nick makes me feel so…" Rachel's voice broke off, and she dropped her dark head towards the half-eaten bowl of cereal not yet cleared up in Carole's pre-school breakfast battle with her children. There was a long, uncomfortable pause, and Susan and Carole shot each other a concerned glance. Then Rachel raised her head, defiantly. "He makes me feel so undesirable. I know I'm not the shape I used to be and I do dress for convenience" – she looked down at her tracksuit bottoms and navy jumper, bobbly and shrunken from an accidental machine wash – "but if he doesn't approach me and hug me and make me feel like a desirable woman then how can I suddenly turn into a raving siren? I mean, by the time we go to bed I'm so tired I can hardly make it up the stairs, let alone burrow into my underwear drawer and throw on a wisp of chiffon. And I'd be so embarrassed anyway – with my stomach and thighs I'd look more like a small performing elephant than the object of male fantasy."

"Has he said something?" Carole ventured.

"Oh no, he doesn't have to say anything, he just doesn't try any more. It isn't just the sex," she added, shaking her head, "it's the touching. It's the him coming up to me and hugging me from behind when I'm cooking, like he used to, or the holding hands when we walk along. That's really all part of it, isn't it, the need to feel that someone actually wants to touch you. I'm beginning to feel like a cross little island that no-one wants to visit. If I was a tourist attraction I'd be closed down through lack of interest."

Carole narrowly avoided dropping the three mugs she was lifting down from the cupboard. She held back from laughing, though, because although Rachel was smiling depreciatingly, it was a sad smile, a smile that turned the corners of her mouth down, the smile that her daughter Harriet had just before her chin wobbled and the tears came. "How long," she asked carefully. "How long has it been?"

"Oh, a month, at least."

"A month?" Susan's voice was shocked, and they both looked at her enquiringly. She coughed. Carole saw she was twisting her wedding ring round and round her finger.

"That isn't very long," she said, lamely. "Is it?"

"It's long enough to make me feel about as sexy and wanted as a cabbage."

Carole poured the boiling water on to the instant granules, and clicked in sweetener for the three of them. No milk for Susan. She put the mugs carefully down on the table, avoiding the toast crusts piled up by Harriet. "Maybe you should surprise him."

"Surprise him, how? Open the door in nothing but a basque? With my luck it would be the woman delivering the parish newsletter. Whatever, I'd feel ridiculous. What about you, anyway, you and your bright advice? What do you and Simon get up to, to keep the spice, as they say, in your marriage?"

"Not a lot. The last time we tried to be inventive we drank a bottle of wine first. I remember nothing after that but the next morning I woke up wearing a bobble hat and hold-up stockings."

Rachel choked on her coffee. "And did it last? Did it herald a new dawn of passion?"

"Hardly. Simon laughed so much finding me lying next to him looking like a stripper with a passion for rambling he put his back out and we didn't do it for weeks."

"Perhaps I need to invest in underwear. Men do seem to be obsessed with knickers, don't they? Why is it? It's not as if we're passionately interested in the contents of their underwear drawer. Why should they be allowed to dress for comfort in large boxer shorts when we're supposed to feel comfortable trussing ourselves up in thongs? It isn't fair. I ought to suggest that if Nick expects me to waft about like Mata Hari in lacy dental floss then he ought to invest in leather briefs."

"But would you find it erotic?" Carole raised an eyebrow, and took a sip of her coffee.

"No. I would enjoy seeing him look ridiculous, though."

"I don't think we're getting to the nub of the issue," Carole said, sternly. "Do you feel that your marriage is being adversely affected by the general lack of intimacy?"

"Yes," Rachel said, conclusively. "It is. But the longer it goes on the harder it gets. We're like ships moored in different harbours. There's a big divide between us and neither of seems to want to bridge that."

"And sex would be the bridge?"

"Sex is the bridge."

"Do you love him?"

Rachel tipped her chair back on to two legs, and regarded the ceiling. "I don't honestly know," she said. "He's the father of my children, and he makes me laugh sometimes and I can remember when I did feel excited to see him but now, well, now, he's just there. Like the washing machine. I don't think I could do without him, but I don't know if I need him."

"How does he feel?"

"Oh, who knows. When was the last time Simon opened up to you about his feelings? They don't talk, do they, men, about how they feel."

"But how would you feel if you didn't have him?" Carole persisted.

"That's a good question," Rachel said, slowly. "I would feel there was a – a gap."

"A gap's a start," Carole said. "Gap is good. You would miss him."

"I'd miss the washing machine too," Rachel pointed out.

"I know. I think you have to try. Reach out to him. Hug him, little things, if you can't face suddenly whipping off your clothes to reveal exotic lingerie."

Rachel made a face. "That's going too far. I might cook him a nice meal, buy a bottle of wine and try and hold his hand across the dinner table. Tonight. I shall try tonight."

"Good for you. He is a lovely man, and you don't want him to go off and be someone else's gap, do you?" Carole drained her coffee. "You're very quiet, Susan. Is this all a bit much for a Monday morning?"

Susan looked at them both, her closest friends, and her eyes were full of tears.

"It's been seven years," she said, quietly. "We didn't talk, I didn't talk, to anyone. We both left it too long, and now there is no bridge."

There was a long pause, and Carole and Rachel looked at each other in horror.

"We had no idea," said Carole, falteringly. "You didn't say…."

"Well, it's not exactly the sort of thing you boast about is it? The fact that my husband gave up showing me affection years ago."

"Did you?" Rachel hesitated. "Is it you? Or him?"

"A bit of both. After Clemmie was born I kind of went off it, like you do, when you're breast feeding and you feel that your body is being invaded quite enough anyway, thank you, and then there's the total exhaustion which comes with being woken by a child fifty-six times a night. Things just drifted and I didn't lose all the weight very quickly and I felt pretty unattractive. You get out of the habit of touching, too, don't you? When we first married we touched all the time, not just sexually, but holding hands and hugging and kissing hello and goodbye, but then that disappeared and I stopped missing it, really. I –" she paused, and the tears ran down her face. "There isn't really anything left, now. I don't think he actually sees me anymore."

"But you're gorgeous!" Carole was outraged.

"Not gorgeous enough, obviously. He must be having an affair, I think, but I can't face asking him about it. And everyone thinks we have the perfect life, while I lie in bed reading chick lit and he lies in bed reading thrillers and there is a yawning, cold divide between us."

"Do you want to be on your own?" Rachel asked. "I know I don't, which at least is something."

"No, I don't. The thing is – I do still love him. I look at him and I see the man I married, and I find him attractive but I can't pluck up the courage to reach out to him."

Carole raised her eyes to heaven. "So much for having it all," she said. "What we should do is tie ribbons in our hair and whip out the lacy knickers. What price liberation now? We're all sex starved."

"It's men's fault too," Rachel pointed out.

"Yes," said Carole, patiently. "But the point is that we're brighter than them, aren't we? We drive relationships. Men just trundle along, like little railway carriages, and they don't notice anything unless they actually hit it."

"Is subtlety the key?"

"Oh, sod subtlety. We've got to let them all know that we think they're the best thing since sliced bread and virtually throw ourselves at their feet."

"I think I better wait until the children are in bed," Susan said, with the beginnings of a smile.

Carole grinned triumphantly round the table and looked at her watch. "Right, girls. We've got a week to sort this out. We shall reconvene at exactly this time next week and I want detailed reports from both of you. This is a campaign, a kind of reverse women's liberation. We re-invent ourselves as sexy women. Never mind the wobbly bits, men hardly notice them anyway, especially when they're encased in black nylon."

"It goes against everything I've stood for," Susan said.

"Good," said Carole briskly. "I'm a bit bored of trying to be superwoman. Let's try pussy cat for a while and see where it gets us."

The next Monday. The same coffee, the same table, the same debris. Only this time there were three women with shining eyes, shining hair and a languorous look about them.

"To the spice of life," Carole said.

"I'll drink to that," the others joyously replied.

"Anyone want to borrow my bobble hat?"

Mapping Out The Future
Christine Emberson

Ella Fitzgerald's 'Everytime We Say Goodbye' is playing and I can't help but think it's ironic. As you hold me and brush away my tears I'm crying more than just a little, sorry Ella. In fact I'm sobbing. Big huge chest-shaking sobs and I sense you becoming more and more uncomfortable. My tissue is saturated and proving useless. It is November and we're staying in a beautiful woodland cottage and you've just put out the fire in more ways than one.

"Come on now, come on," you cajole "It's not that bad, I'll see you again in a couple of weeks." You proffer up some kitchen roll, not quite the white handkerchief.

"I know, it's just I hate this bit. All the planning that goes into these weekends, and then it's all building up to saying goodbye again."

"We have to say goodbye so we can say hello again next time." You immediately realise this is a silly and garbled thing to say. I smile through the tears.

"That's better, that's my girl," you announce, making me feel fifteen years younger than I actually am.

"OK," I announce. "I'll get on with work and stuff and yes, before I know it we'll be together again." You're nodding now; I'm saying what you want to hear. You're a lot happier hearing the familiar words and you won't leave until I'm settled. It is all part of the routine, our routine.

"Good, I'll pop a map in the post then?"

"Yes," I nod, smiling.

It's your idea of excitement, a different place to meet every time. So efficient, the accommodation booked, the perfect table reserved at an elegant, expensive restaurant. And, just so I'm never late (you abhor tardiness), a map with directions. I don't object, who would? You are everything I want, an astute businessman, the perfect gentleman; you're beautiful, stylish but regrettably married. Very much married but there has been no pretence, no lies, the facts laid before me, right from the beginning. I could never accuse you of leading me on; you are a gentleman, albeit an adulterous one.

You are gathering your things together and making a feeble attempt to straighten the bed. The sheets are far too crinkled to smooth out; each crease has become a memory of our time together. How you carry and lower me to the bed, undress me gently, paying equal attention to every part of my body, kissing and caressing expertly. How you whisper and kiss my hair, and how I smile, urging you on. How I watch your face and gauge your breathing and then, after, when we sleep, how our bodies curl into each other and our legs intertwine. I'm looking at the pillows now, they remain sunken slightly where both our heads have laid, our noses tip to tip, your steady breathing just tickling my face. It is hard to walk away from this cocoon, a safe haven from our different worlds, but we do, every time we have to.

It is three weeks later and for the third morning running I fling open my front door and pounce on the postman. He shakes his head nervously. I'm confused, perplexed and bewildered to have received nothing from you. This has never happened before. I've gone through all emotions. Anger: because I made a scene last time you cannot cope any more. Worry: I've phoned your office pretending to be someone else in case you've fallen under a bus. "No, Mr Jones is absolutely fine, very busy in a marketing meeting at the moment." Now I don't know what to do. I've phoned in sick at work and immediately regretted that too. I've got too much time to think and worry now. Perhaps I'll drive past your house (again) on the off chance you'll be getting into your car. Acting casually, as if I'm always driving this way at this time of day. No, I can't, this isn't going to work. I have to be positive, make a decision. Right, retail therapy, I decide. I just pray I don't bump into anyone I know from work.

I'm in a fitting room with an array of outfits all on particularly nice ribboned, padded, coat hangers. This is what the doctor ordered. Part of me momentarily wonders what the point is of buying more new clothes, since I don't know if I'm going anywhere yet. But then I decide a new outfit will always be sensible. I need to look nice for you. I need to dress appropriately for all the beautiful hotels and restaurants. In fact, I think, admiring myself in the mirror from every angle, this trouser suit is perfect. I'm feeling better and thinking far more positively – it is amazing what a new outfit can do. I'm going to go home, take a bath and have an early night. I needn't worry, the post is dreadful these days, always a delay. It may just bring something tomorrow.

Arriving home I realise moodily there are no parking spaces; my road is a driver's nightmare. Victorian terraced houses line each side. Tarmac has been placed over the original cobblestones. It's no wonder we all jostle for spaces: the road was originally constructed for horses and carts, not Hondas and Audis. I have to park in another side road and I'm walking head down, craving my warm bath and a glass of chilled wine. I'm virtually at my door when I realise a figure is sitting on my front step. I focus and, startlingly, realise it is you. You're here, smiling cheekily but somehow looking distinctly odd, like finding a polar bear in the Sahara desert.

"Why… why are you here?" I stammer.

Immediately you take charge of the situation, jumping up, waving an envelope animatedly at me.

"Decided to hand-deliver the map." You offer it to me and I take it gingerly.

"Open it!" you say, a little too loudly. Suddenly, getting caught up in your enthusiasm, I rip open the envelope. Split-second images of far-flung places pop into my head. Perhaps the Caribbean? I know it has to be special. And there it is before me, but for a moment I can't fathom it out. It is a plain old Ordnance Survey map of my town. My eyes zoom in, my road is circled in red ink with the word 'home' written boldly across it. Confused, I stare at you.

"That's it, my love, I've done it, I've come home to you." You are grinning broadly and then step forward to sweep me up into your arms, gripping me firmly. You are not going to let go.

"Great." I am completely stunned by this revelation.

"Isn't it wonderful," you go on, cuddling me tight. "No more having to go off to hotels, woodland cottages, all those blasted expensive restaurants, having to get all dressed up, at last we can be here, together – forever!"

"Yes, unbelievable," I answer, allowing my designer shopping bag to drop to the ground. It lands with an almighty thud.

The Dog's Blanket

Ruth Joseph

What constitutes infidelity? Two hands touching like the brush of a lace-wing, as they reach for a phone? A walk in the park together, oblivious to the world? Or a look, an exchange of glances that goes beyond starriness to a deeper constellation? And why suddenly turn from a life that seemed good (well, averagely good) and follow temptation? What is the trigger that banishes loyalty and suddenly exclaims, "Why not!"?

I thought I'd been enjoying my life at home with a husband and two children. Time had moved on and the children could look after themselves if they were off school, so it was time to return to the job market. I wanted a job with variety. I could type but wanted to escape that life, so I'd started working for a small paper and sold advertising space.

I've tried to think why it happened. Matthew and I were happy with each other – we never rowed. Well, not major rows. There was the odd niggle if he forgot the wine for a dinner party, or arrived home two hours late because he had to keep some of his pupils in and didn't think of ringing and I'd made something special and was playing the oven game moving things up and down – a barn dance with the shelves. But there was nothing major. Sex was still good, though less frequent. He was a considerate lover and I never felt rejected. But maybe after fifteen years of pushing the same buttons and pulling adequate stops, there wasn't that spontaneous got-to-do-it-now feeling. Sex had to fit in with timetables, when the kids weren't in the house. A routine, maybe, like going to Sainsburys early on Monday to miss the rush, or filling up with petrol before the weekend.

One evening, I spoke to him about it. Tentatively, because we never did talk, not in detail, like we talked over the new shed or the summer holidays. I suggested we took the old blanket and a picnic, took a trip up the Abergavenny Canal as we had in the old days when we'd moor the day-boat after a while and walk hand in hand in the forest. I kissed his ear. "It's years, love, since you laid me down on the blanket in the midst of pearl-white anemones, banks of moist moss with the fragrance of blue bells scenting our movements… you and me…"

Matthew turned to me in horror, as if those people hadn't been us but others he'd tsk tsked about in his newspaper. Matthew was very conscious of his position as the deputy head, wanting and hoping to be head in five years. His spontaneity and passion had been washed away in a flood of school reports and marking.

"It's too risky," he scorned.

"But we're married. So what if there was a headline in the *Western Mail* or the *Penarth Times*, that Matthew Thomas and his wife were caught in flagrante, in the woods near Abergavenny?"

But he gave me a look as if I was a sixth-former caught smoking in the toilets.

Another time, just before Christmas, after a day's shopping, I felt a closeness helped by a couple of glasses of red. I whispered to him that I might dress up as a tart and sit in a hotel bar, and that he could pick me up and take me back to his room. But there was that face again. So I gathered up my fantasies, popped them in the loft of my mind – well, tried to – and made do with long walks in the park.

So we muddled on. He became more involved with his see-saw work life: the government inspections that terrorised our lives before they happened, and the elation when all had gone well. It was simply the way we lived. But the school was in a good catchment area and the children's parents were motivated. I think, overall, he was content.

But then it happened. It was waiting in the wings of my life. I suppose I had been feeling like an understudy with that starring role just out of reach. The office decided that they would do a regular feature on antiques that would appeal to their AB readership and wanted me to try to rustle up the advertising. I'd scanned Yellow Pages and planned my campaign but many of the antique shops were closed and those dealers I'd managed to see were either suspicious, thinking I was from the police or trading standards, or just gruff and uninterested. So when, on my last visit of the day, I pushed through the stacked frames and dusty chairs and tables, waiting to be attended to "out the back", I was surprised when a tall middle-aged guy, late forties with a crinkled face, smiled at me and asked how he could help.

"I'm from the *Penarth Mirror*," I said, offering my card and unnerved by his bright, blue-eyed stare. He understood that it was advertising and, yes, he might be interested, and give him a few minutes to get the waxes off his hands, and we'd go for a coffee to discuss details. His name was Jed. I looked in his eyes and something was triggered in a lonely space. Those emotions that I'd so tidily wrapped up were forcing their way out. I tried to convince myself that I was just excited, that after a grey wet day when the predominant answer had been no, someone was interested in doing some business. And if he was pleasant-looking, it made my job easier. But my frustration had been simmering for years. I stood at the back of the shop listening to running water and ignoring my conscience. Jed, even in worn beige chinos and an old blue sweater, looked so good. We walked to a small coffee shop and sat in the corner. I tried to concentrate on my business patter, while admiring the turquoise and lilac décor and the bleached wood floor and the single orange gerberas arranged in sandblasted glass vases.

"It's very pleasant in here," I murmured. Pathetic platitudes.

"Yes," he said, crinkling his eyes, his mouth dancing with humour. I laid out my papers to show him the rates for full, half page etc.

"Yes," he said, his eyes fixed on my face and totally ignoring my spiel. "Whatever it costs, I'll do it. But you must sort out the layout. I don't want any pimply adolescent coming round to finish the thing. And if I give you a series of half pages, then you must come with the copy each time."

I nodded, heart pounding, thinking that there would be at least five more occasions when I would see him. I had to steady myself before I could climb into my car with a modicum of decorum. Damn it! I was kidding myself that this was work. My thoughts were no better than all those men 'playing away' that I'd ridiculed in the past. It was dark by the time I got home. But, really there was nothing to blame myself for; a little flirtation with my eyes, maybe.

Matthew was angry. He said he was worried and that I always rang when I would be late. He wanted to get on with a report but the children – aged fourteen and thirteen – had cornered him. They had heard about this giant Schnauser puppy for sale. We had promised them a dog on Alex's fourteenth birthday and that was in three weeks time. I'd been thinking more of a Westie or even a rescue greyhound. But the two boys, and even Matthew, ruled me out.

"They're women's dogs," they chorused.

"It still has to be manageable," I argued. But my voice was lost. Here was the perfect dog, they claimed, and the winter holidays would be a good time for them to get to know each other.

"And Mum. You promised. You said that if we got up every day before school and walked it, then popped in lunchtime –"

I saw a very large animated noose in front of me. This animal would ultimately be my responsibility. I was angry. I looked at Mathew's expression and was dismayed to see a light of triumph. Perhaps he'd even like it if I had to give up work.

The next day, after a trek to Petsmart for collar, lead, worming tablets, toy and basket, the puppy arrived. It already seemed the size of a large dog – a tangle of pepper and salt fur and bright blue eyes that glinted with devilment.

"It needs something nice and soft to put into the basket," shouted Mickie wildly.

Matthew had caught the children's enthusiasm. "There must be an old rug or something in the airing cupboard for him – something snugly." He rushed upstairs to root in the depths of the airing cupboard. After dragging out an old electric blanket that was too good to throw away, and a pile of grey towels bought by mistake in the sales, he found our rug. Yes, our rug, safely put away for sentiment, for me to get out now and then and remember sweet times. It was wrapped in a bag with a few of the children's first babygros.

Don't be pathetic, I told myself. It's a rug. It's a tatty tartan thing – well past its usable life. But I still felt betrayed. He was able to discard our rug – and give our past – to a puppy who happily spent the next hour shredding the damn thing. So in the end, we had to use the grey towels in his bed. The whole incident was ridiculous and maybe it was just hormones but I was devastated. And now I could feel Jed's eyes, and feel the wanting like it used to be.

I'd arranged to meet Jed as soon as the layout was sorted. "He's a special client," I muttered in the office. "Went for a series of six half pages straight away." I tried to look casual, pretending it was business, but when I picked up the phone to make the appointment to see Jed, my heart was thudding in my chest.

"Great," Jed said warmly. "Let's do it over dinner."

Why not? With any other client it would mean nothing. I agreed to go to the shop and we would go on from there at seven.

Matthew was working late and the children had swimming club and chips after with a friend. It was all too easy. I took time dressing, putting on my new black trouser-suit and a bright top underneath. Why did I bother to put on my best underwear? How sure was I?

Jed had bothered. The battered chinos were replaced by a smart pair of dark cords and a bright shirt. The thick mass of hair looked as if it had been washed and he smelt of expensive aftershave. He was waiting at the door of the shop when I arrived and produced a bunch of gerberas.

"You liked these in the coffee shop."

"But it's not a date," I whispered.

He guided me carefully to a small bistro at the end of the road. A thin wire hummed between us. I was afraid to talk. He had reserved a table and we sat opposite each other. My briefcase containing his artwork seemed a redundant prop in the play we were acting out. We both knew that it would happen. We ate very little – a few mouthfuls of pasta and some red wine. Then in a husky voice he said, "Come home, will you… please?"

And in that second and the perfectly delicious moments that followed, I felt no guilt. None. I buried it snugly, with the shreds of a tatty tartan rug.

Mad For Seafood Risotto

Mo McAuley

Ham lay back on his pillows and thought about the woman he'd wined and dined the night before. Angelica. Dear, big-hearted Angel. But not big-hearted enough to come home and spend the night with him in spite of the designer meal he'd shelled out for. He sighed at the waste of money and unnecessary change of sheets and snuggled down under the duvet.

He was immediately overwhelmed with guilt. He should be getting on with his novel, not wasting time like this. He sat up and leaned over to pick up his laptop. He'd just switched it on when the phone rang beside him. With relief, he picked it up.

"Ham?"

"Angel?"

"You know damn well it's me."

"Are you all right?"

"Of course I'm all right. I'm ringing to check on you."

"But I only saw you last night. What's with the solicitousness?"

"Jesus. Solicitude. How can you write a book without any command of the English language? No wonder you're in a mess."

"Well, actually I didn't think I was in a mess until I saw you."

There was a snort down the phone. Ham decided not to challenge it.

"I've been thinking about our conversation and I've decided you need me. I want to get involved with this book of yours, to keep you on course and watch over your progress."

"A sort of guardian angel."

"Sort of."

There was a silence. Ham felt ashamed. "I've booked a hair cut," he said lamely.

"Good, you looked like a sheep, or should I say a ram. When shall I come over? Are you in today?"

It was an unusual suggestion for Angel. She normally preferred neutral territory for her dealings.

"Fine, I'm here. Come about eleven thirty. I'll make brunch." Ham put down the phone.

Ham. She'd always called him Ham. Most people on the newspaper had called him Ham although his full name was Hamamelis. He always called her Angel unless he wanted to rile her. Then he called her Ange to remind her of the Essex roots she'd so carefully buried from public view.

Was it the names that had drawn them together all those years ago? Two columnist hacks named after plants. It was pretty unusual. It was only later he'd discovered that Angelica, the gossip columnist, was really plain old Angela and had no plant connections at all. Whereas he, Hamamelis Mollis, son of a loopy garden designer and equally unhinged sculptor, was a witch hazel through and through.

"And what are your children called?" she'd asked after finally wheedling out of him that he was indeed married and therefore, officially, unavailable.

"David and Susan."

They had been work friends and occasional bed friends ever since.

Ham looked at his watch. It was eight o'clock. There was time for an hour on the novel before nipping to the supermarket. He opened his manuscript file and scrolled to the last chapter.

Solomon remembered his scratched and callused hands holding the plump whiteness of her. He felt ashamed and then ashamed at his shame. She was his mistress and he was her slave to use as she desired, yet still he felt the pride of his ancestors coursing through his veins.

He read the last line with horror and imagined Angel doing the same. Had he really written that? Obviously, yes. There was no-one else to blame, no sub-editor or editor re-writing and refining. The familiar justifying argument began in his head. Wasn't this what readers wanted, what publishers wanted? But what sort of readers, what sort of publishers? Epoch Erotica readers and publishers for a start. They were gagging for it, according to the editor's response to his synopsis and first three chapters.

"It's set in Virginia," he'd explained to Angel when pressed on the subject over dinner. "It's about exploitation, slavery in the early nineteenth century."

"Sounds impressive. Back to some serious principles then."

Ham re-read the sentence on the screen and floundered on in his lonely vindication. At least he was still a member of Amnesty International and he did occasionally read the *Guardian.* On the other hand, why shouldn't a big subject be made accessible to all? It was a noble cause.

Exonerated at last by his own mental rhetoric, Ham set about moving Solomon's muscular, ebony physique nearer to the enchanting, slight figure in the pale green dress.

It was nine thirty before he made it into the shower. The water fizzed around the holes in the silted up showerhead before jetting out at peculiar angles. Only the odd needle of hot water actually reached his head. He ducked about trying to catch the maverick spray so he could wash his hair. He would have a quick shop, prepare brunch, then make a start on a new chapter before Angel arrived.

"So when will this magnum opus be finished?" Angel had nagged over dessert last night. "You've been at it for ages."

"I'm stuck," he'd replied and received another lecture for his flippancy.

At one point in the evening he'd wondered if chastisement was the only reason she'd phoned him up to suggest dinner. It had always been an integral part of their relationship but it was usually light-hearted, delivered with a helpless shake of the head and a wry smile. He often felt he was a child substitute for Angel, a naughty, wilful child that needed constant admonishment. No, it was more likely to be ghoulish curiosity that had brought on this new flurry of interest in him, to see how he was getting on in his new life of isolated, 'serious' writing. Perhaps she was secretly working on a novel herself. She'd taken quite a lot of time off recently he'd heard. Not that anything had been mentioned over dinner.

The funny thing was, her haranguing had suddenly turned into tears. One minute they were sitting at the table embroiled in their usual verbal sparring, the next she was weeping into her hands. It had thrown him completely. He was the one who'd been kicked off the paper – surely he should be in tears rather than she. Perhaps it was because the seafood risotto was off the menu. Angel was mad for seafood risotto and she'd been looking forward to it all day, apparently. But that was a ridiculous notion, even more so in retrospect.

Even with her mascara running she'd looked attractive. Angel always aroused him and she knew it. He'd had the same effect on her when he was younger, a good fifteen years younger. But then he'd been saddled with stroppy teenage children and a flat-chested wife he felt obliged to love and cherish until death – or a dandy publisher, as it turned out – whisked her away. Now, when he was free and on the scrap heap, Angel wasn't interested, of course. Young men. That's what successful, middle-aged women wanted. He'd read it time and again in her own column.

The doorbell rang. Eleven thirty. Dead on. Angel liked to be punctual. Ham stopped at the hall mirror and checked his appearance before opening the door. Angel stood on the step looking awkward and Ham suddenly felt pleased at the novelty of the situation. He waited for her to comment on how smart and attractive he looked but she just held out a bottle of champagne.

"An apology, for my rudeness last night."

"Good grief. Come in before I faint."

He had laid out a continental feast for them – croissants, petit pain, fruit, ham and cheese. Angel smiled at the display and wondered aloud who else might be coming, a French football team perhaps? She had lost weight he noticed, quite a lot of weight. It hadn't shown in the murky lighting of the restaurant. It suited her in some places, but not in others. Her face looked gaunt. She was wearing a purple-three-quarter-length dress with long black boots. Sexy-boots she always called them. Large hoop earrings dangled from her ears and she wore a brightly coloured scarf arrangement about her neck and shoulders.

"Shall I take your scarf?" Ham asked.

She shook her head and wrapped the scarf tighter around her although the room was too warm as far as he was concerned. Her huddled, quiet demeanour unnerved him.

"Sit down," he said. "I'll make some coffee."

"Do you have any herb teas?"

"Herb teas? Me?"

"Don't worry then. Coffee's fine."

She moved over to sit on the sofa.

"Help yourself to food," he called over his shoulder from the corner of the kitchen area.

"I don't mean to be ungrateful," she said, "but what I really fancy is some eggy bread. Do you remember when I made it for you that morning for breakfast? You said you'd never had it as a child. I felt so sorry for you. All that privileged background and education but no eggy bread."

Ham forced the plunger down in the cafetiere. Why was she bringing up that night together at her place, the one and only time she'd allowed him into her own bed and into her carefully guarded private life? She'd refused to talk about it ever since, giving him short shrift when he introduced the subject on a couple of occasions.

He began to whisk some eggs. Angel took a pan down from its hook. She poked around the kitchen looking for what she wanted – a knob of butter, a slosh of olive oil. They gossiped about the paper as they cooked, she dipping the bread, he flipping and checking until it was nicely browned. At last they sat opposite each other at the table, eating. Ham looked across at her. Her face was flushed and there was a sheen of sweat on her forehead.

"Take off that scarf thing," he said and heard the irritation in his voice. "You're obviously hot."

She stopped, fork raised, mouth slightly open. Her round, owlish eyes stared across at him. Oh God, she was going to stab him or throw the eggy bread in his face. Instead, tears filmed her eyes. She put down her fork and raised her hands to fumble with the clasp that held her scarf in place. Slowly she unwound it to reveal her lower neck and upper chest. It was bright red and the texture of her skin seemed different too, sort of gathered and almost translucent in its thinness, as if it might split at any moment.

"Jesus. What happened?" he said.

"Radiotherapy."

"But why?"

"Why on earth do you think." Her voice faltered.

"Angel, I'd no idea."

"Of course you didn't. I never told you."

"But where is it, was it?"

She touched her breast in reply.

"Shit."

Ham continued to gaze at the raw neck, its redness deepening to brown into her cleavage. Her breasts looked normal, slightly smaller than usual but still Angel's beautiful breasts. Angel, breast cancer. The words just didn't fit together.

"They're still there, you idiot."

"And is it all right now? Are you clear?"

She shrugged. "So they say. But time's suddenly become pretty precious I can tell you. And eggy bread."

She wrapped the scarf carefully around her again and carried on eating. Ham continued to gaze across at her, his own meal cooling on the plate in front of him.

"I'm changing my ways," she said. "I'm becoming a health fiend. I'm learning to relax, to prioritise, meditate and appreciate – all the stuff they dole out these days because they've no idea if the medical treatment will work.

And I haven't had a fag for over two weeks. I can't believe you haven't noticed."

"That's wonderful."

"Don't patronise me."

"I'm not. I'm trying to say the right thing but I'm not sure what it is. I want to help though, if you need any help."

She smiled across at him.

"I sort you out, remember. Now open that champagne before I become maudlin and flood the place out."

Ham set out the champagne flutes and popped the cork. Champagne's such a happy drink, he remembered her saying at a press awards night where she'd scooped the Columnist of the Year. He'd had an awful job getting her home afterwards.

They drained their first glass quickly. Ham filled them up again and they sat in silence, sipping at a more moderate pace.

"Are you ever lonely, Ham?"

"Me? No. I'm better on my own. You know me."

"Do I? I'm not sure anyone really knows anyone in our business."

He looked at her with surprise. "But we're straight with each other. We know us. Don't we?"

She didn't reply. Her face suddenly turned pale. "Oh God, I feel all dizzy. I think I'd better lie down."

She stood up and leaned against the table as she wearily ran her fingers through her hair. "At least I'm still hanging on to this mop so I suppose I should be grateful. They have this new method, a cold cap thing you wear during treatment that's meant to stop it falling out. Bloody excruciating, though." She set off towards the hall and the stairs. "First left isn't it, after the two steps?"

Ham nodded, unsure whether to offer help or not. He listened to her footsteps ascending the stairs then decided to wait a while. He finished off the bottle of champagne as he tidied the kitchen. Angel. Breast cancer. It didn't make sense no matter how often he repeated it. Angel was beyond such things, probably immortal. Any alternative had never crossed his mind. It felt as if he'd rubbed the surface of a precious object and found something suspicious, maybe totally fake, underneath.

He went up to check on her. She was in his double bed but not asleep.

"Have you changed the sheets recently? You men develop such grubby habits on your own. Like little boys."

"Thanks. I have actually, not that I expected you to end up between them."

"I didn't expect to either but I'm just so cold and shivery."

Ham scurried to check the wall timer and feel and fiddle with the radiator, eventually deciding there must be an air blockage that he had no idea how to fix. He found a spare blanket and brought up a hot water bottle.

"You make a wonderful nurse," she said. "Come and lie down with me. I promise I won't tell matron."

Ham lay on top of the bed next to her like an effigy on a sarcophagus. After a while he glanced in her direction. She had one arm across her brow and eyes. Her other arm lay across her chest, as if protecting it.

"Ham?"

"Yes."

"Do you think I'm a failure?"

"You? You're a total star. I mean look at you, you're successful, you're popular..."

"Popular for what, successful for what? For being a tough-assed, witty bitch who terrorises and amuses people in equal measure. It's just a performance. That would be okay but it's all I've got, this performance. What if I can't keep it up?"

"Angel, please, this is too much all at once."

"Why?"

"I don't know. Because we don't normally do serious I suppose. Why didn't you tell me you were ill?"

"I don't know. I just couldn't."

They lay together quietly for a while, she with her eyes closed, he staring at the patch of damp in the corner of the ceiling. At last, Ham pulled the edge of the blanket over himself to keep out the cold. Angel stirred and patted the bed next to her.

"You're cold," she murmured sleepily. "Come inside."

Ham slipped in beside her.

"Angel?"

"Mmm."

"You know this business about the book..."

"Don't worry about it. I'm fine to help. I want to help."

"No, it's not that. There's something I need to tell you. It's important you don't have any great expectations about it. It's not exactly, you know, James Baldwin or Harper Lee or anything. I do have a publisher though and I know it will bring in decent money so you mustn't ever worry about that sort of thing, not that anything's going to happen to you or you're going to need me at all. But just in case you did, I want you to know I'm always here. I suppose I'm just not the thwarted high flier I always thought I was, or you seemed to think I was."

"Why would I think that?"

"Eh?"

"Never mind, Ham."

Under the bedclothes her hand fumbled to find his and give it a squeeze. They lay side by side with their fingers locked, listening to the sounds of the neighbourhood ebbing and flowing through the window – the wedding bells in the local church, the drone of Saturday traffic heading into town, the clamour of children playing in the park.

As the morning shifted into afternoon, a sullen October rain set in, dripping steadily on the sill and splashing off the laurel bush pressed up against the window. The room became warm and still and Ham drifted in and out of sleep, listening to Angel's deep rhythmic breathing and taking comfort from its strength.

It was dark when he finally awoke, proper evening dark. Their hands had unclasped and Angel had rolled on her side away from him. Ham slipped quietly out of bed, tucking the duvet in around her. Downstairs he put the kettle on to boil then opened the fridge and took out a medley of seafood he'd bought at the supermarket that morning. He flicked through his new Italian cookery book until he found the recipe he wanted.

Heart Cry

Caroline Praed

Karen is waiting, awkwardly, in the hallway when I emerge with skin paler than a bridal gown and my social smile pinned as tightly to my face as a wedding corsage to a lapel. Her answering smile is rather more shaky, but she manages what she can. And, after all, I've had by far the more practice.

I usher her past the extravagant display of long-stemmed red roses. Harry never forgets Valentine's Day. And then I make some excuse about the exhausting tour and picking up a stomach bug, and she grabs at the explanation. Karen was always prepared to follow my lead, as befits the younger.

That's the unfairness of it. I'm the elder, the planned child, the special first-born. Karen is my little sister: dignified, unassuming and unjudgemental. Not plain, exactly, but somehow featureless so that people can never describe her except in 'she's sort of average' terms. They chat to her, then they gravitate to me.

I'm tall and slim and always elegantly clad and shod. Karen, in her baggy jumper and leggings, looks more like a teenager than a twenty-eight-year-old. As I usher her to the door, she apologises.

"I should never have come rushing over, not when you're so tired, only just back. All that travelling. I didn't think, just wanted to tell you our news, I'm so very sorry, Chrissy."

Graciously I assure her that the news couldn't have waited and that I'm delighted she came over to tell me. "I'll be fine after a little nap." With a quick glance in the mirror to check my appearance, I walk with her to her elderly car, painfully conscious of my own new, gleaming, silver sports car.

Those who don't know me well would comment that I am over-fastidious about appearances, but it's part of the job. Paparazzi would joyfully sell pictures of me looking anything but perfect, if I gave them the opportunity. I hope Karen understands that.

She's never challenged my right to be the first, the best. Never – until now.

People make assumptions, interpretations, based on bias, usually. Oh, I know that you don't and I don't, but people generally do. They assume, for example, that I am content, even happy, with my life and lifestyle. They think that reaching the top of my profession must be fulfilment in itself.

Harry guesses the truth I always deny. Sixteen years ago he spent our first night exclaiming over my 'long, clever fingers' and kissing each in turn. His was the energy and commitment behind organising my first Royal Festival Hall recital, and our careers and lives have flourished and grown together ever since. It broke up his marriage, but I've forgiven myself for that many years past.

I didn't have to become a virtuoso violinist, you know. I won a place at medical school, but chose the more uncertain profession and thrived. Harry says I'd have reached the top of whatever career I'd chosen. I always act modestly whenever he says that, but I believe it to be true. Don't hate me for that self-assurance, it's all that I have.

You don't know how I ache, weep (in secret), for a child of my own. Mine and Harry's. I've almost accepted the stark improbability of it now, though a tiny irrational part of me goes on hoping. But now we're in our forties, and too old to be considered suitable first-time parents by any agency.

A foreign child, you say? A deprived child from the third world? Don't think I haven't been tempted, touring abroad, by innocent, trusting, dark eyes. But, even if I could bribe my way through the paperwork, it doesn't seem right – not for us.

And so you see, Karen announcing that she's pregnant ... just two months after the wedding; I can't help the jealousy. I'll never be complete the way she will be. And all the public adulation and champagne receptions and pampered travel, and even the more private and sincere adoration of Harry, none of it matters. Not compared with a priceless child.

Tell me I'm wrong. Tell me to concentrate on what I have and not on what might have been. Tell me about all the people worse off than myself, who dream of having even a tenth of what I have. Tell me as often as you like – it makes no difference.

Ask my parents who it was played with the dolls, dressing them and nursing them.

"Chrissy," they'll say, "it was Chrissy".

But perhaps Karen has forgotten. She's so much younger. I'm sure she came round today not to gloat, but to share her wonderful news. I'll be a godparent, I hope. I want to give this child every possible advantage.

Just think – Harry, an uncle! I'll tease him about that, tonight, when I've accepted it, when I'm able to joke about our coming niece or nephew.

For a moment a vision of Karen saying, “You have this baby, you've always wanted one,” fills me. I know this thought is destined to return and haunt me throughout her pregnancy. Right now, it heats me through in seconds until I explode with rage at my stupidity.

I vow never ever, consciously, to covet this child.

I've asked Karen all the right questions. When is it due? Do they want a girl or a boy? What would they like as a christening gift? Oh, I can afford to be generous. I might not have children of my own, but I know how to spoil them.

'Good old Chris never forgets a birthday', and is sure to think of an extravagant present. Each such date is acid-etched into my memory, every gift selected to a poorly-stifled refrain: *What if this was my child?*

I collapse onto the king-size bed in my designer bedroom and weep, head buried in the pillow, although there is nobody to hear my sobbing. Then:

“Anyone home on Valentine’s Day?” bellows Harry.

He's back! I rush downstairs, still leaking tears, desperate for my lover's embrace. I was going to prepare my words, set the scene oh-so-carefully, but I find myself blurting out the news to a now damply-jacketed shoulder.

“Harry ... we're going to be uncles!”

Seascape

Jane Bidder

For as long as anyone could remember, Miss Margaret Offord had lived at Seascape. Not number 19, as it should have been known, being squarely placed between number 18 and 20. But Seascape. A house number would have been far too ordinary for the likes of Miss Offord.

Since we lived at number 18, I frequently got the opportunity to observe Miss Offord through illicit means. I would spy on the unknowing spinster through chinks in the wooden fence that divided our semi from hers.

My mother used to tell me sharply that I allowed my imagination to run riot. But so, surely, did Miss Offord. Who else would live in a boring North London suburb which was as far flung from rocks and waves and crabs and buckets and spades, as you could possibly be – and still call your house Seascape?

"Did Miss Offord give the house that name or was it there when she moved in?" I asked my mother.

"Lord, child, how would I know what that eccentric woman did?" she said, bundling my sister into the canopied pram before putting her out in the garden with the washing. "Ask your grandfather. He's lived here all his life."

This was a sore point and one which, even at my tender age, I was well acquainted with. When my mother had married my father, she got Granddad too. My father put it differently. "I couldn't leave him on his own. Where's your heart, woman? Besides, we couldn't afford a place of our own – still can't."

The rows taught me that everyone had their own way of doing things. Take Miss Offord. For a start, as I peered through the fence, I could see that she dug sandcastles in the garden out of earth. Now I should confess here that I had never actually dug a sandcastle myself although it was one of my dearest wishes to go to the seaside. But I would experiment in my garden and feel the earth trickle through my fingers. Miss Offord did the same. Squatting on her haunches, her long skirt bunched up like a mermaid's fan, she shovelled earth into a brightly coloured pail, and then inverted it before topping off with a small paper flag.

"Did Miss Offord once live by the sea?" I asked my grandfather, one evening when we were curled up on his sofa, watching television.

"Why do you ask, Poppet?"

"Because Miss Offord digs earthcastles in her garden and puts paper flags on top."

"Does she, now? Wonder she can get through that clay. Must be stronger than she looks. My grandfather sucked at his pipe. "Maybe she misses the sea."

"Is that why she called the house Seascape?"

"Perhaps."

You had to pick your times with adults to hold a sensible conversation and this clearly wasn't one of them.

Fortunately, the opportunity arose the following week when I came home from school to find that the front door key wasn't under the stone by the front door. Nor was Granddad who was usually sneaking around my parents' front room when they were out. My mother always used to say that in case of emergency, I should go next door. By that, she meant number 17, not the other way. But Mrs Holmes wasn't in either.

There was only one option. Excitedly, I approached the stone wall that ran along the front of Seascape. It was made of tiny pebbles and at the top was a row of shells, firmly embedded in the concrete. How had she found so many shells? Or had she sent the builder to the seaside with a lorry? The front gate creaked as I opened it and I walked past a wonderful bush with long blue flowers, smothered with Red Admirals. (We never got butterflies in our garden.) Then a funny thing happened. As I knocked on the door, I caught a whiff of fresh salty air, the kind that I instinctively knew belonged to the seaside, even though I had never been there.

Maybe she wasn't in. Perhaps she and my parents and my grandfather and number 17 had all been called to some big adventure and I was the only person left in the road – maybe the world. But if that had happened, wouldn't there have been a clue? Then I saw it. A big pink shell, sitting by the plastic milk crate that said 'one pint please'. I put it to my ear and immediately the door opened.

"Yes?"

Miss Offord stood in front of me, wearing a black swimming costume.

I looked again and she was wearing a plain black skirt with a white ruffled blouse with a brooch at the neck. On the brooch was a little blue boat. I thought that might disappear too, but the more I stared, the more it twinkled on a little black line of a wave.

"Can I help you, child?" said Miss Offord softly.

So I explained about my parents and the missing key and the big adventure and her eyes sparkled. "Would you like a glass of lemonade," she said, leading me into her kitchen. "I make it myself, you know."

It was delicious, just like the warm Victoria sponge that she produced out of the oven as though she'd known she was expecting guests. And after I'd eaten enough to banish that gnawing, empty feeling you get in your stomach after school, we talked in her front room which had a telescope and a pretty little mother-of-pearl box that I would have loved to have opened. Afterwards, we went into the garden. "Do you like my pond?" asked my hostess.

It was amazing! She'd dug a hole and put some black polythene lining in and then some water and now there were water lilies on top. "Granddad was right. You must be very strong," I said.

"Explain," commanded Miss Offord. So I told her about looking through the fence and watching her build earthcastles and asking my Granddad if she'd named the house after the sea. Her eyes sparkled blue as the butterfly bush. "I did, indeed. I used to live by the sea. Every day, I would walk with my betrothed who loved me more than all the pebbles on the beach."

She put her hand on my arm and we both held our breath. "Never believe dull people who tell you that love doesn't last, Poppet. It lasts for ever."

"How did you know my name was Poppet," I whispered.

"I've heard your grandfather through the fence. Chinks work both ways."

I was about to enquire about the whereabouts of Miss Offord's betrothed when I heard my mother's voice. "Well, she's got to be around somewhere. I was only a bit late. Monica, where are you?"

"I prefer 'Poppet'," said Miss Offord. "Off you go before they get worried. Come to tea next week."

But I never did. The following Saturday, there were all kinds of activities at Seascape. Two cars pulled up outside, and one blocked our drive which made my father cross. Then next door's blue upstairs curtains were drawn. And then came a knock on the door. "That was Miss Offord's niece," said my mother, bustling into the kitchen where Granddad was helping me with geography homework. "Miss Offord died in the night. Probably a heart attack."

"She can't have," I said horrified. "I've only just met her."

"What do you mean?" asked Granddad quietly after Mum had bustled out again. So I told him how she'd taken me in and explained why she'd changed the house's name from 19 to Seascape to remind her of her betrothed. "I meant to ask why she didn't live near the sea if it meant so much to her," I sniffed.

"We often mean to ask people something but time runs out first," said Granddad solemnly.

I wasn't allowed to go to the funeral because it was too upsetting for someone my age. But I was permitted to attend the funeral tea. "How long did Miss Offord live by the sea for?" I asked her niece, who was grey and fat.

"Live by the sea, love? Lawks, she never lived by the sea. A Wembley girl, born and bred she was. But grant you, she seemed to have a fascination for all things nautical. The agent says we're going to have to get rid of the shell wall if we're to sell the place – and repaint from top to bottom. Every room in the house is blue!"

So the wall came down and a fence rose up and the blue rooms became magnolia and the new people made Seascape into number 19. But I never forgot what the house, or its owner, had really been like and I wrote about them both in English, the only subject I shone at. I had recognised a kindred spirit in Miss Offord; we might only have met briefly but I suspected her imagination had run riot too.

Then, years later, when I was home from university, Granddad got ill. I sat by his side and read to him. Even Mum had red eyes. “Don’t know why that woman thinks I’m on my way out,” he muttered to me, one evening. “Can’t go yet. Got to see the sea first.”

“The sea? “

“Got to take Margaret Offord,” he said, looking me straight in the eye. “The girl next door. I loved her more than all the pebbles on the beach. We were going to live by the sea, just her and me. But then I got tricked into marrying your grandma. Still stayed next door, she did.”

“But Granddad, why didn’t you move if she upset you?”

He grinned. “Margaret didn’t upset me. We were there for each other. We made our own seaside right here instead. Our escape. That’s why she called the house Seascape. There couldn’t be any funny business when your gran was alive of course. But afterwards, well…” And his eyes twinkled.

Granddad died that night. It wasn’t until after the funeral that it seemed right to ask my father. “There were rumours,” he said quietly, “and I know my parents *had* to get married…”

My grandfather left me a small legacy, which allowed me to go travelling after my degree. I went to places that Miss Offord and I had talked about during our brief afternoon together and to countries Granddad had spoken of during geography homework. It was in Africa that I met Carlos. His English and my Spanish were both basic, but as we sat by the sea, I kept making earthcastles in my head.

“It’s just a summer romance,” I insisted, against my better judgement.

"Is it?" he asked, his eyes soft with hurt.

When I got back, my parents had decided to move. "We've been clearing up," said Mum, "and we've found a box that Granddad left you, with your name on it."

It was the same mother-of-pearl box that Miss Offord had had in her front room. Inside, were two faded yellow tickets for deck chairs and a tiny black and white photograph of a woman in a black swimming costume and my young Granddad smoking a pipe. At the bottom of the box was a brooch of a blue ship on a black wavy line. Sail away, whispered Miss Offord. Take love when you find it, whispered Granddad. So I phoned Carlos. And I said one word.

"Seascape?" he said, mystified. "What is that?"

"It means yes," I said. And at precisely that moment, I felt the sea singing in my head and Granddad holding me tight.

Betty, Christine, The Thug and James Bond

Suzanne Gillespie

"Oh sugar." I'd reversed and, BANG. Into another car. I could feel my heart disappear into my boots. My first accident in my first car. Disaster or what?

I opened the door, slow and careful. I peered at the other car first. It was black. I recognised it. It was the car of my dreams, the one on my wish list, the one I didn't get. A Ford Escort RS 2000.

"I'm really sorry," I said, looking ruefully at the dented bumper and glaring smashed headlight. "Betty didn't mean it." I patted my car. I finally dared to look up at the face of the young man hovering over me.

Oh wow, he was as dark and sexy as his car. My tongue stopped working, or maybe my brain was too busy drooling.

"Who's Betty?" he said. He sounded amused rather than cross, even though I'd caused the accident.

Betty was my car. A sky-blue Hillman Imp. I'd named her after her previous owner. One little old lady who had a Pekinese dog. I never did manage to get all the white dog hairs out of the black carpet. Betty and I had a love-hate relationship. I loved her for being my first car and giving me independence, but I hated what she was. I'd really wanted a flash car, like his. Betty, with her 875 cc engine, just didn't have street cred.

I'd reversed into Paul. He was fantastic. He fixed the damage himself and I only paid for the parts. He was nineteen to my seventeen and studying engineering at the local college. We spent an afternoon together, getting to know each other. Coffee, cars and James Bond were part of the conversation. I told him I fancied his car. I fancied him too, although I didn't say that out loud. He told me the car he really wanted was Bond's Aston Martin. Then he asked me out to dinner.

I said no. Thanks. Regretfully.

Why?

I was engaged to Mark. We'd been a couple ever since third year at primary school and we'd fallen in love over a game of kiss chase in the playground.

My second car was a navy-blue Chrysler Sunbeam. I carried on that love-hate thing with her. She was a hatchback, not trendy enough for a nineteen year old, and I guess I hurt her feelings when I told her. She got called a lot of names. Sunbeam wasn't one of them. In two years the car had seven punctures, ate fifteen cassette tapes, refused to acknowledge first gear existed every Tuesday, and blew the head gasket halfway to London. And they were just the major things. So the name that finally stuck was Christine. After an overdose of Stephen King.

When Mark and I got married Christine moved on, probably to terrorise her next unsuspecting victim. Sorry, driver. Along with marriage, kids, one of each, jobs, houses, and holidays we had a procession of standard, faceless, family vehicles. None of them were ever christened.

After twenty years of marriage, I found myself with Honey, my eighteen-year-old daughter. Sean, my seventeen-year-old son. A divorce and no hard feelings on anybody's part.

I'd also built up an impressive lingerie business and just survived my fortieth birthday.

The time had come for me to indulge my fantasies.

I gave myself a full make-over. I had my hair cut and styled. I bought a new wardrobe. I redecorated the house and bought the kids a Mini Cooper S to share. They say lots of good things come in small packages, at least that's what I told the kids about the Mini.

I suggested they name it Mickey, but was outvoted two to one. In the end they agreed on Charlie Croker, after watching *The Italian Job*.

My real love was my new car. My fantasies still included James Bond, so I bought myself a BMW Z8. The sport convertible in metallic silver with all the must-have extras: alloy wheels, Sat Nav, CD player, air conditioning and leather interior.

Driving the car, hearing the throaty sound issuing from under the bonnet, feeling the heavy beat of the engine throbbing right through me, and being in control of all that power, was like sex on wheels.

I named the car 'The Thug'.

I'd only ever had that one accident twenty-three years ago, so when the car queuing behind me bumped into the back of The Thug, my language was unrepeatable.

I jumped out and stalked round to the battle area. The thought that the world was *really not big enough* kept drumming through my mind.

"How could you hit The Thug?" I said despairingly whilst stroking the wing of my car.

"I'm really sorry," he said "I wasn't looking."

I did look. Wow, Pierce Brosnan look-alike. Gorgeous and sexy, just like The Thug. His eyes crinkled up as his mouth widened with a long-remembered smile. Paul!

"So this one's called The Thug." He laughed. "Appropriate." He slid his hand along the front wing of his own car. It was the same model, in a gun-metal grey. "Looks like we still have Bond in common."

For an instant, I was seventeen again. Until I realised that the only male in my life now was The Thug. And Paul was even more interesting than I remembered. A few strands of grey in his hair coordinated with his car and gave him that suave, distinguished look.

"Looks like this one's serious." I smiled. "I think it might take a long afternoon with lots of coffee and conversation to sort it all out, if you're available, of course."

The horns started honking around us. We were holding up the queue.

"Oh, I'm available." He grinned. "Are you free Friday?"

I grinned back. "What time?"

"I'll pick you up at seven."

"Seven's a bit late for coffee, isn't it?"

He laughed again. "Not if we have that dinner first. Followed by a nightcap. Shaken, not stirred, of course."

Thanks to the Thug, I managed to snare my very own James Bond.

The Association of Bit-Part Players
Sally Quilford

It was always a certainty that my beautiful friend and flatmate, Rosalynde, would get married first. She is twenty-six years old, blonde, perky, quirky and as nutty as the whole of Brazil. She is also kind, loving and generous.

It is fair to say that if we were in a film, she would be the beauty who won the heart of the handsome leading man, and I would be her plain, but loyal, best friend who dried her tears during the inevitable misunderstanding that tore them asunder until the last five minutes of the film. It is in life as it is in art. I have dried her tears through many heartbreaks, but she has also nursed me through a long period of ill-health that put my career, and subsequently hers, on hold for some time.

Rosalynde and I, if you had not already guessed from the previous analogy, are actors. We met in drama school at the age of fourteen, but whereas Rosalynde (not her real name) is now setting the London stage alight in *As You Like It*, I due to ill health, have only ever been a bit-part actor. I have bought mints in Rita's Kabin on *Corrie Street*, played a corpse in *Morse* (my face was made up to be so disfigured that even my own mother said she would have had a hard time identifying me), and I once booked into the Crossroads Motel, just before Jane Asher woke up and realised it was all a dream. I like to think that if she had dreamed on, I might have turned out to be her long-lost daughter.

A heart problem put paid to my dreams of stardom, leaving me bedridden for some time. Rosalynde was at my hospital bed throughout, nursing me, keeping up my spirits and crying the night she thought she had lost me forever. A heart transplant later I was on the road to recovery. When I was well enough to return home, she went back to work, and very quickly found stardom in the West End.

Rosalynde had only been rehearsing her role in *As You Like It* for a few days when she came home, her face aglow.

"No?" I said, with mock surprise, when Rosalynde told me she was in love.

"No, really. It's my Orlando. Oh, you know who I mean."

I did indeed. Tall, dark, ruggedly handsome with vivid blue eyes, he was, according to one celebrity magazine, the new Jude Law, and the new Jeremy Irons according to another. Either way, his ascendency to Hollywood and regular roles as the British baddie, could not be far off.

I did not want to suggest to Rosalynde that Orlando might not be around much longer – she had already lost two boyfriends to Hollywood (she was always attracted to the most talented actors), so I listened patiently while she extolled his many virtues.

"He bought us all a Danish pastry for breakfast."

I agreed that he must indeed be a god.

I was surprised to learn from another friend that the 'god' had actually only bought Danish pastries for Rosalynde, after she had mentioned a passion for them. It was she who had shared them amongst the other cast members.

However, when Orlando turned up at our door with flowers a day later, it became clear to me from the glazed expression in his eyes that he was as smitten as she. So our roles were set. Hero, heroine and the plain but loyal friend who facilitated their romance by disappearing to the pictures for hours on end, awaiting the moment when my skills in the supporting role would be needed.

The catalyst to their first argument was a revelation in a Sunday tabloid. Orlando, it transpired, had been married once, and had not thought to mention this to Rosalynde the day he asked her to marry him. She was devastated. She wanted to believe that she was the first woman he ever wanted to marry. I tried to tell her that as he was in his thirties, it was hardly likely that she would be his first anything, unless he had spent his formative years in a monastery only emerging to play his first starring role. But she was not moved, and said she would never forgive him for his deceit.

So followed the first meeting of the Association of Bit-Part Players. Orlando, it turned out, also had a plain but loyal friend, Oliver, another bit-part actor, who, when we first met, bragged (his grey eyes twinkling… now I come to think of it, he was not that plain…) that he had played the hand under the patio in *Brookside*. I doubted it very much, as Oliver's fingers were long and strong. The hand under that patio had been decidedly chubby.

"He didn't mean to deceive her," said Oliver, over coffee at the National Theatre. "He was very young, only eighteen when he got married. They were divorced less than a year later. Everyone is entitled to one mistake."

"You're preaching to the converted," I told him. "I understand, but Rosalynde is a true romantic. She wants to be his first great love."

"She is. Honestly, she is," said Oliver, emphatically. "He's going mad without her. And he's driving me mad in the process."

I knew exactly what he meant.

"Could we do something to get them together for a chat?" I suggested.

We came up with a plan. I would persuade Rosalynde that she needed a night out (*As You Like It* had come to the end of its run so she was 'resting'). Oliver would do the same with Orlando and we would bring them together.

"How about coming to the theatre tonight?" I suggested to Rosalynde the following evening. "We hardly ever just go to watch nowadays."

"Oh, darling, that's a wonderful idea and I'd love to go with you, but I'm seeing my Orlando tonight. He phoned me this morning. It's all forgotten. I love him so much. I'm so happy." She kissed me warmly, then left me alone, scratching my head in amazement.

So, two hours later, Oliver and I were sitting alone in the stalls of a theatre, watching some American star of a teen soap who had decided he was not a real actor until he had played Hamlet on the London stage. There was much tearing off of his shirt to dènote the Dane's descent into madness. We could hardly hear Shakespeare's sacred text due to the army of fifteen-year-olds sitting in the front rows who sighed and squealed loudly every time the fabric tore, but it made us laugh so much that we left the theatre believing we had seen a good play, and enjoyed each others' company.

There were several more break-ups and make-ups that kept Oliver and I very busy, but the next great drama came when Orlando finally got the call to go to Hollywood. Rosalynde was working on an Andrew Lloyd Webber musical (did I tell you that she could sing too? Please try not to hate her for being so lovely and talented) and could not accompany him, so there were dozens of heated arguments carried out over the phone, with Oliver and I trying our best to calm the storm between them.

The storm became a hurricane when a young Hollywood starlet claimed in another Sunday tabloid article to have spent a 'night of passion' with Orlando, in which he made love to her a record ten times. I must say I was impressed, but, of course, very angry for Rosalynde's sake. The big romance was all over. Unsurprisingly, a heartbroken Rosalynde called off the wedding.

Oliver and I struggled to find a way through this one. Fortunately we were now working together. We had both landed very good parts in a television medical drama, Oliver as a dashing consultant surgeon, and I as the paediatrician he was enjoying an illicit romance with, so we had plenty of chance to put our heads together.

"I don't condone Orlando's behaviour," said Oliver, whilst we were rehearsing our lines together. "But I honestly can't see him behaving like this, even given the opportunity."

"He's in a new country, where he's being treated like a god," I said. "He'd be inhuman not to be tempted."

"Mmm," murmured Oliver. "It's not like him. He's had girls throwing themselves at him all his life, and he's always been the monogomous type… Do you think we should kiss before you say that line, or afterwards..?"

Then, before we were able to come up with a solution, the Hollywood starlet was charged with drug trafficking, video footage showing that she had actually been selling dope on Sunset Boulevard on the night she claimed to have put Orlando through his paces. She had simply used him for her alibi, believing he would be too grateful to have his name linked to hers to deny it.

I cried tears of happiness for Rosalynde as I put her on the plane to Los Angeles. Orlando was waiting for her at the other end and there were rumours in the Sunday papers that they were planning to tie the knot in the same Las Vegas chapel where Billie Piper and Chris Evans had married. They did not. They wanted to be married at home, with all their family and friends in attendance.

Now, I look around the room full of wedding guests and smile. Oliver and I are dancing.

"Well," I say, smiling up at him. "It took us some time, but we're here at last."

"Yes," replied Oliver. "I suppose this signals the end of the Association of Bit-Part Players. They won't need our help anymore."

"Thank God!" I laugh. "I'm a nervous wreck."

"Are you, darling?" he asks, a worried expression crossing his handsome face. "Has today been too much for you? Do you want to sit down?" I shake my head and he kisses me tenderly. I am so happy that it is some time before I am aware that people around us have burst into a round of applause. I pull away, blushing, and look around at our family and friends who are all laughing and mockingly sighing in relief.

Our very special friends, Orlando and Rosalynde, are also applauding. Orlando makes a very handsome best man, and Rosalynde, who is wiping a tear from her eye, a stunning maid of honour (though Oliver told me, with all the blindness of a man in love, that she is not as beautiful as I am today). They are planning their wedding for when we return from our honeymoon so that we can perform the same duties for them.

It always seemed certain that Rosalynde would marry first, but as actors we know better than anyone that scripts are liable to last minute changes, especially when a happy ending is called for.

Beach Watch

Nina Tucknott

It's the fourth day of our holiday. The sun's beating down and I pick up my paperback and put on my new sunglasses. Great things sunglasses – you can sit back and watch people without them realising what you're doing. And on this holiday I've been sitting back. Sitting back and watching a hunk further down the beach. Watching him quite a bit, as a matter of fact.

He's been in the same spot every day and I get a feeling he's interested. He's got shades on as well but he keeps looking my way. He makes me feel all funny inside. I call him D&H – short for Dark and Handsome. Talk about temptation with a capital T...

I'm so glad I came... Only a few months back I was fighting tooth and nail *not* to join Claire and Pete on this holiday. I was sure they only asked because they felt sorry for me, and being the third wheel under the cart was definitely not my idea of fun. Even if it meant getting away from a wet UK.

But when Zoë said she'd come along too, I changed my mind. Zoë's OK, a bit wild for my liking, but at least with her around it meant I wouldn't have to sit and look at Claire and Pete cuddling all the time. They've been together for yonks but they still act like it's their first date.

I guess I'm only envious – after all, not so long ago Dave and I did the same. But not any more. Now there's just me – Dave having decided that a curvaceous Rosie was more to his liking.

The funny thing is, I didn't see it coming. When he confessed I was totally flabbergasted. How foolish of me to think we'd be together forever, eh?! Stuff like that only happens in books... maybe even in the one I'm pretending to read...?

Claire and Pete were great when it happened. As soon as they heard, they rallied around, bringing other friends too, not to mention a bottle or three. Sitting cross-legged on the floor long into the night, we laughed and cried, cried and laughed, guzzling red, white or rosé. The morning after I'd wake with a mega hangover but feeling it'd been worth it, knowing so many people were rooting for me.

During one of our sessions Claire mentioned Tenerife and a nice little hotel they were going to, and asked would I like to come too. "No way!" I protested to begin with. "I don't think so," followed later. But once Zoë had booked her ticket it changed to: "Well… if you're really sure..."

And here I am – getting bronzed and feeling almost on top of the world. Dave's face has become a blur and I don't mind watching Claire and Pete being all soppy. In fact, my only problem's Zoë. She's taken it on herself to be with me every minute of the day. Quite infuriating, particularly with D&H so near. She's cramping my style.

Yesterday I swear he almost came up to me but then Zoë appeared with two ginormous ice creams and that was that.

Today I've decided to give him three hours and if he doesn't come near me I'll stride up to him. After all, we've only got three days left!

Glancing at my watch I realise his time's almost up. I guess it'll be up to me then... I'd like a date with him and hopefully he'd like one with me too. I'm pretty sure he's English – he's read a different English newspaper every day. And if he isn't, well... it's his loss!

My only dilemma now is how to get rid of Zoë. Claire and Pete, on a trip to a parrot park, won't be back until at least six. What a pity Zoë refused to go along too. I feigned a headache, saying that I'd spend the day in bed but she wouldn't have any of it. She chucked two paracetamols on my bed, gave me half an hour and then dragged me down to the beach. Knowing D&H would probably be there, I didn't protest too much.

Rooting around my beach bag now I find my purse with a wad of euros. Maybe a trip on a banana boat will keep her out of my sight long enough? I know she'd love to have a go but too much clubbing's left her dangerously broke.

"Zoë..." I squint against the bright sun. She's just come back from a quick dip. "Why don't you have a go on one of those?" I point into the distance. "My treat..."

"Cool!"

"I'd better stay here," I offer, "watch our stuff, like..." She's not listening. Grabbing the money, she's off, racing along the sand like a little kid, reaching the yellow inflatable banana-shapes in no time at all.

A plan's already been forming in my head. Once she's seated I'll pretend I want to take a photo of her. It'll mean having to get close to the water's edge. And how strange... but that'll be exactly next to D&H's spot!

Grabbing my camera I get up. Half-smiling, I pretend to wave towards Zoë while taking in D&H all along. He looks my way and smiles encouragingly.

Suddenly I feel all nervous and tongue-tied. Having been with Dave for so long I'm rusty when it comes to chat-up lines. "Do you come here often?" doesn't quite go on a beach in Tenerife, does it? While "Hot, isn't it?" seems totally corny.

Zoë would have no such problems, she'd know what to say. I've been watching her in the hotel bar. Rico, our waiter, is practically eating out of her hand every night. "Hi–i gorgeous" seems to be her standard phrase. Perhaps I could try that?

And then, when I'm almost by his towel, Zoë comes racing towards me. "Nan... Nan!" she shouts. "Come and have a go... they need one more."

Honestly! Such a spoil-sport! Oh well... there's always tomorrow...

Biographies

Penelope Alexander is a teacher. Born in Bristol, she is married with two sons and lives in Northamptonshire with her husband and various pets. She writes poems and articles and helps run a writers' group. Penny has written stories ever since she can remember, and occasionally sees them in print.

Diana Appleyard, a former BBC Education Correspondent, is a novelist, journalist for national newspapers and women's magazines and she is a regular guest on national radio. She and is currently working on her fifth novel. Diana lives with her husband and their two children in Oxfordshire.

Lynne Barrett-Lee lives in Cardiff with her husband and three children. As well as numerous articles and short stories she has published four novels, her fifth *Wild About Harry* published by Bantam is due out in September 2005.

Jane Bidder trained as a journalist and has written for several national newspapers and Woman's Weekly. She had a series of children's books published by Franklin Watts called *Family Memories*. Her first adult novel *The School Run* comes out in August, published by Hodder, under her pseudonym Sophie King. Jane is married with three children and a dog.

Simon Brooke was born in Yorkshire but now lives in West London. After various employments he finally became a journalist in 1995 and writes about travel, fitness, style and 'blokes' stuff' for the various national broadsheets. He has written two novels, *Upgrading* and *2cool2btrue* both of which are published by Orion and he is currently writing his third.

Christine Emberson is National Ford Fiesta Short Story Writing Competition winner. She lives in Kent with her two young sons and three cats. She works part time in the City, tutors for Kent Children's University and runs on her own children's party business. She is working on her first novel.

Gemma Forbes is the pseudonym of Valerie Bartholomew. She has been married twice and has two children. Having managed her own manufacturing business for 21 years, she re-trained to become an aromatherapist. She has written for pleasure for many years and has now joined joining a writing class which has provided the motivation to get stories published.

Della Galton's passion is writing. She lives by the sea with her husband and four dogs and works as a full time writer. She has sold in excess of three hundred short stories to Women's magazines and also writes serials and features. She has two novels awaiting publication.

Suzanne Gillespie loves reading all genres especially whilst enjoying sun, sea and sand but only recently started writing. She lives in Bournemouth with her husband and two dogs.

Josephine Hammond grew up in West Africa and has four adult sons. She now lives in Pembrokeshire. Previously published work includes newspaper and magazine articles as well as contributions to the Arvon Foundation Mini Saga book. Jo is currently studying for a MA in Creative Writing.

Zoë Harcombe read maths at Cambridge University and has worked in blue chip organisations since. Zoë's diet book, *Why do you overeat? When all you want is to be slim* was published by Accent Press in 2004.

Sarah Harrison has written sixteen best-selling novels as well as children's books, short stories and non fiction. She has three children, two grandchildren and lives in Hertfordshire.

Sue Houghton is married and the mother of four children. She has won a number of writing competitions and is internationally published in women's magazines. She was highly Commended in the PBD/UK Great Read Competition.

Dawn Hudd lives in Hereford with her husband and three young sons, along with numerous pets. As well as writing she works part time as a support worker in a local school and is doing a BA in Creative Writing at Birmingham University.

Christina Jones had her first short story published when she was fourteen. She has been a best-selling novelist for the last seven years, has had countless articles and stories published in magazines and newspapers, and has won several awards.

Jan Jones is a member of the RNA and has had short stories published in a variety of women's magazines. Her first novel *Stage By Stage* is being published by Transista in October 2005. Jan lives in Cambridgeshire with her family and would like to dedicate her story to her brother-in-law, Mike Jones, who died last year following a heart attack.

Ruth Joseph recently graduated with a M.Phil. in Creative Writing. She was won various prizes and been published extensively in Wales. Ruth's first solo collection *Red Stilettos* was published by Accent Press Ltd in September 2004. Ruth lives in Cardiff with her family.

Rosemary Laurey is a retired special-education teacher who lives in Ohio and spends her days writing. She is a USA Today best-selling author and has been a finalist for several awards and won the PRISM for Best Paranormal Novel and the PRISM Best of the Best for 2002.

Carolyn Lewis lives in Bristol with her husband and two cats. Carolyn has three daughters and two grandchildren. A graduate of the University of Glamorgan's MPhil in Writing, she has won various competitions. Currently she is working on her second novel whilst tutoring part-time in creative writing.

Rachel Loosmore graduated from London College of Fashion in 1997 before inadvertently entering a career in licence trade management. Having undertaken correspondent courses in Creative Writing and Proofreading Rachel changed her career path from pubs to publishing and started work for Accent Press Ltd in September 2003.

Carole Matthews is the internationally bestselling author of nine romantic comedy novels. Her books feature on the Sunday Times and USA Today bestseller lists. She has three films in development in Hollywood

Mo McAuley has an MA in Creative Writing and has won several prizes for her short stories. She was a supplementary prize winner in the Bridport Competition in 2003. Her work has appeared in anthologies and magazines and she is now working on a novel.

Lauren McCrossan has written three bestselling novels for Time Warner – *Water Wings*, *Angel On Air* and *Serve Cool.* After studying for six years to become a lawyer, Lauren succumbed to her true passion and now works full time as an author and freelance magazine journalist.

Catherine Merriman is a novelist, editor and a short story writer. She is also a university tutor and a director of the New Welsh review. Her first novel, *Leaving the Light On* won the Ruth Hadden Memorial Award. In 2004 she was the editor of *Laughing, Not Laughing*, a collection of autobiographical writings by women on the subject of sex.

Linda Povey's first success came with the publication of verses for greetings cards. She now writes short stories for popular women's magazines. Linda is involved in running residential courses for writers. She works as a part-time teacher in Shropshire.

Caroline Praed is the 2003 winner of the Katie Fforde Bursary and a member of the RNA. She has had short stories published in national magazines as well as being commissioned to produce a non-fiction book on education for children with autism.

Sally Quilford was born in Wales, but now lives in the Peak District, England. She's been writing for ten years, and has had had over forty articles, stories and poems published both online and in print. Sally recently came second in the Derbyshire Literature Festival 1-2-1 writing competition, and was a finalist in the 10th Too Write competition.

Angie Quinn was a journalist, feature writer and organist in Ireland before she moved to France and then to Wales where she now lives. She teaches Creative Writing and has had both short stories and poems published. She is on the Novel Writing MA at Manchester Metropolitan University and is co-editor of Borderlines Poetry Magazine.

Kate Roberts has worked as a theatre practitioner for twelve years. She is the director of drama4singles, a drama dating company. Kate has written two plays, *Cut Up* and *Closure*. *A Foreign Affair* is Kate's first published short story. Kate lives with her daughter in North Wales.

Rachel Sargeant was born in Lincolnshire. Now living in Shropshire, she is a full-time mum. A former winner of Writing Magazine's Annual Crime Story competition, she is currently working on her second novel, a whodunnit.

Jill Steeples lives in Leighton Buzzard with her husband and two children. Her stories have been published in the popular women's magazines and she was recently a prize-winner in a Writers' Forum poetry competition. Jill is a member of her local writers circle and a international online group.

Ginny Swart lives in Cape Town, is married with three children and has been writing fiction for three years. She is a member of an Internet writing group. Her stories have appeared in high school textbooks, anthologies and women's magazines. She has just started work on a novel.

Phil Trenfield was born and raised in Cheltenham. He now lives in Cardiff where he works in event management, whilst spending his free time creating the short stories he loves to write. He is currently writing his first novel that he hopes to have published soon.

Nina Tucknott writes monthly gardening and cookery articles and has written hundreds of articles and short stories for magazines and anthologies. She is presently working on her first novel. Nina is a Swedish-speaking Finn who now lives in Brighton with her husband and two teenage sons. She has taught creative writing and is the current chair of West Sussex Writers' Club.

Fiona Walker began her writing career at just twenty one and had instant success with her first novel. Since then she has written six best-sellers, most recently *Lots of Love.* Fiona devised and co-edited the *Girls' Night In* series which raised over half a million pounds for War Child. Her latest novel *Tongue In Cheek* is published in May 2005 by Hodder and Stoughton.

Jane Wenham-Jones is the author of two novels – *Raising The Roof* and *Perfect Alibis* – both published by Bantam. She also writes for women's magazines and the national press and has a humorous weekly column in her local newspaper. She lives with her husband and son in Broadstairs, Kent.

Dawn Wingfield has written several short stories. She lives in Colorado with her husband and children and when not helping with homework or struggling with something in the kitchen is usually to be found with her nose in a book or working on a novel.

Jackie Winter started writing when she was seventeen with pieces in Jackie magazine. Five years ago she joined an inspirational creative writing class and since then she has had some success in competitions and had several stories published in various women's magazines.

A Message from
British Heart Foundation

The facts about Heart Disease

- Every two minutes, someone in the UK has a heart attack.
- More people than ever are surviving after heart attacks and surgery and there are currently 2.7 million people living with heart disease in the UK.
- Heart disease is a long-term debilitating condition that significantly affects the quality of life of patients and of those who care for them.
- Heart disease could affect any one of us, whether we are seven or seventy, male or female.

The work of the British Heart Foundation

- The aim of the British Heart Foundation is to play a leading role in the fight against cardiovascular disease so that it is no longer a major cause of disability and premature death.
- The British Heart Foundation is leading the way in heart research, education and patient care.
- The BHF has set up 372 cardiac rehabilitation programmes while BHF nurses provide specialist care and support to heart patients in their own homes.
- £1500 can fund a year's worth of training and support for a BHF nurse.

"I'm so full of confidence with my BHF nurse. The attention I'm getting now is terrific. He's got time to talk to me. He's medicine himself." Patient of a BHF Heart Nurse.

Why we need your help

The BHF can currently only fund 180 specialist BHF Heart Nurses – 1 nurse per 15,000 patients. We urgently need to dramatically increase this number to ensure that we provide care for heart patients – we must do more than simply keep people alive.

Look after your heart

Be smoke free... from the moment you stop smoking, the risk of heart attack starts to reduce and is halved after one year of stopping smoking.

Avoid stress, take time out and relax… it is important to 'break the cycle' and find ways to manage your stress. There are two main ways to tackle it: try to tackle the source of your stress; change how you respond to stressful situations.

5 portions of fruit and vegetables a day… there is good evidence that eating a diet that is rich in a range of vegetables and fruits lowers the risk of heart disease.

Take regular exercise… half an hour a day makes all the difference and this can be included in your daily routine. Start off gently and build-up gradually.

Reduce salt intake to keep blood pressure down… it is important to try to eat only the recommended amount of salt (less than 6g per day). This could help you to keep your heart healthy.

We have a selection of literature on healthy eating, getting active and giving up smoking. For more information please visit www.bhf.org.uk/publications

The BHF needs your help

Please accept my donation of £................
(please make cheques payable to 'British Heart Foundation')

*Or debit my credit/CAF card no: ....

Expiry date....../...... Amount £.......... Issue No ... (if switch /solo)

Signature.....................................

Name...

Address...
....Postcode.............

Email...
* Credit Cards Taken: Visa, Amex and Mastercard.
Debit cards taken Visa Delta, Switch, Solo, JCB, and Maestro

Gift Aid declaration

If you are a UK tax payer please tick the first box so we can claim back **28p** for every **£1** you give **at no extra cost to you.**

GA1 □ Yes, I am a UK tax payer and would like the BHF to reclaim the tax on all of the donations I have made since 6th April 2000 and any future donations I may make*.
*For the BHF to reclaim the tax on your donation you must be paying at least 28p in UK income or capital gains tax for every £1 you donate.

GA2 □ I am a non taxpayer.

What happens to your personal information
The BHF values your support. We will use information provided by you for administration and marketing purposes. We may contact you by post, or occasionally by phone or e-mail, and include new and information on the BHF's charitable work (eg how your money is spent, heart health information, BHF events) and related products and services from our subsidiary companies such as Christmas gift catalogues. Please tick the box if you do not want to hear from the BHF at all [ ] S
Occasionally the BHF may pass on your details to carefully selected third party organisations we are working with, for them to send you information on their events, products and services. Please tick the box if you do not want your details passed on in this way [ ] MP2

Please send this page to:
Sexy Shorts for Lovers. British Heart Foundation,
14 Fitzhardinge St, London. W1H 6DH.

bhf.org.uk Registered Charity Number 225971

The 'Shorts' Range
Of Charity Books

Accent Press Ltd produce two charity books each year.

Saucy Shorts For Chefs in aid of Breast Cancer Campaign (Reg Charity # 299758) published in October 2005. A delicious combination of raunchy reads and scrumptious recipes.
ISBN 0954709292 £6.99

Previous titles still available from www.sexyshorts.info…

Scary Shorts For Halloween
This collection of true, contemporary ghost stories will send a shiver down your spine while raising money for Breast Cancer Campaign (Reg Charity # 299758)
ISBN 0954489942 £6.99

Sexy Shorts For Summer
Another sizzling selection of short stories in support of Cancer Research UK (Reg Charity # 1089464)
"Sexy, funny and page-turningly good…the perfect beach read" Katie Fforde.
ISBN 0954489934 £6.99

Sexy Shorts For Christmas
Filled with fresh, fun fiction the perfect stocking-filler benefiting Breast Cancer Campaign (Reg Charity # 299758)
"Sparkling stories, perfect entertainment." Jill Mansell
ISBN 0954489918 £6.99

More Titles
From Accent Press Ltd

An Eye Of Death by George Rees ISBN 0954709276
This stunning historical novel has everything: humour, romance and a brilliant murder mystery plot.

The Fevered Hive by Dennis Lewis ISBN 095486736X
A cutting edge collection of Cardiff-based, urban writing.
(Available from April 2005)

The Last Cut by F.M. Kay ISBN 0954867378
A powerful and provocative collection of erotic poetry
(Available from April 2005)

Red Stilettos by Ruth Joseph ISBN 0954489977
An intriguing and provocative collection of short stories by a Cardiff-based Jewish writer.

Why Do You Overeat? By Zoë Harcombe ISBN 0954489933
After twenty years researching the causes of over-eating this book explains the three reasons why people struggle to lose weight.

Notso Fatso by Walter Whichelow ISBN 0954489969
A tongue-in-cheek, ruthless and very funny take on the world of dieting.

How to Draw Cartoons by Brian Platt ISBN 0954709209
Fun, simple and entertaining – this book will help even the complete novice turn out professional cartoons in minutes.

Triplet Tales by Hazel Cushion ISBN 0954709217
Beautifully written in rhyming couplets with full colour illustrations, this book is sure to be a children's favourite.

Titles Available By Post

To order titles from Accent Press Ltd by post, simply complete the form below and return to the address below, enclosing a cheque or postal order for the full amount plus £1 p&p per book.

	TITLE	AUTHOR	PRICE
☐	Sexy Shorts for Christmas	Various	£6.99
☐	Sexy Shorts for Summer	Various	£6.99
☐	Scary Shorts for Halloween	Various	£6.99
☐	Why Do You Overeat?	Zoë Harcombe	£9.99
☐	How to Draw Cartoons	Brian Platt	£7.99
☐	Notso Fatso	Walter Whichelow	£6.99
☐	Triplet Tales	Hazel Cushion	£5.99
☐	The Last Cut	F.M. Kay	£6.99
☐	The Fevered Hive	Dennis Lewis	£7.99
☐	An Eye of Death	George Rees	£7.99

All prices correct at time of going to press. However the publisher reserves the right to change prices without prior notice.

PO Box 50, Pembroke Dock, Pembrokeshire, UK. SA72 6WY
Email: info@accentpress.co.uk Tel: + 44 (0)1646 691389

Cheques made payable to Accent Press Ltd. Do not send cash. Credit/ debit cards are not accepted.

NAME ____________________

ADDRESS ____________________

POSTCODE ____________________